HOLLOW VENGEANCE

TOM RICHMOND

PUBLISHED BY FIDELI PUBLISHING, INC.

Hollow Vengeance

Books may be ordered through booksellers or by contacting:

Fideli Publishing, Inc.
119 W Morgan St.
Martinsville, IN 46151
888-343-3542
www.FideliPublishing.com

Cover imagery © Thinkstock.

ISBN: 978-1-60414-995-1 (soft cover)
ISBN: 978-1-60414-996-8 (eBook)

Library of Congress Control Number: 2013923161

Printed in the United States of America.

PROLOGUE

Frank Barrett, a shavetail second lieutenant, walked along Ft. Walton Beach, Florida, deep in thought. He wanted to speak to a shapely brunette but couldn't land on the device to overcome his shyness. Then suddenly, he had an epiphany. On his next pass he blurted out to the girl on the blanket. "How did you know I'd be here?"

Ramsay rose halfway from her beach blanket, startled by his question. She must have thought he was suffering some delusional case of mistaken identity or sunstroke.

What started as a quiet day was suddenly punctuated by this unexpected strange young man standing over her. He stood six foot with sandy brown hair poking out of his navy blue ball cap. He possessed a lithe, tanned body hardened by physical training. He shielded his eyes from the sun's rays. She guessed that he was about to ask another irrelevant question.

How did I know? Ramsay thought to herself.

She spoke coolly. "I'm sorry, you must be thinking of someone else."

He smiled. "I could have sworn you were looking for *me*."

Undiminished, Ramsay parried with a withering question. "How could I be looking for you when I don't even know you?"

Unruffled, he rebutted proudly, "Oh, but you should, I'm 2nd Lt. Frank Barrett, United States Air Force."

Confused, the twenty-year-old shook her long hair loose from her ponytail with a thoughtful look, trying to make sense of his last remark. Lifting her sunglasses, she took a good look; in doing so, she revealed her sparkling azure eyes. In sunlight they twinkled brightly against the backdrop of white sugar sand.

Unforgettable, he thought.

"Lieutenant Barrett, I hope you'll forgive me, but I really do *not* know you, and I *certainly* had no intention of finding you here either."

Frank persisted. "Well, now that you know my name, what's yours?"

Ramsay was not some dim-witted coed stalking the beach for bachelors. In fact, she only recently graduated summa cum laude, from Florida State University with a double major in English and physical education. A break before braving the job market was her only intent at present. Now she was facing a come-on from some young U.S. Air Force officer.

"I'll tell you what," she quipped. "I'll tell you my name if you admit this isn't the first time you've tried this."

Frank took the liberty of sitting on her blanket.

"Okay, you got me. I might have tried this approach before, but I can't remember when."

Ramsay cocked her head. "Have you had much success?" she asked.

Sheepishly, Frank replied, "No, not yet. Actually, I was hoping it might keep me off the streets."

Ramsay raised an eyebrow and gave Frank a wry smile. "Oh, really, just what's that supposed to mean? Just what *is* your job in the U.S. Air Force anyway, public relations?"

"Ah … no, actually," Frank replied. "I'll be a real fighter pilot when I finish training. You know, I can't help wondering why I've never seen you here before."

Ramsay narrowed her gaze.

She said, "My father was a fighter pilot."

Frank laughed. "Wow, that's uncanny, so was mine; see, we really *do* have something in common. Will you hold that against me?"

Ramsay started wagging her finger defensively, but Frank interrupted. "Hold on, no fair—you haven't told me your name yet."

She settled back, decidedly admiring his verve. "It's Davis. Ramsay Davis."

"That's a beautiful and different first name. I like it."

Ramsay countered, "Well, it keeps me off the streets."

He smiled genuinely, another thing she liked about him.

Their conversation ambled amicably with small talk as he learned of her future plans. Clearly, within the hour they both sensed something good was happening to them. Before the sun simmered into the gulf, they walked hand in hand along the beach, sharing longer stories of their youth. It was the beginning of a love that would blossom into their very hearts' desires. So far they were convinced completely, hopelessly in love. Ramsay replaced every reservation Frank ever held about marriage with heartfelt joy. She was invariably filling his thoughts with songs of endearment. In Frank's mind, he felt if she was not with him, he could not be himself. Whenever she was near him, she sustained him. Now he wondered how he could possibly ever leave her.

She had him speaking words like *always, all,* and *forever,* and he really meant them this time. Before they were just words, but now it was different. They took root in meaning the more he endeavored to take her heart away. Truly, they each found a place in the other's heart. But Ramsay also made it clear there would be a courtship. Frank had to work at their relationship for a year. Finally, Ramsay knew there was no doubt in her mind the time to marry was near.

In the meantime, Frank finished his first phase of pilot training, and Ramsay found a job. She loved teaching English at Fort Walton High School. Next there was the beautiful wedding ceremony provided by Ramsay's parents with a reception held at the Officer's Club on Mac-Dill Air Force Base in Tampa. As they say of weddings, it was a beautiful affair, and a good time was had by all.

Frank's bachelor party was distinctly different. Drinks spiked with moonshine rendered a night dimly recalled. You might say it was a little drunk out that night. His buddies celebrated by raising Frank's pants on the flag pole at Peter O. Knight Airport across the bay from Mac-Dill—so much for decorum. Married life fared better.

Frank and Ramsay lived in a tiny base apartment on Eglin AFB. Soon, Frank managed to land a staff job in his fighter wing. He also kept his hand in flying Phantoms.

Those were days of beach sunsets, quiet romantic dinners, toasts with wine, and sharing the love that made them happy. They agreed to keep a year to themselves before raising a family. After all, there was plenty of work and love to go around. That year was a blissful blur spent entirely on exploring their dreams.

Predictably, the war in Southeast Asia caught up with them. Frank received orders to proceed to Nellis AFB in Nevada for advanced combat training. He was assigned to the Seventh Air Force, Eighth Tactical Fighter Wing where he would continue flying F-4 Phantom jets.

In mid-June, Frank would leave for Nellis. Frank and Ramsay agreed it was best for him to complete advanced combat pilot school alone. For the next six months, Frank was subjected to rigorous training, including escape and evasion, resistance to interrogation, and survival school, all preparing him for the war in Vietnam.

In the meantime, Ramsay taught high school in Tampa while residing with her parents. In December, they all hopped a flight to Las Vegas to attend Frank's graduation from advanced combat school. Sadly, Frank's own family would not be in attendance. They had perished when his dad's plane crashed in the Rockies ten years earlier.

Ramsay's blue eyes widened as her pulse quickened at the sight of the bright lights of Las Vegas appearing on the horizon.

"Look, Mom," she said excitedly. "My view is absolutely dazzling. Can you feel it? We're letting down now. We're finally landing."

Her folks across the aisle watched with hope in their eyes as her anticipation grew.

When they arrived, Frank escorted them all to the fabulous Desert Inn to share a night of reunion and celebration. The clubs in Vegas after dark never disappointed.

After graduation, Frank said his good-byes to Ramsay's parents, knowing it would be the last time they would see him for at least a year, maybe longer. Ramsay stayed on for three intimate days in Vegas before dutifully shouldering her own burden of separation. The course Frank finished was intense, demanding, fast-paced, and success oriented, yet nothing prepared him for the heartbreak and frustration of parting from Ramsay's side. He felt he was tearing away from his soul.

The Air Force taught him to be confident, quick, even a minister of death, but it never prepared him for the heartache welling up inside as Ramsay kissed him good-bye. A surge of feelings rushed into his heart as he pressed her lips hard against his. In that same moment, she stiffened, staring back at Frank through teary blue eyes.

She spoke firmly. "Now I must prepare for *my* duty to wait, while you do yours alone."

Hearing those words melted his heart as he forced himself away from her embrace. He turned and climbed the ramp of the C-130 transport taking on replacements. At the top of the ramp, he turned to blow a kiss. Then he saluted and disappeared into the aircraft's yawning belly. The ramp rose, slowly squeezing the light out of his former life. It was nearly Christmas 1970.

1

They say the journey is long but the mountains are patient. Frank's flight from George AFB, California, to Ubon Royal AFB, Thailand, felt like that journey to the mountains. Crossing the Pacific with his GIB (guy in the back), 1st Lt. Chad Grin, they met their first challenge. It was in-flight refueling. In training, it gave Frank the golden heebie-jeebies. Everything must be so precise. One good slip could result in a midair collision sure to ruin everybody's day.

Across the Pacific, they topped off repeatedly in their fuel-guzzling F-4C Phantom II aircraft. Each episode left Frank so uptight you couldn't pull a needle out of his ass with a tractor. Yet, by the grace of God, and superior training, the flight saw the verdant serpentine mountains of Thailand.

In fact, they arrived just in time for Vietnamese Tet. Frank knew it was more than just their lunar New Year's festival. He and his crew mates heard on Stars and Stripes radio it was an all out strike coordinating North Vietnamese and Viet Cong forces up and down the map in South Vietnam. These strikes were nothing new. In 1968, they broke in to the U.S. Embassy along with multiple strikes in South Vietnam.

Frank's inbound flight covered ten thousand miles of ocean, making landfall once at Clark AFB in the Philippines prior to their final destination at Ubon Royal Thai Air Force Base in Thailand.

Fatigue built to where crew members were like zombies, desperately seeking sleep. Every man on that flight felt grateful he did not have to deal with the enemy under those conditions. Fortunately, Ubon was hundreds of miles from Vietnam.

That first night, the pilots were bused to the quarters they would occupy for the duration of their tour. The goal was to complete one hundred missions; then, by the grace of God, they could return to the world as they knew it.

Frank stumbled into a wide, bunk-lined bay. Ceiling fans slowly revolved above him. Other replacements wavered under the weight of their overseas bags as they entered. Frank plopped down on a bottom bunk. The others shuffled by, finding a bed of their own. Other pilots tried sleeping through the seemingly endless shuffling of boots on the wooden floor. As tired as they were, they were just too keyed up from their last mission for a good night's rest.

What will it be like in this new world? Frank wondered.

Chad took the bunk above Frank's in a bay of twenty beds that were neatly lined up in two rows.

Interrupting Frank's thoughts, Chad said, "Whadda ya think this place will look like in the morning, Frank?"

"Not much, now let's try to get some sleep, partner. I know we're going to need it tomorrow," Frank answered.

"Roger that, Frank. I just hope they don't feed us to the wolves right away."

For the past six months Chad and Frank did everything together. They ate, slept, exercised, studied, and flew. Sometimes they even shared the latrine together—in separate stalls, of course. Frank felt confident that when the time came, they would perform their duty with distinction. With thoughts of the impending conflict churning in his mind, he drifted off into a restless sleep.

Frank awoke to sunlight streaming in through the wooden slatted windows. His first sensation of Ubon RTAFB was the stench assaulting his nostrils. It was more than just an effusion of modern base smells and Thai living.

The sooty oily scent of expended jet fuel (a high-grade cousin of kerosene) mingled with fumes of generators run on diesel that kept the electric grid alive. Then, there was the underlying smell of old cooking oil mixed with garlic and soy sauce. But, the coup de grace was the stench of burning raw sewage just off base. It left a lingering bouquet of feces strong enough to gag a maggot. Frank thought, *How could all this have escaped my senses the night before?* Then, he realized the final ingredient was missing in the night—the oppressive, unrelenting heat of the sun was changing everything.

The heat felt like a blanket donned in a sauna. Everyone sweat with no effort whatsoever. Outside, there was background noise intruding from all sides. Jets taking off, landing, and running up all created a back drop for dozens of vehicles racing to and fro on the flight line. Through it all, Frank faintly heard a strident voice in front of their quarters. It was their flight sergeant calling everyone to report outside.

Frank and the others hadn't seen him in the light of day. He wore a bush hat, a T-shirt, and khaki shorts. He stood at attention as he looked over a group of disheveled pilots and co-pilots in various states of underwear trying to hold on in formation.

"You gentlemen didn't require C-130 transport like the rest. Since you delivered us ten new Phantoms, you've earned a night's sleep before reporting for duty."

Frank told himself, *At least that long flight over the Pacific sure paid for something.*

The sergeant continued, "You new guys will reform the 555th squadron. Aside from KIA and missing, you're replacing those who've reached their one hundred mission mark. Now, it's your turn. Good luck. Now, gentlemen, line up to receive your orders for the day."

Every replacement pilot received a to-do list. A report to the base commander, Col. Ryan Young, topped that list.

Colonel Young's office had a set of wide wooden stairs leading to double doors with sandbags all around it. A sign above was stenciled: Cmdr. 8th Tactical Fighter Wing. As everyone entered, the company clerk waved the group in, so they proceeded. The men came to attention before Colonel Young, briskly snapping off salutes. Frank and Chad allowed their eyes to wander a bit, taking in the scene of Colonel Ryan behind his desk. Behind him was an assorted collection of aircraft pictures. One showed him posing atop an F-4 painted in a spinach-and-sand camouflage paint scheme, as were all Phantoms on base. It was clear—five little red airplanes painted neatly beneath a gaping shark mouth appeared on the Phantom's nose.

An Ace, Frank thought, *impressive for an old man in his thirties.*

When it was their turn, Frank announced, "First Lieutenant Barrett and First Lieutenant Grin reporting for duty, sir."

Colonel Ryan replied, "Very well, as you were."

Frank and Chad smartly dropped their salutes while remaining at attention. He was a sturdy-looking, no-nonsense individual with crew-cut brown hair and searching green eyes. When he fixed his gaze upon them, it stuck. He began reciting his routine greeting pumped out for all the rest, when suddenly he halted midsentence. He cocked his head to one side with a look of incredulity.

"Wait just a damned minute here. You mean to tell me you two are lieutenants Grin and Barrett?"

Frank stated, "Yes, sir".

"You gotta be joshing me! Oh, this is priceless."

Suddenly, it dawned on Frank. He saw how before their names had always been paired alphabetically. Throughout training, their names were never paired the other way around—like then. Just then, Frank caught Colonel Young wiping his hand slowly over his handle bar mustache, neatly disposing a smile. Quickly, he reclaimed his sense of decorum.

He remarked, "For a second there, I thought you two gentlemen were sent over here by the USO."

For some unknown reason, having said that, he lifted himself off his swivel chair and then dropped back with a thump.

"Well, if that doesn't beat all, Lieutenants Grin and Barrett. Tell me, gentlemen, where are you two from?"

Frank said, "Sir, we completed our combat crew training at Nellis."

"No, I mean where were you born and raised?"

Frank said he was raised in Tampa, Florida, in an Air Force family. He hoped that last part might garner approval.

The colonel looked right through him, narrowing his green eyes. "An Air Force family, huh?" It sounded as if that made Frank keenly suspect in his eyes. "I suppose your daddy was a pilot too? Well, don't go thinkin' that makes *you* the best there ever was. *I'll* be the judge of that, Lieutenant Barrett."

"Yes, Colonel Young, sir." Frank responded. Suddenly, Frank felt he was no longer making a good impression.

"What about you, Grin? Where the hell do you hail from?"

Chad puffed out his chest, speaking in a southern drawl. "I'm from South Kareolina, sah, born and bred, sah, a graduate of the Citadel."

Colonel Young barked, "A rebel huh? Well, you'll get no sympathy from me. I'm from Ohio, and my daddy was a pilot, too. You see where it got me?"

Then he leaned forward, placing both hands on his desk. "Here in the Eighth Fighter Wing, it is our duty to interdict the enemy at any opportunity, but our primary mission is to escort bombers to their targets. Mostly, you will be flying combat air patrol known as MiGCAP. You will be responsible for providing air cover for our bombers against MiGs in the target area. Also, you will drop ordinance on selected targets prior to your MiGCAP duties. In addition, your objective is to knock out any potential threats to ongoing missions, such as SAM sites and antiaircraft batteries when encountered. That's it in a nutshell, gentlemen. You'll get further details down the line from your flight leaders. I'll be joining you from time to time, so stay sharp. Are there any questions?"

They replied in unison, "No, sir."

He admonished, "Then, get to it, dammit!"

Frank and Chad each snapped off a salute, turned smartly, and left.

It was only ten thirty in the morning, and the rising temperature kept pace with the stench off base. Its environment was distinct, to say the least. We were surrounded by primitive drainage systems. Ponds known as klongs connected by canals made the unmistakable smell of decomposing sewage and daily burning of human feces prevalent.

The next stop was "new guy school" (ngs), which was attended faithfully for three days. Most ngs stuff was superfluous, to say the least, like descriptions of the base and local flight patterns. Other parts seemed to serve the enemy more, like indoctrination in the rules of engagement. There was, however, some value in training on weapons release and improved radar warning receivers. These also enhanced the effectiveness of the EB-66 jamming aircraft we would fly with.

When it came to fighting MiGs, we relied on aggressiveness and instinct. Nevertheless, the saying still applied, "You can tell a pilot, but you can't tell him much." It wasn't long before the new guys encountered the worst when they faced the enemy without a gun.

2

ost off- duty time was spent sleeping or becoming acquainted with other pilots at the officers' club known as the F&R (short for front and rear). It was an inauspicious amalgam of Americana and Thai good intentions put up in teak. For the most part, it was a drinking club for pilots with a flying problem.

The establishment stood for no-holds-barred camaraderie. The only problem was, it catered to veterans of the conflict. To gain admittance, new guys not only had to swear loyalty to the squadron, but they must also have experienced aerial combat. Newbies, in the meantime, were to buy vets rounds whenever the brass bell above the bar rang.

Frank found it easier to hang out above in the air traffic control tower.

"Tower, this is 'Hot Sauce' Howard on final approach. I have no-gear-down lights, and I'm critical on fuel. I took some AAA over the IP. I'm requesting a confirmation of gear down."

"Roger, Hot Sauce. You're approved for that low-level flyby. Bring it in for a look-see."

"Roger that. Hot Sauce will be coming by."

Frank stood in back of the controller with a ring-side seat for the action. In less than a minute, Hot Sauce Howard was flying his plane over the runway, closing in on the tower at near-stall speed. Frank reached over the console and grabbed a pair of binoculars.

The tower called, "Affirmative. You have visible damage to your left main gear well. Your main gear are not down. Repeat, your gear is not extended."

Hot Sauce's voice sounded strained. "Roger. I was afraid of that. My GIB does not respond on interphone either. He may be unconscious. Ah … I'm requesting foam on runway twenty-two. Over?"

"Roger, affirmative on that. We have emergency vehicles dispatched."

If he couldn't fly, Frank preferred standing in the tower so he could observe inbound flights. He'd much rather watch and learn in the control tower than pound down shots and beers in the F&R. Of course, to gain a few hours of flight time was taken advantage of whenever the opportunity presented itself. Yet, his commander was holding back new guys until they were thoroughly indoctrinated.

Now, Frank watched closely through his high-powered binoculars as Hot Sauce prepared to grease the Phantom onto the runway. As he flared his plane, holding it off just above the runway, he slowly allowed the midsection of his plane to touch down just where the main gear would have been. It looked like a nice landing from Frank's perspective. Suddenly, a sound louder than the usual screeching emanated from the belly of the stricken Phantom. Part of the gear door had jolted loose, hitting first on the runway. It provided just enough drag to cause the plane to skid at an angle. The foam only served to heighten his loss of control. The radio crackled.

"Oh God, here we go!"

Hot Sauce Howard was at the mercy of his plane's inertia with no brakes to slow down. Now, the aircraft glided sideways off the runway into a marshy area. Suddenly, it flipped over on its canopy. The result was instantaneous. The weight of the 55,000-pound aircraft crushed the canopies and both men in their seats. There was no time for a zero-altitude ejection. When the plane broke up, it was suddenly engulfed in a huge ball of blackening orange flame. There was nothing for fire trucks to do except pump arcs of water into the twisted ball of melting aluminum that was once Major Howard and Lieutenant Dyer's plane.

The following week, we participated in our first flight with the fighting 555th squadron. It was February 14, 1971.

A massive increase in strike activity was underway. The air force determined to sequentially destroy North Vietnam's industrial base. Part of the plan included destroying power plants, rail yards, and military airfields.

Frank told Chad, "We're finally receiving QRC-160 radar pods. That should get us close enough to the target. Now we can escort the F-105 Thunderchiefs (affectionately called "Thuds") right to the target instead of maintaining an orbit outside SAM areas."

Flying MiGCAP alongside bomb-laden Thunderchiefs (affectionately called Thuds) called for two extra 370-gallon wing tanks and four AIM-7 and AIM-9B air-to-air missiles mounted on stations under the wings. Flying at twelve thousand feet, they looked for MiG-17s. They did not disappoint.

"Do you see them, Frank?" Chad asked.

Chad caught sight of six 17s spaced evenly in a wheel formation. This way they could take advantage of the Phantom's missiles' limited effectiveness at low altitudes while circling to protect each other's tails. The only way to penetrate their wheel was jumping in from above. Frank and Chad would swoop in trying to gain radar lock, launch their missiles, and then get the-hell-outta-Dodge before another MiG jumped on *their* tail.

The voice of flight leader Capt. "Cavalier" Kelsey came over loud and clear. "Don't get spooked, you nervous nellies. We have clear contact on six bogies at twelve thousand feet coming our way. Do not engage—repeat, do not engage—escort the Thuds all the way to the target. Do I make myself clear?"

Frank replied, "Roger, Cavalier. We've picked them up already."

Frank asked, "What if they start climbing toward us?"

"Just keep your cool and maintain formation. Cavalier out."

Frank had his eyes on the MiGs, when suddenly they uniformly initiated a shallow climb.

Frank sounded nervous. "Cav, they're climbing our way, buddy."

"Just maintain number two. You and Chad can get your feet wet on the way back."

Chad called out, "I see smoke trails, Cav, and he's got a lock on us."

Frank didn't wait to hear from Cav. Quickly and quietly, he locked on the MiG now in front of him. In order to gain speed, he immediately dropped tip tanks. Closing fast, he fired two AIM-9B missiles. One hung on its rail; another fell away in a sporadic twirling swirl of smoke, while the other tracked abruptly downward toward the reflection of some lakes below.

They soon learned their missiles were unreliable at lower altitudes. In fact, by early 1971, the AIM-9B had chalked up a 15 percent rate of effectiveness. Unfortunately, Air Force brass insisted there *was* no problem. Naturally, the clear, dry desert proving grounds in Nevada painted an entirely different picture than the lake-spattered terrain of Southeast Asia.

Frank had no time to regret his errant launches. He bugged out toward the wheel, pushing his throttle to military maximum position. It was tantamount to a swift kick in the pants. Simultaneously, he pushed the nose of his Phantom down steeply. These two actions resulted in one helluva fast dive. Nearing mach two under the pressure of high negative Gs, Chad forced out a terse reminder. "Watch your VFE, Frank."

Fortunately, their speed saved them when the remaining 17s launched missiles, while the other three dropped down to the canopy below. The MiGs' missiles took different tacks, staying their course right at Frank's nose. One zipped right over his left horizontal stabilizer, while the other sandwiched by their missed high-speed target. Hurtling away at first, the two missiles then steered around, changing course, seeking the heat of Frank's exhaust. One spent its fuel, causing it to harmlessly drop toward the jungle canopy—just what Frank was hoping for. Now, it was a race between them and the other missiles' fuel consumption.

Frank urged the missile to run out of fuel like an athlete thinking he could out run the fastest man on the team.

"C'mon now, you little bastard, run out, run out. Dammit, at least just run low and get off my ass!"

Just then, the last missile *did* exhaust its fuel, bursting right beneath them!

Chad shouted, "Damn, that was so damn close. I could hear shrapnel banging on our tail. You'd better check your elevators, Frank. I think we might have sustained damage."

Frank rapidly eased back on the throttle and then started gently pulling the nose up, testing his elevators.

Chad cried, "Get us the hell outta here, Frank. I think we've seen enough for one day."

Frank replied, "I will as soon as my best maneuvering speed comes back!"

Cavalier and the others were out of sight, on their way to escorting the Thuds to the target.

"Ah, Chad, we're going to turn back now," Frank said. "Without tip tanks and missiles, we're done. We can't reach the target and get home, too."

Chad affirmed, "Roger that, Frank. It's your call."

Frank bled off enough speed to execute a chandelle and then steadied the nose on a southwest vector.

"Do you think we'll catch hell from Cav?" Chad asked.

"No, Chad, only me."

Frank chuckled nervously as he scrutinized his fuel-consumption ladder gauge.

The rest of the flight home was totally silent. Frank didn't want to talk about how dangerously close things had gotten, and Chad was too busy with his radar and thanking his lucky stars they were heading home.

Frank retraced the highlights of the mission in his mind. *Our number three stayed out of the wheel, confirming our kill. That's good. Cavalier can't fault me for that one. Whadda you know—my first real kill.*

Our number three shouted, "Way to sting 'em, Barrett."

When Frank heard those words in his earphones, he was exhilarated down to his socks.

Frank thought, *Our first kill took less than thirty seconds. Chad's exuberant too, although he's maintaining an even strain. That voice on my earphones—was it our number four? He must have stayed above observing while we went in for the kill. He also confirmed the enemy was breaking off. He said, "It looks like those pecker woods have had enough stinging for one day."*

A new voice interrupted Frank's thoughts.

Cavalier chimed in. "Nice shooting, stinger. We'll have to talk when we get back."

The balance of the mission called for their flight to low-level bomb a key bridge in North Vietnam. Later, Frank was told the Thuds went in strong, but the enemy was ready with blanket AAA at the target. One of the Thuds was hit right away, but managed to make its drop.

That particular Thud called out, "Thanks for the escort, Cavalier. I owe you guys a drink. I'm outta here."

Later, Frank heard he pancaked successfully on a nice bed of foam after finding he couldn't lower his gear.

"Chad, our low fuel level light just came on. Call the tower and let them know," Frank said.

"You think we'll make it? Should I call for foam?"

"Not just yet, Chad. We'll just stay on top of it."

Frank and Chad were doubly grateful when they landed safely. They each checked the tail section, finding both horizontal stabilizers had thirty-millimeter holes the size of tennis balls perforating them.

After debriefing, Cavalier Kelsey's flight filed into the F&R Club. Chad and Frank shared the thrill of ringing the brass bell. Now it was their turn as the rounds were bought for *them*. It was then that Frank received his combat nickname for his first kill.

Kelsey raised his beer to initiate him. "I give you "Bee Sting" Barrett. He stings once and makes the other guy die."

Feeling victorious, Frank greeted each congratulatory salutation from his flight with great relish. His pride allowed him to accept their accolades. Then Kelsey approached. Judging by his serious look, Frank felt some sincerity coming on.

Kelsey said, "Great shooting, partner. I wish I could've joined you."

Frank knew in his heart of hearts that Kelsey sacrificed a victory by following orders.

Frank replied, "Something slipped up there in the heat of combat. I was just following my aggressive tendencies." Frank raised his glass just like Kelsey had, speaking with humility.

Kelsey interrupted. "Yeah, that was plenty nice shooting, partner, or *are* you? You know my training taught me to stick with the mission plan. You know, stay on target? It seems you got a brand-new way of fighting this war. You held your own, and we plastered the target without you, so I'll ease up this time. In the future, it would behoove you to stay on task. That way, we won't be missing anybody when we need 'em most."

Frank backed down, though it hurt his pride. "You kept the mission on task," he said. "We just got lucky, Kelsey."

Chad immediately slapped Frank on the back.

"Luck ain't got nothin' to do with it, partner. I'm the one who was plotting that launch back there."

They all laughed, putting aside their missile issues for another day. That night Frank went to bed a warrior and never looked back. Kelsey's message was lost on him.

Frank wrote Ramsay every day and was especially happy to share news of his victory. He tempered his words, though, so as not to make her worry.

My dearest Ramsay, we proved ourselves today. We flew a routine escort mission and got lucky. We managed to down an enemy plane. Please, no bows. We aren't finished. You ain't seen nothin' yet, baby ...

Frank's next mission proved him right. A week later, his flight interdicted a supply route. Again, they were escorting Thuds—only this time at fifteen thousand feet. Chad spotted MiG-21s near eighteen thousand feet, making a shallow dive toward the Thuds. Frank climbed his craft in a head-on to intercept. When Chad determined the envelope using the symbols on his radar screen, Frank fired two missiles.

Seconds later, they both watched their AIM-7s tracking upward. Their large smoke plumes would normally make them highly visible to MiG-17s or 19s, but the view from a 21 is limited by a blind spot directly behind and beneath the canopy.

Frank spoke. "You watch this, Chad. Our launch will soon pose a problem for that MiG approaching us. Our missiles should arrive right behind the lead MiG."

However, the real problem was the launch envelope displayed in Chad's part of the cockpit. It was inaccurate because the symbols were correct only when the target was acquired in straight and level flight. That was something MiG-21s rarely did.

In the meantime, high humidity was *the* limiting factor for airborne radar. All things considered, Frank had to write Ramsay admitting that he was not some hot fighter jock taking chances.

3

The combination of unreliable radar and missiles was taking its toll, and several pilots felt desperately in need of reliable weaponry to achieve air superiority. After talking it out, squadron buddies voted Frank as their spokesman. Frank agreed that dogfighting with cannon was the answer and further agreed to approach the commanding officer along with the other pilots.

On the following evening, ten flight officers walked the wooden planks to Colonel Young's headquarters. They stuffed themselves into his cramped office, while Frank made his pitch.

"Colonel, you've been on beaucoup missions. You know the score. We're up against MiGs armed with thirty-millimeter cannons. Now, we all agree the F-4 is a fine aircraft, with some exceptions. We feel our craft needs to be fitted with a gun, so we can dogfight close in. We all feel we can meet and defeat the enemy at close quarters if we can just engage him close in with a real gun."

Colonel Young rose from his desk with a scathing look on his face. "You people walked all the way up here to tell me what I already know?"

Frank stared back in surprise. Taken aback, he said, "You mean you agree?"

Colonel Young pounded his desk with his fist. "Hell yes, I agree! Just tell me who the hell else I've gotta convince in this man's Air Force to make that little dream come true. 'Cause to tell you the truth, when it comes to aerial cannons, I'm just too small to crap one!"

Frank stood his ground. "Sir, if it ain't you, sir, then who the hell is big enough?"

The others laughed nervously, yet they stood firm behind Frank. At that point, Colonel Young's countenance clouded over. His frustration was palpable.

He blurted, "All of you get the hell out of my office. I'll see what I can do. My only promise is I'll keep trying. You men deserve that much."

Thereafter, missions continued as scheduled. Then, Frank got lucky with an AIM-7 launch, downing his first MiG-21 from behind. He was at an advantage when he first spotted the 21. Frank swooped down from 18,000 feet in order to arrive on his six at 12,000 feet, always staying in his blind spot. At the speed he was traveling previously, Frank knew he'd have to giddyap to get where he needed to be.

"Hold on, Chad. We're going inverted."

"Roger that," Chad replied.

Immediately, Frank rolled his craft so he could execute a sharp inverted dive loading on positive Gs instead of negative. Had he done it right side up, they would have piled on too many positive Gs and experienced a grayout. Plastered to their seats for a few breathtaking moments, Frank rolled out straight and level right on his six, while maintaining a suitable envelope for missile launch.

After getting a clear tone and radar lock, he launched one AIM-9 right up his tailpipe. Bingo—he'd scratch one MiG-21. His first one downed and his second kill. When Frank trudged to his quarters that night, he felt out of gas. The strain was sapping him. Not every mission was that clean. He felt sure he was going to screw the pooch one day. *One day,* he thought, *I'm gonna take that golden BB, and I'll be checking in to the Hanoi Hilton.*

After a good night's sleep, he felt better. At least he could face the others at breakfast. The conversation invariably returned to the same topic. This time, Frank listened to Major Foster as he was making his case for cannon-packing F-4s.

Major Foster said, "Hell, look, we all know the F-4 wasn't designed for one, but with some ingenuity we can mount one. If we could only get permission, we could have maintenance cannibalize Vulcan Gatling cannons from out-of-commission Thuds. That way, we can test them and convince the brass they work."

Frank said, "Sure, Sam, we get the picture, but where would you mount a Vulcan (M-61 twenty-millimeter Gatling gun) on an F-4?"

"I'd sling it right up under the nose, so we could use the pipper as a boresight."

"We might as well," Frank said. "There's no such thing as a cannon sight on an F-4 right now anyway."

Fortunately, in the next few weeks two outside factors combined to change everything. Unbeknownst to our little group, the high command was interested in a new form of attack favoring dogfighting. They wanted to conduct large decoy raids into North Vietnam to draw MiGs into a trap. The plan was to have F-4 IIc aircraft simulate large F-105 bombing attacks.

In this way, the MiG-21s would come up to attack what they thought were bomb-laden Thuds, only to find faster F-4s ready for a real gunfight. As luck would have it, the Eighth TFW was about to receive orders for just such a mission. This news led to the second factor. When Colonel Young got the word, he contacted an old Korean War buddy—a major general who just arrived on his first tour.

Colonel Young sat in his office poised on the phone. "General, it is *you*," he said. "I'd recognize that voice anywhere. How the hell are you?"

General Carver spoke. "I'm just fine, Colonel. I want you to know I'm behind this idea of strapping cannons on F-4s. I'd stake my reputation on it. I'm coming over your way after I finish inspection here. Why don't you start cannibalizing what you've got, and I'll come up with some hellfire speech that'll make you guys look like heroes. Whadda ya think, Colonel?"

"I'm a strong advocate of dogfighting myself, general. And with your distinguished record as a double ace, I think we can pull together enough clout to get the air force to *design* F-4s with cannons."

"That's what we need. Fight fire with fire, I always say. I'll be over to inspect your boys in three days. Get off to good start now, Colonel. I'll see you soon."

When Frank heard the news that they were finally getting a chance to prove their tactics, he got his fellow pilots in the squadron to meticulously prepare for a mission that would appear like an F-105 strike. Their plan called for duplication, right down to the same times, altitudes, airspeeds, frequencies, flight names, and even the routes taken. The mission would look, for all the world, like a bombing mission on radar. The recently acquired QRC-160 jamming pods could make them appear like Thuds to Vietnamese radar controllers. In all, fifty F-4s, eight F-104s, and thirty Thuds were prepared for the mission.

The general arrived in time to give a real no-guts-no-glory send-off speech. After the last plane left base that morning, it climbed through a pall of sooty smoke. The F-4 typically leaves a telltale dark exhaust stream behind on takeoff, only this time they didn't care. They were headed for an operational altitude of twenty-five thousand feet.

Free from ground clutter, their radars would operate at peak efficiency. By the time they entered the target zone, they had unlimited visibility on top. Tension mounted as they prepared for a full-blown ambush. Frank's finger was fidgeting on the fire control button of his six-barreled, twenty-millimeter cannon, loaded for action.

The F-4s entered the ambush zone in two forces composed of six flights of four. Each would pose as normal F-105s and use identical formations. Mission support was composed of F-105 Wild Weasels, and B-66 ECM aircraft. If successful, their masquerade should attract MiGs from all four bases in the area for a battle *royal*.

Colonel Young led the mission.

Colonel Young said, "Listen up, men. I'll stay on top and press the attack from there. Remember, F-4s will be the only aircraft in the target area. That means if a plane appears on our radar, it's the *enemy* and can be engaged without visual identification. In other words, men, *there are no rules of engagement!*"

That information was received with a unanimous in-flight cheer. Now, the formations were packed tighter than a Baptist bus. Soon, different flights began peeling off toward Haiphong and Hanoi. Tension was building as the real excitement was yet to come.

Capt. "Cavalier" Kelsey spoke to his flight. "Like the colonel said, you get the picture. Were gonna be the largest force on radar that the North Vietnamese have ever witnessed. Let's keep them crappin' in their pants and get some."

At the initial point, the main formation entered the target zone over Phuc Yen Air Base and then doubled back, descending to attract MiGs.

Chad remarked, "Lord almighty, Frank, would you look at all those sweet little NVA planes down there?"

Just then, it happened.

"Quit looking down," Frank yelled. "There's plenty right up here with us. This is it—they took the bait. There are six bogies climbing, and they're all aiming at me!"

"Roger that, Frank. They're MiG-17s, and those aluminum skins really make 'em shine," said "Devlin" Derek.

"Well, let's just shine them on," Kelsey replied.

He had Lt. "Devlin" Derek tucked in close beside him, while Maj. "Duce" Davis brought up the rear. Frank was the outer point right in his flight of four.

Major Davis's voice crackled over Frank's earphones. "Form up abreast, gentleman, and call out your targets."

The entire formation achieved the element of surprise. Tension mounted as their aircraft hurtled toward the enemy closing at Mach 4. Frank sorted out the farthest right MiG appearing as a dot on his windshield. As the dot grew larger, his butt cheeks clenched while his finger fidgeted on the launch button. Every man was holding on to that proverbial needle with his cheeks firmly clinched.

Major Davis ordered, "Select AIM-7s and fire at will."

Frank selected only one to conserve missiles. Tensely, he announced, "One 7 is away here. Bee Sting out."

Other chatter flooded the air waves despite orders to keep it down. Similar calls went out across the crowed sky as the men of each flight could no longer contain their excitement.

Davis came over. "That's what I call a devastating strike."

MiG parts were flying all over the sky.

"We took all six—six in a row!" Major Davis enthused.

Frank shouted, "Mine's an affirmed kill."

"Hell, they *all* are. Now form up on me at ten thousand," said Colonel Young.

All of the flights re-formed to continue their subterfuge. Then, Frank noticed the jig was up.

He said, "They must have seen something's different up here. I see six more. There are six MiG-21s stacked on my three o'clock."

Frank fired first. "One AIM-7 away. It's tracking straight ahead on target—got 'em."

Immediately, other calls started coming in. The dogfighting 555th was having a field day. Frank's kill lost its tail in the explosion and abruptly entered into a flat spin.

"There, you see," Chad quipped, "planes don't fly without tails." He had watched for a chute and confirmed it. "I see one chute at four o'clock."

Colonel Young broke in. "Gentlemen, that was an outstanding job. I commend you, but there are three more of them about to skedaddle away."

Duce reported, "No joy here. Those gomers are bugging out."

After the mission, Frank learned other flights weren't as successful. Due to delays, miscommunication, and bad weather, they didn't hit the jackpot like Colonel Young's boys. General Carver's new release *Stars & Stripes* wrote, "The mission of the Eighth Tactical Fighter Wing on March 15 dealt a devastating and decisive blow to the North Vietnamese Air Force with a total of twenty kills and three probables." That news spread like wild fire and served as a real morale booster.

Frank laid his copy of *Stars & Stripes* on the bar back at the F&R.

"Now, that's worth at least one big hot diggity damn!" he said.

So it was, that in an aerial combat that lasted no more than two minutes, Frank claimed his third and fourth kill. Meanwhile, Kelsey waxed poetic at the bar, coming forth with an ominous herald.

"So the boastful hunter soon loses his prey. Then potential rises hither to whoop his butt to a fray."

4

Every time a fighter jock gets some, there's never a shortage of pilots who warn not to get cocky. Frank's time had arrived. He sat on a barstool at the F&R, once again, hearing his wingman Kelsey wax on. It was late and Frank longed for sleep, but Kelsey was intent on eloquently endowing him with the benefit of his infinite wisdom. Three bourbon and cokes ago, Kelsey began. "As I was saying, you listen up, 'cause it's gonna save your butt someday, buddy."

For emphasis, he kept poking Frank's chest.

"Every time a man goes up hish days are numbered. Hell, we all know it. But it's the guy who thinks he's gifted or somethin' that gets himself in Dutch. Oh, hell, I know, you've been there, done that and think you know the way back, too. Well, lesh me tell you somethin', ol' buddy palzey. You haven't lived until you've had your tail shot off 'cause you thought you were God's gift to aviation. Yeah, I know what you're thinkin'. Ole Kelsey just dropped the ball; didn't keep his head on a swivel."

Then Kelsey draped his arms around Frank's shoulders, pulling him in close, spraying bourbon breath as he guided him into his confidence.

"There I was thinking I had the world by the tail, racking up three 17s. I thought, *Hell, send 'em all up. I'm unstoppable.*"

Suddenly, Kelsey yanked his arm away, leaning too far back in his chair as he swayed his glass through the air.

"You know what? Thash just wha they did. They launched a butt load of SAMs at little ole me, just as I was headin' home. That, my fine feathered friend, is when they shot ol' Kelsey right in the ass! Yep, just when you think you're on top, cock of the walk, there's always some lil' bastards waitin' down there, itching to tear you a brand-new, double-wide a-hole."

Enough, Frank thought. Ever the smart-ass, he shot back. "Is that why you're not an *ace* right up to this very day?"

Kelsey suddenly grew sullen, pondering Frank's last remark while looking deep into his glass for an answer. Then, he seemed to sober up all at once. Slamming his glass down hard on the bar, he slid off his stool, getting right up in Frank's face *again.*

"All I can say is thish, fly boy; you got one helluva attitude."

With that, he staggered out, leaving Chad and Frank alone in the bar. So far, Chad remained silent throughout Kelsey's harangue. Now he leaned over and spoke with the wisdom of near inebriation. "I'm your RIO, right?"

Frank confirmed. "That you are, Chad my friend. That you are."

"Well, believe you me; all I saw in your dogfighting was intelligent aggression."

Frank raised his glass. "There you go, Chad—discerning achievement through greater understanding."

That night many officers got pretty tightly wound, as one might say. It wouldn't be the last time either. It's just too bad, because the only lesson Frank took away was that his peers were *only* jealous. Frank just didn't do humble very well.

The next two months went by routinely with no kills, just missions flown over friendly Thailand and less friendly Laos while en route to downright nasty North Vietnam.

It wasn't long before excitement came, however, when Chad and Frank had a close call with some SAMs. Frank couldn't help but remember Kelsey's advice. They flew into North Vietnam to bomb an ammo dump near Haiphong. It took two passes to zero in on the target, but they did the job. On egress, Chad sighted a SAM launch to their right. Frank took evasive action, pulling into a tight roll. Fortunately, when he looked down while inverted, he spotted three more flashes on the ground. Pulling the nose over, he hit mil Max simultaneously, pushing their speed up beyond Mach 2 to redline. Going straight down, they grunted like pigs trying to keep blood in their heads as the Gs piled on. It was like riding with a nine-hundred-pound gorilla sitting on your chest that you damn well didn't want to disturb.

Frank imagined that the North Vietnamese ground controllers thought they hit their plane when the first SAM flew right past their canopy and exploded thirty feet away. If not for the speed differential, Frank and Chad certainly would have been flamed. There was no time to think, with three more SAMs on the way. Chad fired all flares, hoping to bait the telephone pole–sized interceptors with enough heat before they locked on.

"On the left," Chad shouted. "One took the bait!"

"Tighten up, Chad," Frank cried. "We gotta pull out."

Losing altitude rapidly, they had to pull out before going over indicated redline. If they exceeded the do-not-exceed airspeed, the wings would rip off if they tried to pull out. Frank couldn't right the plane to punch out; it certainly was no configuration to launch a missile. Instead, he waited 'til the last second, rolling thirty degrees, hoping to diminish his profile to the last two SAMs, which streaked by so close Frank thought he felt heat from their exhaust. Now the ground was coming up fast. Frank glimpsed the whirling dial on his altimeter passing through two thousand feet. Now they had to pull out, or they'd be a smoking hole in the mountains.

Slowly, steadily, Frank applied air brakes until the airspeed bled off ever so slightly to the highest maneuvering speed. Next, both men strained on their sticks.

"Help, Chad," Frank grunted as the Gs made them feel like their eyes would pop from their sockets. Frank forced out words. "Help me! Pull up!"

The stick was heavy. Finally, with both straining on their sticks, the plane started grudgingly coming out of its dive. Just then, filling Frank's windshield were two karsts side by side with exposed craggy faces. They narrowly shot through the V between them!

As they roared out the other side, Chad shouted. "Jeez, I think we just clipped some trees!"

At least they didn't hit a mountain. That was the *best* part of the mission. Later, Frank felt somewhat humbled by the event. It was his true baptism by fire. Thereafter, he refused to be called a red hot pilot *ever*. Frank definitely took this away from their experience. Mountains are where you find them, not where you think they are. Thanks are to God. They only had a few missions left.

Life at Ubon got interesting during those last missions. Frank started thinking Colonel Young had it in for him. The colonel was gunning to make triple ace, yet Frank was racking up the kills. So, whenever hourflight went up, Colonel Young made sure he was first on the scene if there was to be any action.

On one of those days, he outdid himself. It was a clear dawn in September—perfect flying weather and unlimited visibility. Col. "Red Crown" Young was flying that day—in the lead, of course. They were covering a Thud strike force west of Phu Tho when the EC-121 side-looking radar vectored them to intercept MiG-21s returning to their base. The MiGs were approximately three miles away. Red Crown ordered his flight south to intercept. As they closed, he turned left, meeting the enemy head on. He passed the first MiG, knowing from experience there would be a trailing MiG. However, he hadn't counted on four. He passed them, too, reversing course, banking hard left to engage them from behind. The last MiG banked sharply to the right, evading his attack.

Red Crown gained position on his rear quarter, and his GIB obtained a solid lock and tone on him at five o'clock. Firing from the edge of his envelope, both AIM-7s struck home. It was an inspiring sight that no one had time to dwell on. The first MiG was already attacking them from behind, often a fatal consequence of being last in formation.

Chad shouted, "He's on our six, Bee Sting. Make it or break it!"

Frank turned hard across his curving intercept coming out at his five o'clock. The MiG perceived the threat, jinking hard right, and then dived away. *That little gomer is really working for it*, Frank thought. Knowing he didn't have hydraulics like they did, he must have really been straining on that stick. Frank figured he must have been a "Big Charlie."

Chad called, "Let's poke and hope."

Frank fired two AIM-7s at minimum range at the limit of their ability to turn. Expecting them to miss, he was preparing to switch to gun attack when both struck the MiG for his fifth kill. Suddenly, he was an ace and hadn't even fired his cannon yet. Colonel Young claimed his fifth, too, so the intersquadron rivalry continued.

The party at the F&R started early. There appeared two angels before them. Not really, but they did feel really blessed. Colonel Young and Frank stood at attention, while the others held their glasses high. After that, the evening digressed into uproarious affair As tradition would have it, later the Colonel and Frank were snuck up on and thoroughly doused with a tub of ice water. Late in the evening, Frank set off to his hooch, still damp. It was then that he slipped and fell face-first on the wooden planks near the door of the club. Now that was a memory! Although the pain never equaled the embarrassment of having scraped off half his bulletproof mustache, his pride would definitely take longer than the rest of the mustache he'd shaved off to recover.

It's true when they say no two missions are alike. Frank could remember one in particular in mid-November. The monsoon season was upon them, and it was work just dodging thunderheads in the sky. He was up front this time, as his number of missions made him senior pilot in the flight. They were flying in a fluid four formation nearing the North Vietnamese MiG base at Phuc Yen close to Hanoi. The Thuds from the 333rd had already roughed up the area with intense bombing, so they knew to expect action. Because the weather was marginal, they took different flight routes to the strike zone in support of the Thuds hitting the fuel depot near Phuc Yen.

As they rolled in on the target, everybody's radios immediately started jamming up with overlapping calls and incoming threat warnings. The ridge ahead erupted in AAA fire erupting in bright orange and black bursts at their proximate altitude. Then, they sighted SAM trails streaking up toward them.

Apparently, the Thuds did a nice job of pissing off everybody in the valley. Frank keyed his mike, instructing his GIB to man the missiles. Chad wasn't with him; he had contracted a bad sinus infection. Hence, he was off the duty roster. Frank's new GIB was Lt. Bob Sullivan.

He chattered, "I'm on it, Bee Sting. I'm setting up sparrow launches for the AAA site ahead."

Frank couldn't make out the exact target because of all the smoke coming from flak batteries atop the ridge hammering away at them. Instinctively, Frank looked to his right as his peripheral caught something bright bursting into view; it was Cavalier's plane. It was tumbling out of control. In Frank's mind, he was seeing Kelsey's plane coming apart in slow motion in a churning ball of orange flame!

Bob cried, "No chute! They bought it, Bee Sting!"

Frank's heart sank for an instant, but he was too busy to acknowledge. Having rolled inverted, he was pulling his nose down through the horizon in a steep, angled dive. Frank whispered in his oxygen mask. "I'm damned if I'll let those little bastards get a fix on me."

Bob stayed with the target, firing AIM-9s. Frank could see their arcing smoke trails crossing over in front of him.

Seconds later, Bob called, "Bingo. We got 'em."

Frank quickly rolled level, looking back in time to see the ridge where the battery was in flames. He felt some satisfaction, at least, in seeing them go and more in knowing Kelsey and his GIB didn't have to suffer.

Then Bob shouted, "MiGs—all under us."

Frank was now climbing through five thousand feet. Looking down, he saw at least ten MiGs flying in pairs coming up after them. They must have figured the Thuds were going to bomb their air base.

Frank put his nose down, heading for the first two. When he was closing in, he realized they were MiG-17s. They probably knew they were too close for an effective missile launch and continued climbing. Frank opened up with his gun, spraying the first one heavily before the MiG even fired a shot. Immediately, the plane blew up about three hundred yards in front of them. Frank had to maneuver quickly to dodge the flaming shrapnel. The second plane broke hard right. Frank kicked rudder, staying right with him all the way through his jinking turn. As soon as he righted his plane, he sprayed the second plane, too. Trailing thick, black smoke, he rolled over on his back and ejected.

Bob shouted, "Scratch two MiGs—good shootin', Bee."

Just then, Frank felt concerned about the rest of his flight. He took a chance of being overheard speaking on his radio to nobody in particular. "Where'd everybody go?"

Bob answered. "I saw three and four bug out toward some foothills about a mile back. They had several MiGs closing on them."

It was then Frank realized the rest of his MiGs had taken after the others in their flight. Pushing his throttle full forward, he gave chase.

Bob called, "We gotta rock and roll, Bee Sting. It looks like they're starting to engage our guys."

Frank lit the afterburners, leaving the target zone far behind. The MiGs were concentrating on catching the rest of their flight, so Frank slipped up behind undetected. There were eight of them now, and he wasn't sure how he was going to attack with two missiles and a cannon low on ammo. His first problem was how to fire without hitting his own guys.

Frank called to planes three and four over the radio. "Three, break right on my mark; four, you go left. We'll take a missile shot when you're clear." Three and four acknowledged, and Frank counted down.

"Ready now ... *breaks three and four!*"

Frank launched their remaining A-7s; each tracked disappointedly low, disappearing in the overcast beneath them. Now, they were closing on eight MiGs with nothing but a gun. Fortunately, the MiGs hadn't spotted them yet. Frank was in their blind spot. He started firing short bursts to conserve what little ammo he had left. To his surprise, two of the MiGs in the rear echelon sprouted smoke, rolling right, then left, then each went down to the deck. In five seconds, they flew right past the rest of them, rejoining three and four. They poured on the coal and beat it out of the area before the MiGs knew what had passed them. Gratefully, the Phantoms were definitely faster, and the three left lived to tell it.

Losing Kelsey was a blow to them all. Of course, they all knew the risks going in, but it still came as a shock when someone close by got it. That night Frank was feeling really low. Thankfully, he saw a letter from Ramsay was waiting for him on his bunk. He sat in the half light near the generator to read it while others slept.

Finally, Chad was back in the saddle, and all seemed well. With mission number ninety-nine on the preflight schedule, he and Frank sat down for the briefing. Colonel Young was explaining they were to cross over Laos and join up with some B-52s for an escort mission to target Dong Hoi near the eastern coast.

Good, Frank thought, *Another useless dumping of B-52 bombs in the jungle. This should be duck soup.*

However, the weather was all wrong for the mission. It was clear at the target, yet predicted to be socked by the time they got there. Frank didn't care. They weren't going to bomb anybody anyway. They were just gonna escort the flight. After they armed up and strapped in, they started engines and left the chocks at 0720 hours. The whole flight was routine. The B-52s dropped their load in the boonies, leaving moon-sized craters in the dense jungle before heading home. That's when Frank decided to get creative. They hadn't fired a shot all day except to clear their guns.

Frank keyed his mike. "How'd you like to pay a visit to our old friends at Phuc Yen Air Base, Chad?"

"Oh, I don't know, Bee Sting." Chad laughed nervously. "I wouldn't want to tempt fate, you know."

Frank laughed. "Don't worry. We won't out stay our welcome."

When Frank got close enough to the North Vietnamese air base, he spotted a line of MiG-17s still parked in their revetments. Boldly, he rolled in. Succumbing to his salutary side, he put the plane in a slip in order to dump altitude in a hurry. Then, he executed a touch-and-go right in front of the North Vietnamese Air Force's control tower. Departing with cannon blazing, he strafed every plane on the ramp using up the last of his ammo in a one-fingered salute to their air force. Frank enjoyed watching those MiGs flying apart on the ground. As he climbed out at an extreme angle of attack, only Chad could appreciate the sight of their AAA batteries automatically swinging around to automatically line them up in their crosshairs. Frank could hear Chad shouting on the interphone.

"You are one bat-shit-crazy pilot! Get us the hell outta' here before you get us both killed!"

Frank replied drolly, "Why, Chad, you know we're just living up to our reputation. Remember when Bob Hope visited us for Thanksgiving? Did he not say, 'The Eighth TFW was the world's largest distributer of MiG parts'?"

"Frank, consider your part done. Now, let's hump it on home, amigo!"

Frank pushed the throttle up to mil Max and did just that before anyone below could get a bead on him.

Frank said, "Do you know what we should to do for our one hundredth mission, Chad?"

Only the sound of the wind clawing at his canopy returned to Frank's ears. He didn't hear a sound from Chad for the rest of the flight.

Checking the mission board the following morning, there it was next to his name: a small but readable #100. Everybody on base knew what day it was for Frank and Chad. Truth be told, Frank even put in some extra missions with Chad out sick, volunteering to stay on and wait for him just so they could finish together. Knowing this, Chad felt obligated to go along with Frank's plan for a little air show on their one hundredth mission.

At mission briefing, they learned they'd be flying MiGCAP in two flights of F-4s escorting a gaggle of Thuds to a target on the south side of Hanoi. Colonel Young would be flying with them.

Frank was thinking sarcastically, *What a special send-off on our one hundredth mission.*

On the way into the target they got some SAM activity that left them all puckered up. Frank and Chad managed to evade two of the screaming telephone pole-like missiles themselves. When the Wild Weasels and Thuds rolled in, they stayed on top at fifteen thousand, trying to avoid radar-directed AAA. When the familiar bright orange balls of AAA started filling Frank's windscreen, he spoke to Red Crown. "Shouldn't we go down and get those guys?"

Red Crown replied, "Negative, Bee Sting. We stay up here and cover; let the Weasels get 'em."

For a brief instant, the notion slipped back into his head that Colonel Young was trying to pick off a couple of stragglers for himself. Just as he was considering those odds, Frank spotted two MiGs making a beeline for the Thuds below. One of their favorite tactics was slipping up behind when the bombers made their initial point.

Frank spoke to Chad on the interphone as he pushed down the nose. "Green 'em up!"

Chad acknowledged, "Roger, Bee Sting. I have the bogies sighted."

Chad got radar lock on one of the MiGs. He launched two AIM-9s. As luck would have it, one hung up on the rail, and the other went wide. Red Crown saw this and launched one of his AIM-9s immediately. It struck home, creating a brilliant fireball over the target.

Chad called, "That's triple ace plus one, Red Crown. Nice shooting."

Red Crown ordered, "That's it, boys; let's stack it and pack it."

With that order, Frank said good-bye to Hanoi. The flight homeward was uneventful. Soon, it was time to prepare for the final approach to Ubon.

"Bee Sting to Red Crown. I'm requesting permission to buzz the tower."

"Roger that, Bee Sting," Red Crown said reluctantly, "permission granted."

Frank turned in on final, lowering the nose and gently picking up airspeed. Now he was ready. Chad hunched down in his seat, anticipating a wild ride.

"Ubon tower, this is Bee Sting on final for a one hundred-mission pass."

"Ah ... roger, Bee Sting. The pattern is clear for your pass!"

They came screaming in over the treetops. Frank's first pass would only be a wake-up call. At near supersonic, they roared past the tower at one hundred feet! Pulling up sharply at the end of the runway, Frank held the F-4 in a vertical climb, bleeding off airspeed and rolling three and half times. Then, Frank kicked the left rudder, allowing the plane to stall. For a few seconds, it shuddered and then slipped backward. Then, he pushed the nose down in a power dive until it picked up speed. Rolling level, Frank pulled up just above the runway and then flew its entire length, blasting past the tower again, waggling his wings. Breaking out in another tight turn, Frank pulled at least four Gs. Last but not least, he lined up for the runway a mile out, calling the tower.

"Ubon tower, Bee Sting, here. I'm requesting a flyby with a victory roll!"

"Roger that, Bee Sting. You got it, do be careful."

This time, Frank and Chad came in at fifty feet off the deck, flashing past a small crowd of well-wishers. Roaring past, he pulled up steeply and executed a victory roll, pulling another four Gs before going inverted. This time he held it there until they stabilized while Chad fired off four flares—strictly nonregulation. Frank knew Colonel Young would chew their tail for that when they got down, but it was worth every second! On final, Frank called the tower for a gear-down check. "Ubon tower, Bee Sting is on short final with gear down and locked as indicated."

"Ubon tower confirms gear is down. Come on in, Bee Sting."

Upon landing, as soon as they rolled out, Frank and Chad popped their canopies and felt the hot breeze in their faces as fire trucks rolled along each side of the runway, spraying their foam in arcs over them. They taxied to the blocks, parking on the numbers before each snapping off one final salute. It was the end of an experience not everyone gets to live. All the men in their ground crew were cheering for two of the luckiest bastards in the world!

Frank had ordered a case of champagne to christen the celebration on the flight line. As he climbed down the ladder, his crew chief handed him an open bottle. Holding it above his head, he shook it and toasted the crowd with its foam. Chad was right behind Frank, spurting foam from his own bottle. Just then, Colonel Young stepped up to congratulate the two men. He shook their hands and then stood between them, putting his arms around them.

Lowering his voice, he said, "It's a good thing you guys won't be around to pull another damned stunt like that."

Frank and Chad each gave him their best opossum grin. Taking it all in stride, he didn't say another word as the base photographer stepped up to capture the moment.

Then, things reverted back to business as usual. Frank and Chad's moment of glory was fading. Maintenance crews went back to prepping planes for missions as Chad and Frank walked away on November 30, 1971.

We were gonna make it home for Christmas, sure as shootin', Frank thought.

5

Chad had parted from Frank at George AFB, as each headed for home. The holidays were going to be special for both men, and they parted hastily in the best of spirits. Of course, Frank and Chad promised to stay in touch and to keep up with changes in their lives. Somehow, Frank knew things would never change between them. There's something about bonding in combat that never equates to life anywhere else. Chad was Frank's brother-in-arms. He couldn't help wondering where and under what circumstances their next meeting would be. For now, they were both elated to be homeward bound.

The flight to Tampa couldn't be fast enough. Frank smiled, thinking of the U.S. Air Force's way of rewarding his prowess in war. They gave Frank the duty station he requested along with a job he was sure to find challenging. He would be a flight instructor, teaching others what he had to learn the hard way. The job would have a certain amount of gratification. After all, he must have done something right. On his chest, he wore the Distinguished Flying Cross. Frank prayed for a patient temperament to pass on valuable lessons he'd learned over North Vietnam.

Finally, Frank heard that familiar rumbling of gear coming down. He was as excited as a newlywed. Then, all at once, he was standing there on the ramp, and there came Ramsay running from the gate.

Frank thought, *This is it, the big moment!* He stood straight up, feeling weak in the knees.

She attacked Frank full force as she jumped into his arms. "I love you, I love you, I love you! Oh, how I missed you, darling."

After smothering him with kisses, Frank finally let her down to appreciate her pretty white dress with blue trim. Through a mist of happy tears, he felt the warmth of her body pressing against his. It was all too beautiful. She reached around his waist and then stood back in surprise.

"Oh, my darling, you're so skinny. What did they feed you over there?"

Frank laughed aloud, absentmindedly saying, "You should see some of the guys we left behind."

Her sudden look of concern made him realize what he said could be taken two ways. Frank didn't intend to suggest the plight of POWs.

Ramsay smiled up at him. Her feeling of empathy poured over him from deep in her heart.

Frank thought, *How rough it must have been for her, waiting and wondering all this time.* He wrapped his arm around her waist, steering them away from the bustling crowd. "Come on, darling," he said. "We've got catching up to do."

Ramsay walked beside Frank with a quick, energetic pace. She seemed so full of life. Frank was positively on air, trying to take in every detail of the moment. They nearly skipped down the concourse, almost missing baggage claim.

When the couple reached the parking lot, Ramsay had a mischievous look in her eyes. Frank could see excitement building there.

She said, "I've got a big surprise for you."

Frank replied, "I don't think it could get any better than the one you've just given me."

She laughed like a school girl. "Oh, yes … it can … You shall see, my dear."

Taking Frank's hand, Ramsay led him to the elevators. When they stepped in, she grabbed him behind the neck and kissed him again.

As they stepped off at their level, Ramsay teased. "I wonder what we'll drive home today."

Frank suspected she was too giddy when she came to a stop behind a brand-new 1972 sky-blue convertible Ford Mustang. She motioned with a flourish, outstretching her hands.

"Ta-daaa! It's our new car, Captain Barrett."

"What?" Frank cried. "How did you …? How could … where did you … how did we get a new car on a teacher's pay?"

Frank froze for a moment. He wondered how she learned he was promoted.

Ramsay stood proudly by the shiny new car, gesturing as if she were a showroom girl presenting it to the world for the first time. Beaming, she cried, "Mom and Dad bought it for the good captain and his wife for doing their duty honorably."

Frank was completely taken aback. The Mustang had everything on it. All the bells and whistles were in order. It was a Boss 302 cubic inch V-8 with wire wheels and black leather upholstery. It was a car any pilot would drool over. Now, here it was.

Frank wondered, *How did she know I was promoted?*

She tossed him the keys. He opened her door with great flourish. Then, with some fanfare, Frank bowed graciously. "Madame, your carriage waits."

Ramsay played along, stepping daintily into the car with her head held high. She said, "Home, Frank, and through the park."

By the time the couple arrived at Ramsay's parents' home, Frank had learned that her father, Mike Davis, retired USAF colonel, had pulled some strings on base. He spoke with the base commander who was genuinely grateful for Frank's safe return. He let them in on Frank's little secret. Frank's assignment was at MacDill AFB with the rank of captain. Ramsay's parents were ecstatic knowing Frank and Ramsay would be making Tampa their new home.

Ramsay's mother, Jena, said, "It's so nice to know you two will be living close."

Frank said, "Ramsay and I have talked it over. We'd like to search for a home off base. As a matter of fact, we'll be looking at some houses just south of the MacDill in the Interbay area of south Tampa."

Mike winced a bit at the thought of them living in the same neighborhood as the king pin of the local mafia. He overtly took it in stride. "I like that area," Mike said. "It has parks and good schools, and the fishing is not bad off Ballast Point Pier. Just be careful. Don't get in over your heads, kids."

Jena scolded, "Oh, Mike, don't try telling them their business. Frank has a good head on his shoulders."

Frank said, "Well, I do have some limits in mind. We'll start out with something of a starter home. That's what we agreed upon. You know, with the money we've been able to save between Ramsay staying with you and my flight pay, we've already saved a good down payment."

"Oh, that's wonderful, Frank," Jena chimed in. "And you won't have to go far to come and visit."

"Yes, Mom, we won't be far away, and you can come and visit, too." Ramsay pointed out.

Mike said, "Now, who's getting in whose business? Anyway, let's go out and get some lunch. I'm starved."

He added, "I'll buy if you give us a ride in that new car of yours."

Frank smiled, saying, "It's a deal, Joe. You pick the place."

Mike replied, "Say, what about that nice little seafood place, Falgies, along South Bay Shore Drive?"

Ramsay loved Falgies with its Italian atmosphere. She didn't know it was owned by the local mafia capo de capo, Santo Bonocante. All Ramsay cared about was the romantic atmosphere with its glorious view across Hillsborough Bay.

A week later, after some exhaustive house hunting in the same area, Ramsay thought she found something of interest in a book of listings laid out on her lap as Frank drove.

"Frank, take South Bay Shore Drive, like we did the other day with my folks."

Ramsay said. "Now, turn left onto Gandy Boulevard and go to MacDill Avenue. The map says go south on MacDill and then turn right on Napoleon Avenue. I want to see the neighborhood there."

"I'm on my way, dear."

As it turned out, Napoleon Avenue was a broad, sidewalk-lined avenue in a well-established neighborhood of older homes. Most of them appeared to have been built in the late forties. As Frank and Ramsay proceeded slowly, Ramsay kept watch out for realty signs. Suddenly, she excitedly grabbed Frank's arm.

"Stop, stop, look there, Frank!"

Frank hit the brakes, thinking he was about to run over someone's pet. "What is it? What's the matter?" he asked.

"That house," she cried. "It's almost exactly like the one we just saw—only it's for sale!"

"All right, all right, get hold of yourself. We'll stop and have a look-see. Just try not to look anxious in front of the sellers, okay?"

She regained her composure, assuming the look of a detached buyer. Under her breath, she murmured to Frank. "See, honey, it even has a little white picket fence in the backyard."

Frank pulled into the drive at 3113 Napoleon Avenue. He could tell by the look on Ramsay's face that it was love at first sight. It was a small blue home with white trim. The two-bedroom, single-story, wood-frame house looked to be in very good shape.

Frank remarked, "I must say, it is a stylish-looking little home. It looks like the owners have kept it up nicely. What you do say we see if anyone's home? If they are, just let me do the talking, okay?"

Ramsay was already opening the car door. Frank just hoped she could curb her enthusiasm. He rang the bell and soon a spritely looking middle-aged woman appeared.

"Hello, we were just driving by and thought we'd like to see your house. Are you showing it today?" Frank asked.

"Yes, we are. Come on in, please."

"We're the Barretts, Frank and Ramsay."

"It's nice to meet you. I'm Lillie Parker. My husband is not home right now, but I can show you around if you like."

Frank and Ramsay followed her in, listening carefully as Lillie told them about the house.

"This home was built in 1949 as part of this subdivision, so most of the homes are about the same age in this neighborhood. Are you living in Tampa right now?"

"Yes," Frank replied. "We're living on the base."

"Oh, that's nice. We're an air force family too. My husband is about to retire soon. That's why we're selling. We're planning on moving to Arizona. We recently painted the entire home, inside and out."

Ramsay said, "It looks beautiful. I like the shade of blue outside."

"Thank you. Down this hallway you'll find the master bedroom and bath."

The Barretts continued their tour of the home, learning it was 1,800 square feet. It had beautiful cherry wood flooring, one and a half baths, and a large screened-in porch on the back of the house. It was supplied with gas heat and upgraded appliances and a remodeled kitchen.

The fenced-in backyard was a plus, because the couple was thinking about buying a dog. All in all, Ramsay was quite taken with the place. Frank could tell she was definitely interested. She kept her word, waiting patiently for her husband to make the first move. Frank told Lillie they would like some time to think it over. Promising to get back, they said their good-byes.

In the car, Ramsay couldn't wait any longer. "Oh, Frank, it's just perfect for us, don't you think?"

Frank agreed, but thought they should come down from $28,000, and he told her so. "Let's go home and talk it over and see if we can agree on an offering price," he said.

Ramsay looked at him so hopefully with those beautiful azure blue eyes that he had to resist saying yes right away. Actually, he was already thinking about how much the bank would loan him. On the way home, Ramsay couldn't stop talking about the little house. The house itself was a mere quarter mile from the secluded villa of the drug-dealing Bonocante.

6

Frank entered their apartment by the back door, stepping over an overturned laundry basket. Not seeing Ramsay, he called out. "Honey, I'm home. I've got good news for you."

Looking around, Frank was a bit frustrated. "Honey, where are you?"

Frank walked through the kitchen and then saw something that made him stop in his tracks. The small living room was completely disheveled. A cold feeling stabbed at his senses.

Frank yelled, "Ramsay, where are you? It looks like you managed to rearrange everything in the living room." He thought, *Oh my God, have we been robbed? Where the hell is she? I hope she's all right!*

Maneuvering around the overturned furniture and possessions lying on the floor, he ran into the cramped bedroom. "Ramsay, are you all right?"

She lay spread eagled on the bed, moving her head from side to side and groaning. Frank quickly sat on the bed by her side and reached out for her shoulders. Turning her over, he felt her listless weight as he did so. "What is it, honey? Are you sick?"

Then, the smell of hard liquor strung his nostrils.

Frank asked, "Ramsay, what have you been doing?"

She mumbled, "Just leave me alone in my tiny, little apartment. I don't have anywhere else to go. Why shouldn't I get drunk?"

"Oh damn, honey, this is no way to be. What's the matter? You can't stand living here on base, can you? That's it, isn't it? C'mon, let's get up. You gotta get up outta this bed. You need a shower."

"Leavph me be, Frank. I don wanna get up. Ish just the same old crappie plach, clean it or not. Wash the diffrence? Ish just the same ol' stinky crap hole. Why? Why should I bother?"

Frank tried to be understanding. He knew she'd have to shower off and sober up before she'd feel any better. He regretted that she'd had to put up with the rundown housing they were provided. As it was, the waiting list for better housing was long with all the personnel coming and going on tours overseas. Vietnam just wasn't enough. Now, there were incursions into Cambodia that had to be attended to by the secret little war planners, who cringed, fearing their dominos were about to fall in Southeast Asia.

The living conditions were taking their toll on Ramsay. She was entirely frustrated and had begun taking it out on herself. Frank managed to get her undressed and into the shower. It seemed as good a time as any to break the good news.

He smiled at her sitting under the shower head with water bouncing off her head on to him.

"Honey, we finally got our loan approved by the bank." He didn't tell her he resorted to asking her father to co-sign on the loan. Otherwise, the bank told him it was just too risky for a pilot and a school teacher in the current military situation. Swallowing his pride was a blow to Frank's overinflated ego, but he did it anyway.

"Washh did you jus say?" Ramsay asked.

Frank spoke clearly in her face. "We got the loan. We can move now, honey."

Ramsay swung her arm up, trying to reach his neck, slurring, "Come down here, baby. Let's celebrate!"

Frank laughed. It felt good, and he needed the comic relief after the day he'd been through and then finding Ramsay in her condition.

The next day, work schedules continued unabated. Only the very young could possess such stamina and fortitude as they demonstrated in the hectic days ahead. Ramsay was so enthused with the reality of their leaving the apartment that she went out and bought a little brown-and-white fox terrier. That night, she introduced Barkley to Frank.

"Won't he be happy in our new fenced-in backyard?" she said.

When all was said, signed, and done, the puppy did take to his backyard right away. When scampering around, he only stopped to mark his territory. In the weeks to come, he would get all excited whenever Frank mowed the backyard. He did not like the sound or smell of the lawn mower. Running circles around it as Frank pushed, he ran so fast his little paws trimmed the grass, too.

For weeks, Frank was immersed in hectic training as he prepared his men for Operation Linebacker II. Amid that intense preparation, Frank was also called upon to attend to domestic responsibilities. While at home on a Saturday, he received a call from Chad.

"Well, hello, old buddy," Frank said. "It's good to hear your voice. Where are you?"

"I'm at home, Frank. I just started my vacation."

Frank's mind raced. *Good Lord, he did say he would start vacationing in August? I wonder if he's coming our way.*

Chad's voice interrupted Frank's thoughts. "You did get my letter, right?"

Frank assured, "Yeah, Chad, we got it."

"Well, I haven't heard from you guys. Is it still okay if we come for a visit?"

"Sure, Chad, I'd like nothing better. My schedule's busier than ever, but I'm sure Ramsay can show you guys around until I get home from the work scene. I'm sure you remember the way the air force works their pilots."

"Hell yes, I do. That's why I went civilian. At least I've got a union watching out for my bacon. On the other hand, the air force treats pilots like citrus fruit. They eat the flesh and throw away the peel."

Defensively, Frank replied, "Well, it's not as bad as all that, Chad. Actually, Ramsay and I are quite happy here. Once you're out of combat, it's a pretty darned good life."

Chad preempted, "That reminds me why I called, old buddy. Peggy and I want to size up the work situation at Tampa International Airport. Pan Am and Eastern Airlines both offer service there. We decided if we like what we see, we might make it our home base. What do you say to that, ol' buddy? Can you put up with us for a couple of days while we check it out?"

Frank's mind drifted back to the time Ramsay and he were at the breakfast table reading Chad's letter about he and his wife Peggy wanting to make a new home in Tampa. He recalled Ramsay saying she was all for it. She looked forward to having new friends in town to share things with.

7

As the main gear scorched the tarmac leaving puffs of pale blue smoke drifting over runway thirty-six, Frank's pulse quickened. Chad and Peggy were down in town. The reunion with Frank's war buddy was happening. Ramsay wore her pretty blue flowered print dress and a white sun hat. She stood anxiously at Frank's side awaiting Peggy and Chad at the gate.

Frank caught sight of Chad and Peggy exiting the 727. They both looked like tourists wearing shorts, polo shirts, and wraparound sunglasses stuck on tops of their heads. Their flight was on time, and Ramsay was excited about meeting Chad and Peggy for the first time.

Frank stepped up to Chad, slapping him on the back and giving him a brief hug. "Chad Grin, you old son of a buck, how the hell are ya these days?"

"I couldn't be finer, ol' buddy." Then he turned, gesturing toward Peggy. "Mr. and Mrs. Barrett, I'd like you to meet my wife, Peggy."

Peggy was a petite little blonde-haired, blue-eyed beauty. It was clear Chad had done well for himself. She stood five foot six, with ample curves in all the right places. Reaching forward, she shook Frank's hand firmly, leaving him with the impression she was fit.

Chad remained his old accommodating self. Frank recalled countless times he went out of his way to be the congenial Southerner he was raised to be.

After they got settled in, the days seemed to pass by quickly. Frank went to work each morning at five o'clock. Later, they went house hunting. As it turned out, they were amazed at how much lower the cost of living was in Florida. Chad was enthusiastic about their prospects in Tampa.

In the meantime, Ramsay couldn't be happier having new friends who shared so much in common. Each evening, Frank would get home about five thirty, and they'd go out to some place different to eat. Chad and Peggy contacted their respective airlines and set the paperwork in motion for their transfers. Best of all, they found that special house they could not live without. That very night, they celebrated.

* * *

Later that evening, not far away, Little Eddy emerged from the misty, shrouded docks of Port Tampa making his way toward the ships moored at dock. Dressed in black, the slight man carried a briefcase. He gingerly stepped over the grimy, uneven brick-paved streets in his $200 Italian goat-skin loafers.

He forced his attention on the dimly lit Panamanian registered ship looming forty feet above. The fully laden *Corrina* undulated slowly against a row of tire bumpers lining the dock as the tide slowly lifted her hull. After off-loading, she would take on a load of phosphate in Tampa's deep, dingy channel behind Peter O. Knight Airport. The next day, the *Corrina* would depart for South America, passing through the Panama Canal on its return to Buenaventura, Columbia.

Presently, her cargo was six hundred metric tons of fertilizer. Eduardo A. Torres was not interested in fertilizer. He was the local mafia's courier. His immediate responsibility was the briefcase he carried. He was there to purchase the latest shipment of pure cocaine concealed in the shipment of fertilizer. Everything about this deal was risky. The captain would deal with him as independently as a hog on ice. Risks were grave in this life.

Little Eddy moved with a heightened sense of awareness, having snorted a line of high-grade Columbian cocaine in his car only moments earlier. Exuding boldness, he strutted up the gangplank. It was business as usual for him. Encountering the first guard aboard, he spoke fluent

Spanish, indicating he was there to see the captain. Perfunctorily, the AK-47-toting guard performed his duty by thoroughly frisking Eddy before allowing him to board.

Eduardo Torres, aka Little Eddy, resented being frisked by the guard, a fellow Panamanian. *Don't they know me by now?* he thought. Proceeding with a sniff, he stepped through the open hatch into a darkened passageway. Although he knew the way, he never liked navigating narrow passageways on shipboard. It always made him feel as though someone waited around each corner, lurking in the shadows, hiding there to strike him over the head and steal his briefcase tightly packed with Benjamins. Eddy's addiction naturally made him a little paranoid.

His line of work was considered inherently dangerous not only because it was illegal, but also because he was a Panamanian illegal alien. Consequently, he spent a lot of time looking over his shoulder. If it weren't for the relative safety of his day job chauffeuring members of the mob, he probably would have been deported by now. Presently, his loyalty to the mafia-operated so-called legitimate shipping company garnered him protection in spite of his immigrant status.

Warily traversing the labyrinth of hatches and stairs and crossing catwalks deep in the bowels of the freighter, Eddy finally reached the captain's cabin. Rapping on the door, he sounded out SOS in Morse code, believing it added a touch of glamour and intrigue to his work. Captain Diaz answered quickly.

"You're late."

Little Eddy shrugged. "Yeah, well, I just got held up."

"Where did you get held up?"

Noting his look of surprise, Eddy said, "No, not I got held up, like stick 'em up—bang, bang. I mean I had stuff to do, all right? Don't get all uptight. I got the money right here. Maybe you'd like to count it, no?"

Captain Diaz allowed a wide grin to form out of his old and cracking lips. He stood five four with a losing boxer's face and frame. No one in his right mind would ever take him for tough. Presently, he raised his eyebrows and smiled tolerantly as if to say, *What do you think?* Just then, a muscular, heavyset crewman entered the low-ceilinged cabin through another door and silently took a seat at a table behind the diminutive captain.

"Put it on the table," the captain directed. "Arturo and I will start counting."

Eddy set the case on the table, producing a key attached to his belt and unlocking it. Raising the lid, he revealed the money. Captain Diaz turned to open a cabinet behind him and removed two counting machines. Arturo took them and set them up on the table. Swiftly dumping the bills on the table, Little Eddy let them begin their counting process. Captain Diaz sat down and began stacking bills into his own machine.

"Do you want some coffee while you wait?" he asked Little Eddy.

"No, I'll just have a smoke." Eddy slipped his solid gold lighter from his vest pocket and lit up, blowing his first puff toward the gently swaying lamp above the table. In due time, $500,000 in fresh, unmarked bills were counted and stacked. Looking pleased, the captain waved Arturo out of the room. He then kneeled before his safe. As Eddy looked on, he cupped his hand over the combination knob as he dialed the numbers. Pulling open the heavy steel door, he transferred the Benjamins into his safe. Just as he finished, Arturo reappeared with a fifty-pound bag labeled, "Fertilizer Product of Buenaventura, Columbia."

Eddy crushed his cigarette out on the floor and stepped forward as Arturo dropped the bag on the table. Now, it was Little Eddy's turn. Pulling a shiny stiletto from his breast pocket, he slit the bag lengthwise. Reaching in and deftly removing eight black kilo blocks of cocaine, he placed them on the table. He then wiped them clean with a rag before placing them in his briefcase.

Another transfer complete; these bricks would soon be delivered to the local mafia. The profit from the sale of these drugs on the streets of Tampa would be deposited into the accounts of Mr. Santo Bonocante.

Little Eddy reattached the chain to his briefcase and saluted. "Hasta luego, Capitán."

"Si está bien y adiós, mis amigo," Díaz muttered under his breath.

Little Eddy made his way back through the darkened ship. Once outside, he hurried to the safety of his car. Glancing at his Rolex, he noted the time was 12:30 a.m. *Time for another snort,* he thought. Sitting behind the wheel of his 1963 gunmetal gray, turbo-charged Studebaker Avanti R-4, he opened a bejeweled pill case. It contained two ounces of pure white blow. Looking both ways, he lowered his right nostril to the silver coke spoon hanging around his neck. Holding his other nostril and eye shut, he snorted pure Columbian. Suddenly, he sat back rigidly as if frozen. Shivering with his head held back, he felt the rush coursing through his entire body. Seconds later, he felt a deep sense of satisfaction rocking his world. With heart racing, he turned over the key and heard the throaty roar of his super-charged Avanti coming to life. Soon his taillights disappeared into the mist-shrouded port.

8

Ramsay and Frank truly enjoyed showing their friends around town. This time it would be their treat. As Frank drove Chad and Peggy along Bay Shore Boulevard, Ramsay pointed out several highlights as the skyline of downtown Tampa came into view. The summer sun had just dipped below the horizon. Across the bay, a long, tree-lined island appeared paralleling their drive.

"That's Davis Island just across the bay, Peggy. That's where a lot of rich people live. Do you remember that TV Western series, *The Rifleman*?"

Peggy replied, "Sure, it stared Chuck Connors."

Ramsay pointed. "Well, that's where he lives—right over there."

Frank cut in. "They have a nice little civil aviation airport at the southern tip of the island. It's called Peter O. Knight Airport."

Chad looked out over the water of the becalmed bay in that general direction.

Frank continued. "Yeah, funny thing is, one of its runways has the same heading as our main runway at MacDill just across the mouth of the bay. The difference is their runway is 3,000 feet, while ours at is 11,500. One foggy night, a Canadian National Guard four-engine bomber tried an instrument landing at Peter O. Knight by mistake."

Chad said, "Whoops."

"They'd already touched down in that soup before realizing their mistake. Both pilot and copilot rode their brakes until they burnt out. Then, they retracted their gear to slow down. In a shower of sparks, they slid down runway three until they ripped through the chain-link barrier fence at the end. When they came to a screeching halt, the nose of the bomber was poking ten feet out over the shipping channel bordering the other side of the airport."

Chad's eyes went wide. "Good Lord, that must have been a harrowing experience."

Frank kept a straight face. "Yes, I'm sure it ruined their whole evening," he said. "Not only that, they had to dismantle the plane and truck it off the island."

Chad said, "That must have cost them a pretty penny."

"It's safe to say it did. They haven't been back since."

Just across the bay behind Peter O. Knight, the *Corrina* slipped along the shipping channel leading out into Hillsboro Bay bound for Buenaventura, South America, with another load of phosphate.

Frank said, "Here we are. This is the restaurant. It's called the Colonnade; it's been here since the thirties. Seafood is their specialty. I think you and Peggy are really gonna like it. The view across the bay is spectacular."

Frank turned in the drive alongside the restaurant and parked his Mustang in the rear.

Ramsay suggested, "I like the grouper sandwich here. You should try it, Peggy; it's delicious."

Frank suggested, "Why don't we take you lovely gals to a movie after dinner? What do you two say to that?"

Ramsay turned to Peggy, confiding in a whisper, "Now we're getting somewhere."

Speaking aloud, she answered, "I think that's a fine idea. What do you think, Peggy?"

"It's got my vote," she replied.

Chad lifted his Coke and took a sip. Suddenly, he stopped. "There's something in my glass. I think it's a cherry."

Fishing it out with a spoon, he discovered it was an olive. "Now that's odd. The bartender must have dropped this in my glass."

Frank corrected him. "Nope, they put an olive in every Coke they serve here. You see, it's sort of a tradition. Back in the fifties, a lot of young folks made the Colonnade parking lot their local hangout. Back then, they had carhops who served customers outside. The story goes; the owner noticed teens sneaking alcohol into their drinks. To show them he was aware of their little subterfuge, he started putting an olive in every Coke, like a martini. It caught on, and they've done it ever since. Some customers even ask for the olive if they find it missing from their drink."

Peggy quipped, "I think I'll ask for an olive in my drink."

The four friends had a wonderful time enjoying the view along with their meal while discussing plans for fixing up the new home Peggy and Chad had just purchased.

On the drive home, they agreed to have a drink at the house. Frank put on some records.

Frank suggested, "You really ought to hear this; it really makes a statement."

The cut was titled, "In My Life." As it played, Peggy and Chad listened attentively. When it came to the instrumental section, Peggy asked, "Is that a harpsichord I hear?"

"Yes," Frank replied. "It makes an interesting effect, don't you think? These guys are so diverse. You never know what they'll take up next."

When the song ended, Peggy spoke wistfully. "That's a beautiful love song. What's the name of that album?"

Frank held the cover up for them to see. "It's titled *Rubber Soul* by the Beatles. I've kept it around since back in high school. It marks a departure from their previous stuff. Don't you think so, Chad?"

"Well, it certainly is more sensitive than 'I Wanna Hold Your Hand.'"

Ramsay was quiet. Frank could tell she was tearing up again.

Frank teased, "Oh, there she goes again. Love songs always make her misty."

Suddenly, she stood up and headed for the kitchen. "Just leave me alone," she said.

Chad rolled his eyes. "Now you've done it, buddy boy."

Frank ignored Chad and quickly followed her into the kitchen. He found her dabbing her eyes with a dish towel. Frank tried apologizing, telling her he didn't mean to make fun of her in front of the others. When she looked up, her eyes told a different story. She wasn't really mad at him at all. He could tell it was something else.

"What's the matter, honey? Was it the song or something that was said?"

She turned around and embraced him, putting her head on his shoulder and sobbing. Now Frank knew for sure that there was a deeper matter.

"What is it, honey?" he pled. "You can talk to me."

She continued sobbing, allowing tears to dampen his shirt, and then she pulled away as she regained her composure. She looked deep into Frank's eyes before blurting out, "Oh, honey, I'm pregnant."

"What?" he cried. "What did you just say?"

She stammered, "I said, I'm pregnant, darling."

Later, Frank learned from the doctor that Ramsay was ten weeks pregnant. Ramsay was told her due date was March 31. Frank told her jokingly that anything but an April Fools' Day baby would be fine with him.

Each passing day of her pregnancy, Ramsay and Frank found new things to talk about. Naming the baby became a favorite pastime. Her father even got into the act, insisting if it were a boy, his middle name must be Franklin, like his grandfather before him. Her mother stayed out of the debate, saying as long as the child was healthy that was all she wished for.

Choosing a proper name was one thing. Making room for the baby was quite another. Frank wanted them to get a bigger house, while Ramsay wanted only to add a room to the back of the house. After

Chad and Peggy put their two cents in, it seemed the only one left without an opinion was their little terrier Barkley.

By the time winter rolled around, Frank was well into his second combat training class, and Ramsay was getting bigger. She was happy and healthy, though, and pleased she wouldn't have to go through her final months of pregnancy in the heat of summer.

Christmas was very special for the couple that year, as they both looked forward to the new arrival. Then, Chad and Peggy brought in the New Year with them.

Chad raised his glass. "I propose a toast to the unborn pilot-to-be and the newborn 1972!"

"Here's to the son of the year," Frank said.

With that, the four friends all turned up their champagne glasses and then sang "Auld Lang Syne." After Chad and Peggy left, Ramsay and Frank turned in around two o'clock in the morning. Ramsay lay there in bed almost asleep.

She asked, "Do you really have your heart set on a boy?"

"I never said that. I just want a healthy baby, just like your mom does," Frank answered.

"Okay, Frank," she whispered softly. Her voice trailed off as she drifted into sleep. "Just wondered, that's all."

9

Ramsay was now in her eighth month of pregnancy. She'd be leaving work soon to be a stay-at-home mom. Her English classes chipped in to buy her a set of English classics, *Chaucer to Churchill*. It was a very special day for her. After opening her gift, she addressed them in the auditorium.

"My students, my dear students, you are an inspiration. I shall never forget this day as long as I live. You make a teacher proud, and I love you all for it. I've read that knowledge is power; if you are so inclined, use that power to write a poem about what's inspiring you right now. I know I feel I could write reams of poems about you all. I'm grateful for your vibrancy—every one of you. I'm looking forward to seeing you all graduate. Good-bye, good luck, and God bless you."

Tucking the card with her students' signatures in her book, she pressed back tears of joy as she left the stage. It was February 6, 1972.

* * *

Santo Bonocante and his henchmen waited for their chauffer, Little Eddy, to bring their limo to the parking garage beneath the office building they had just exited. In the privacy of their underground guarded garage, it was cold.

They looked forward to arriving at Licata's Restaurant. They knew its atmosphere would be warm and exclusively inviting, filled with the aroma of savory garlic-flavored steaks. Licata's was famous for its premier steaks. Founded by Victor Licata in the thirties, it became the unofficial headquarters for the Tampa mafia. If anyone of note wanted something fixed, Licata's was the place where plans were laid. The high-backed booths and dedicated servers assured privacy in every respect. When they met at Licata's, whatever transpired remained within its walls, including some recalcitrant customers it was rumored. If a cover-up was necessary, it was conceptualized in this establishment. Never mind there was great Italian steak, in the main it served as a convenient and secure place for Santo Bonocante to confer. He remained secure in the fact that Licata's employees were tasked with security. If it meant searching every booth at night for wires, it was taken care of.

Santo spoke. "Okay, now we can talk right here where nothing ever happens, right, gentlemen?"

Three of Bonocante's capos nodded from across the booth as the tall, swarthy capo de capo spoke. Nobody tapped Licata's. Santo referred to the place as his culinary inner sanctum. Santo preferred to sit by himself, making the other large toughs stuff themselves into their places.

Santo said, "First, I want you all to understand your responsibilities. You gotta watch these collections closer. There's been some skimming goin' on, and it's not gonna be pretty when it all shakes out."

The middle-aged Santo enjoyed the finer things in life, and it showed. Sometimes he enjoyed fine things that weren't always his. This was especially so with women, but he never tolerated anyone caught on the take. The nervous looks all around were reason enough for him to suspect, yet Little Eddy had already informed on the man before him who was guilty. Now, Little Eddy stood straight up like a marionette facing the table beside Santo. His eyes did not betray that man; he only stared coldly into the darkness surrounding him.

The candle in front of the three capos wavered as the man in the middle spoke. "Capo of all, you know I always give a good count to Little Eddy. Have I ever held back, Little Eddy?"

Little Eddy maintained his cold, emotionless stare, not responding to the question. The man on his left spoke out. "I don't think he's gonna answer you tonight."

The man on his far left looked up at Santo. His eyes danced back and forth in his head. His right hand moved instinctively over his left, which was trembling on the table. It was time to move on. Santo cocked his head and stared at the man directly across from him and nodded. The other man's eyes ceased to dance when Santo suddenly snatched his napkin off his lap and quickly tossed it over the man's hands. His eyes grew wide in shock. There was no time to jerk his hands away before Little Eddy's stiletto whooshed down, swiftly pinning them both to the table. The dark red napkin revealed a darker spot growing larger by the second. Santo leaned forward and addressed the stricken man in a low, guttural tone.

"*Mine! Bastardo, mine*! Never take what is mine!" His chocolate eyes darted from one capo to the other seated before him. When he smiled, which was rare, the scar etching the right side of his face from the top of his nose to the corner of his mouth stretched. It was a scarlet reminder left by his father for straying from the Catholic faith *once*.

"Little Eddy, show Oscar to the back door," Santo directed.

"Sure, boss. I understand."

Before the other two men could compose themselves, Santo spoke to the man directly in front of him.

"Tony Scaglione, I want you in charge of the north side now. Your headquarters will be Char Pal's Liquor near Busch Gardens. Be careful with distribution and collections, right?"

"Right, boss. I got it," he said shakily.

Santo said, "All you need to do is make sure you got a good count on the stuff when Little Eddy comes by, right? Joe Cangelosi, you hear what I just said?"

"Absolutely, boss. I heard you."

"Then, it's the same with you. Got it?"

Both capos nodded in agreement as Little Eddy shoved his charge out the back door.

"Be sure you guys have the money counted and ready to make the exchange real smooth like when Little Eddy comes back, okay?"

Again, the capos nodded in agreement. Then, Santo sat back in the booth and produced a Cuban Monte Cristo from his Burberry coat's pocket. Leaning forward, he allowed Tony to light it up. Sitting back puffing, he blew smoke upward toward the Tiffany glass lamp hanging above their booth, creating a pall over the Mafioso before him.

"All right now, gentlemen, that's it. Let's have some wine."

* * *

Frank scurried about the house searching for car keys as Ramsay snatched her favorite pillow off the sofa along with her purse and headed for the car. He continued rummaging hopelessly for the only means of their timely departure. Packed bags waited with the car in this well-choreographed departure scene. Now, the last part was up to Frank.

Keep it together, Frank, He told himself. *It's not difficult. The keys are obviously lying on a flat surface somewhere, while she's in labor. Now, logically, where can they be?*

His eyes traced nervously across to the mahogany nesting tables near his easy chair where he cleverly placed them the night before in case of emergency.

Yes! he cried. *And there they are!*

Snatching them up with due dispatch, Frank followed his waddling wife out the door before racing ahead with his prize in hand to unlock the car.

The next few seconds suddenly became a hellish nightmare. Neither one of them remembered exactly how it happened, but Barkley shot out the front door and raced into the street. Ramsay waddled instinctively after, trying to capture him. Frank was now in the car starting the engine. As he looked through the windshield in disbelief, he watched as his wife stooped in the wet street to pick up Barkley. He remembered thinking, *It's raining. She has no business doing such a thing in her condition.* Then, it happened in a heartbeat, right before Frank's eyes.

As if in a dream, he sat in horrific shock viewing the scene framed by his windshield. His legs trembled as he struggled to climb from behind the wheel. He wanted to run, but his brain would not send the message. In shock, Frank's brain would not accept what just happened. First, his wife and dog were in the air, and then, a gray car flashed past. Next, Frank witnessed Ramsay's broken body lying in a heap on the wet brick pavement in front of him. He thought, *Dear God, pregnant Ramsay is lying near Barkley in the wet street!*

I gotta get these damn cops off my ass! Little Eddy thought to himself as he rushed down MacDill Avenue trying to escape, after running a stop sign. In his coked-up mind, it seemed the right thing to do. In his paranoid state, he schemed. His plan was to ditch his briefcase full of coke. He thought, *If I can just get out of their sight long enough, I'll sling it in some bushes and then pull over.*

His Avanti careened around the corner onto Napoleon Street. He suddenly realized his mistake. *Oh, hell. This is a straight street! If I can just toss this bitch before they make the turn, I'll be in the clear!*

In his cocaine-clouded, panic-stricken mind, he floored it, hell-bent on out distancing his pursuers in his super-charged R-4 Avanti. As the siren wailed behind, he had blocks to go before reaching a clump of bushes. Two seconds later he slung the briefcase into the bushes and then slowed his car and submitted to his arrest.

Little Eddy knew full well there were judges bought by the mafia to rule over such cases. He was confident he'd make bail by dinnertime. Now that the briefcase was gone there was little else to fear, yet his heart was still racing at the thought of what had just happened.

What was that loud *thumping noise on Napoleon Avenue? Could it have been that stray dog in the street? Who knows,* he thought. In his mind, he couldn't process the rapid succession of events as they forced their way back into his conscious mind. With red lights flashing near him, try as he might, he couldn't remember what had just taken place. It was a strange sensation as if something serious happened, but he couldn't put it together in his coke-ravaged brain.

Rain was spattering on his windshield and mixing with blood when he finally rolled to a stop.

What was the plan? Is that blood?

He put his head down on the wheel searching his coke-numbed mind over again. Now, slowly, it trickled back. In his escape, he drove the overpowered Avanti into something he thought was a dog.

Waiting and watching in his rearview mirror, he saw the red lights, and then another image rushed into his mind. It was a woman in the street with a dog in her arms; she was staring saucer-eyed at him through his windshield. He put his head on the wheel again with arms draped over it.

What the hell was she doing there? Why are they pulling me so hard?

The wet brick pavement made a sled out of his skidding Avanti. When the wheels locked at sixty miles per hour, he drove the woman and dog she was holding straight up and over the streamlined Studebaker.

10

Tears can never wash away pain. Frank knew that. But as much as he wanted to wash away the damage to Ramsay's racked and battered body, it remained. It seemed heartache, pain, and sorrow would always be Frank's constant companions.

The traumatic event of seeing his wife being struck could only be relived in short bursts of memory. Images his mind allowed the subconscious to release would come slowly when he was ready. He recalled his neighbor running from her home to the scene. She'd heard tires squealing on wet pavement, and then, the dull thud.

How could anyone say it wasn't hit-and-run? How can you mend a broken wife? When the police cruiser returned to the scene, there was another eyewitness in the back. Frank's neighbor testified as to what she heard and knew Frank must have seen. By then, Frank and his wife had left in the ambulance.

Unfortunately, the police never found the briefcase. Frank was concerned with Ramsay's condition and gave no thought to the driver's situation. Ramsay's injuries were starkly apparent. They masked the damage done to Frank's unborn son. Unconscious, for the time being, she was shielded by nature from her blunt trauma.

Later, they told Frank he had carried her in his arms, her femur protruding from her right thigh. Frank told himself he must wait for the ambulance. He retrieved a blanket from the trunk and tried to stop blood pulsing from the deep gash in her thigh. Pressing hard against her most obvious wound, Frank stared into space as he sat on the curb in the rain with Ramsay's head cradled in his arms. The reddening contusions were banding-up across her torso where the bumper struck. Elevating her head slightly, he looked into her blue eyes, which were infused with blood. His gaze fell upon little Barkley's lifeless body lying nearby. His tongue protruded through clenched teeth, eyes wide and glazed in a dead dog stare.

He thought, *Good-bye, little friend. At least you didn't have to suffer.*

When the ambulance arrived, one attendant quickly started bandaging Ramsay's thigh and then placed an air split around it while the EMT started an IV. When he finished, they gingerly slid her onto a spine board and then gently lifted her on to a gurney. Intently, they focused on stabilizing her wounds. The two attendants paid little attention to Frank as he looked on in helpless silent shock.

Finally, the EMT looked directly at Frank. "We're ready to transport. Do you want to ride in back?"

He nodded numbly, climbing in the van in a trance-like state, sitting beside her and watching her taciturn face covered by an oxygen mask. The rest of her body lay draped in sheets. Her blood was slowly seeping through them. There was nothing he could do except for hold her limp hand as they rocked to and fro racing to the hospital.

Looking back, it was worse than a nightmare. It became one huge, confusing dream that lengthened as memories faded in to consciousness. At first, Frank didn't recall entering the emergency room or speaking to doctors there. But, he *could* remember being forcibly separated from her side as the doctors fought to save her. Hours later, another doctor pushed through the doors of the waiting room, giving Frank a grave look. His scrubs were besmirched in blood.

"Captain Barrett, I'm so sorry. We couldn't save your son." The doctor paused a moment, allowing the devastation to settle in Frank's brain before he proceeded. "Your wife is still in critical condition, yet her vitals are slowly beginning to stabilize. There was massive internal bleeding from the spleen, pancreas, and upper intestine, but we have her on a heart pump, and the bleeding is under control now. You'll be able to see her in intensive care tomorrow. Right now, she's unconscious, so she won't know you're there even if you did visit her. I suggest you go home and get some rest."

Frank asked, "What are her chances of recovery, Doctor?"

"Now, I'd say they're about fifty-fifty. Until we get more results from her blood work, we really can't say for sure. There is a high risk of infection, because the wounds she received from the impact were contaminated. We'll be checking her vitals around the clock until she stabilizes. Right now, my prognosis is time will tell."

Frank didn't remember thanking the doctor for his efforts. He was too numb from the shock of losing the son he never saw—a son cheated from drawing a breath, denied a chance to see, walk, love, experience, or even exist. The heartache that came much later was almost unbearable. If he had lost Ramsay, then he would have done something rash right then and there.

For the next three months, Frank doted on Ramsay, spending hours at her side and committing his prayers to her survival and full recovery. He was, of course, dreaming and praying for a miracle. Somewhere inside he sensed there was little possibility of a complete recovery. As if God wanted to finalize that notion, Frank heard from her doctor.

"I'm truly sorry, but your wife fell into a coma this afternoon just after surgery."

Ramsay remained in a coma for three months.

Then, one morning Frank entered her room just after dawn. Sunlight filtered through the shaded window facing east where a more fortunate patient might be afforded a view. Frank detected a slight movement of Ramsay's hand. He really thought for an instant he had just seen her right hand move.

Frank thought, *Was that just my imagination?*

Generally, he always trusted his eyesight; it always served him well in a tight spot. Good eyesight in his profession was crucial. There it was again—movement. Nearly imperceptible, nevertheless, it *was* there. He bolted from the room and ran up the hall to the nurse's station.

This was the first movement he'd seen of any kind emanating from the rhythmically heaving mass of tubes and hoses slaving in symbiosis with his wife.

Frank shouted, "Come quick, nurse. There's movement!"

The ICU nurse on duty rose from her chair with a cloud of doubt troubling her face. She'd seen hundreds of false alarms in her time. Then, upon seeing Frank's total expression of joy, she exclaimed, "That's incredible!"

She spun on her heel, trotting from her station. Reaching the threshold of Ramsay's room, she watched and waited. In a moment, she saw for herself.

"Yes, her right hand is really moving along the edge of her bed alongside the metal railing."

Frank told himself, *She's sensing the cold metal bed railing restraining her.* He dared dream. *Maybe she wants to get up?*

The nurse phoned immediately, alerting the doctor's ready room. She insisted, "Yes, now. I don't care if he is asleep. Tell him I need him up here right away. Do you hear?"

Hanging up, she shot Frank a look of assurance. "Dr. Addison is the specialist on duty tonight. He'll be right up. I know he'll do the right thing."

Frank's mind buzzed. *The right thing? What the hell is the right thing? It's been months of comatose existence for her and misery for me. Now what the hell will be the right thing?* As he waited, Frank's mind drifted back to a place in time when he certainly witnessed the *wrong* thing. In a court of law, it's called a travesty. To him, it was yet another night-mare. It happened when he was in court to see the illegal Panamanian recruit of the local mafia appear before a judge on charges of vehicular manslaughter, assault with a deadly weapon, aggravated assault, hit-and-run, attempted evasion of arrest, driving under the influence of cocaine, and failure to observe a control device.

He was arraigned in a stupor and spent one hour in jail before his attorney posted bail. For his trial, he was provided with the best defense attorneys money could buy. They would work for the mafia as defense representatives for Eduardo A. Torres, making their client appear as if he were the finest piece of work ever to hail from Panama.

Strings were pulled, and the powers that be set plans in motion to free the little bastard. Someone might ask, in the name of humanity and justice, why? In a word, Frank already knew.

In the interim between Little Eddy's arrest and trial, Frank befriended Detective Sergeant Chalmers of the Tampa Police Department. He was assigned to Eduardo A. Torres's case. He confided that he had his doubts from the outset that Little Eddy would ever be convicted of any crimes simply because of his nationality. He was also aware of his relationship as an employee of Santo Bonocante as his personal chauffer.

He told Frank that Little Eddy was an *embarrassment,* a boil on the nose of the mafia's entire organization. He could not be tolerated or entrusted to custody. In that environment, who knew what he might divulge about certain people connected to their operations. Hence, it was a foregone conclusion since they received word of his arrest. Now it was a mere formality.

Of course, the justice system in Tampa would be expected to do its part. That's where Judge Harry Lee Cowen entered the scheme of things. He was just another official who remained resolutely tucked in the back pocket of the local mafia. He had been on the take for the past twenty years. Now, he was looking forward to a comfortable retirement after presiding over one last case.

Frank suffered the indignity of witnessing the results of the political chicanery and bribery that took place in and out of the courtroom, allowing the outright miscarriage of justice that was Little Eddy's so-called day in court. Exactly three months and five days after the hit-and-run, Frank was there to see justice done.

Instead, he sat astonished as Judge Cowen handed down the heart-rending verdict. "I find Eduardo Alfonso Torres guilty of being an illegal alien residing in the United States of America. As such, he is not subject to any federal or Florida statutes. Instead, he is subject to the jurisdiction of the Immigration and Naturalization Service. Thus, he will be remanded into their custody immediately with the recommendation that he be deported to his native country as soon as possible."

Frank's mind was reeling at the sham of the devastating decision just rendered for Little Eddy. Free to go, he strutted down the isle of the courtroom like a banty rooster. Halting his bailiff alongside Frank, he boldly lit up a cigarette and clicked his solid gold lighter shut with a snap. He cocked his head to one side, giving Frank a quizzical look before he smiled his wide, gold-toothed grin.

"Señor, I have many friends in the fertilizer business. Perhaps when it comes time to plant your withered wife, we could be of service."

The bailiff tried hustling him away, but Frank muscled past him, grasping Eddy's throat with both hands. He throttled the shrieking little drug dealer as the judge stridently banged away on his gavel shouting.

"Order, order! I'll have order in this courtroom! Bailiff, arrest that man attacking the defendant. He's in contempt of court. Arrest him immediately!"

As he choked on Little Eddy, Frank could hear the Judge's *order*, which enraged him even more. At that point, order in the court was irrelevant. Instead, injustice was served with Frank being held for contempt of court. He remained incarcerated until he was deemed safe to be a motorist and citizen again. Three days later, when Frank left his cell, he was both bitter and disillusioned.

Ramsay's doctor did do the right thing, which entailed more months of painfully slow progress in physical therapy. At first, there were moments of glimmering hope punctuated by bouts of marginal blood pressure and then relapse and plenty of despair for everyone. Then, incredibly, Ramsay finally reached a point where she could barely write. It was with steadfast effort that she made a pencil move communicating her thoughts. To Frank, this was a triumph! He could almost envision her coming home one day. Hopes kept him falling forward.

Then, one evening when Frank arrived at the hospital, Terry, the R.N., was on duty. She was the red-haired little firebrand that stayed by Ramsay's side as she came back out of her coma. The look on her face that day spoke volumes. Frank could tell she had been crying. Her eyes were red-rimmed and puffy. Nurses on the floor had come to know Ramsay. They cared deeply, not only because of her condition, but also because of her spirit.

Terry said, "Ramsay's trying to communicate. I've done all I can to make that possible."

Frank turned toward her room, squeezing the rose stems tightly and feeling their thorns enter his flesh. As he crossed the threshold, he swallowed his fear. Terry was right behind.

She offered, "I clipped a yellow writing pad on an open chart by her arm so she can reach it with her hand. I think that works for her."

That same hand was atrophied and gnarled from months of disuse. Terry made it possible for Ramsay to extend her tube-laden arm and grasp the pencil with some deliberation. Just holding a pencil was a feat some doctors previously thought impossible. Now, with seemingly tireless, lucid effort, she appeared determined to make her thoughts known without interruption. Frank knew she never gave up on anything in her whole life.

> *My Darling Frank,*
>
> *Tomorrow I most likely will be gone. Last night I had a visitor. It wasn't bad. Didn't realize we were given notice. Maybe my case is special. I'm sad I'll not see you again in this world, but I know there is another. You'll see. When you do, we'll be together again, you, Frank Junior, and me ... how happy. When I look into memories of our life, I find beauty ... moments that never leave. Love from my heart. I implore, my beloved, think on happy times, promise me ... do not cry, promise me. We will all meet again when the time is right.*

Frank looked up at Ramsay for some assurance. She wore an odd look of mixed emotion on her face. She seemed worried for him, yet somehow at peace. It seemed contradictory, but it was clear as day.

Frank swallowed hard and kept reading.

> *My beloved darling, you must stay behind. Remain a person of value. Make moments count, promise me that, please promise. Future is in your hands. Bye, my love. I kiss you tender last time.*
>
> *Love, Ramsay*

When Frank finished reading, his knees buckled. He found himself kneeling besides her, whispering over and over, "I promise, I promise."

Terry rushed forward, trying to help Frank up, but he froze, unwilling to move. Stricken with grief, tears welled up, but he dared not let Ramsay hear him cry. So, he buried his head in his arm to stifle his sobs.

He couldn't fathom how little five four Terry did it, but she lifted him up off the floor under his arms and then dragged him across the room. Just outside, she plunked him down in a chair and spoke sternly in his face. "Captain Barrett, I read that letter, too. Is this what she asked for? Well, is it, captain?"

He shook his head dumbly.

"Well then, get hold of yourself. Buck up and get back in there and give that lady what she truly deserves. Am I making myself clear?"

Wiping tears away with his sleeve, he did as she said. He nodded affirmatively, attempting a smile to show gratitude for her strength. Taking a couple of deep breaths, he raised up and headed back into the room. As he did, Terry collapsed in the chair behind him.

On Ramsay's yellow pad, Frank found more words: "It's about time. I never figured you to be a quitter."

The back of his throat ached as he tried mustering an answer. She stopped him, shaking her head ever so slightly. Her eyes were sparkling like they used to as she forced a crooked smile. Then she began to write again. It took her quite awhile.

"I want you go Falgies. Look across bay for me, okay? Then come back. I'll be waiting for you."

Frank shook his head, no not wanting to leave, but she shook hers back.

"Dammit," Frank cried. "I don't want you to wait for me. I want you here with me—now."

Her reply was clear. No. She gave him a wan smile and motioned to the paper with her fingers. He wanted to refuse, to protest. *Screw this,* he thought. *It's not real. She was just scarred by some silly dream. She's hallucinating from the meds.*

He took her hand. "You'll be fine, you'll see." But his words rang hollow. Her fingers twitched in his hand. She focused on her letter..

"Please don't cry for the sake of our love. Live life to the fullest; don't waste it on empty tears and regret."

Frank felt that was easy for her to say. He was the one being left behind. She was leaving, while he would be stuck there all alone.

Now, Little Eddy was taking everything from Frank. The thought of his leering gold-toothed face burned in his mind. Shaking his head, he then bent down and kissed her cheek once again.

"Good-bye for now, my sweet," he said.

He stepped reluctantly into the hall where Terry was waiting. He turned to her with a contorted look on his face. "You're not going to believe this, but she's requesting I go to a seafood restaurant we used to frequent."

Terry replied in earnest, "Then do it. I get lots of crazy requests around here. If it makes her happy and you can do it, then so be it."

Frank departed on his mission. While he was gone, Terry kept *her* promise to Ramsay. When he returned, he found she had put on makeup and had done Ramsay's hair. She even folded her hands just so over her withered waist and then turned down the lights and lit some candles. Ramsay did look peaceful lying there in the flickering candlelight, but she was gone. Frank didn't cry. Seeing her there in repose for the last time, he remembered, *A promise is a promise.*

11

The next few days following Ramsay's death were a complete blur for Frank. He barely remembered her funeral service, except for the burial. Chad gave the eulogy. Afterward, he nearly fell into her open grave while carrying the casket as one of the pall bearers behind stepped too far forward. There was a brief stir among the crowd, creating a dim memory for him.

From that day on, his existence fused with an all-consuming passion for revenge that haunted his very soul. There was such a void in his life that he allowed the quest for vengeance to enter his being until it burned his very bones, blocking any passage of forgiveness that might dare take its place. He did not fathom the wisdom he might have found in the words of the ancient philosopher Confucius: "Before embarking upon the path of revenge, first dig *two* graves."

He was on that path. Frank found himself sitting in his living room staring at pictures of him and Ramsay in all their favorite places. He shunned the thought of taking out their 8 mm projector (a wedding gift from Mike and Jena) and running home movies for fear in his drunken state he would hear her happy voice. He even refused himself the opportunity of calling her parents. Instead, he called Chad, because he had something horrid on his mind.

"Frank, how the hell are you? Have you decided to go back to work yet?" Chad questioned.

"No, my commander gave me thirty days bereavement leave."

"Well, that makes good sense. What are you doing with that time? Something constructive, I hope."

Frank replied, "Could we meet somewhere today?" It was Saturday, and Frank had called because he knew Chad would not be working.

Chad had bragged earlier, "I managed to land a regularly scheduled route with Pan Am. My flight runs out of Tampa and then round-trip from Miami to Panama with a final stop-over back in Tampa, giving me the weekend off."

Frank remembered commenting. "Nice work, if you can get it."

Chad replied, "Sure, I could meet you over at Lois's Drug Store for coffee if you like. Unless you wanna go and get fancy on me?"

"No, Lois's is fine," Frank agreed. "How about ten o'clock?"

"Yeah, that's fine. Is this just me, or should I bring Peggy along?"

Frank deliberately sounded casual. "How's about making it just us guys on a Saturday morning, okay?"

"All right, sure. I'll see you there, ol' buddy."

Frank hung up. *Lately, everyone is watching me like mother hens,* he thought. *It's like I'm some ticking time bomb. I remember Trudy's undue concern as she watched me from across the yard as I took out the trash. She's even studied my consumption since the funeral. Coming to my doorstep under the pretense of retrieving her casserole dish—ha—I know what she's up to. She wants to view the contents of my refrigerator. I presumed she was looking to see if I was eating enough. Maybe I was being a little paranoid, but damned if I didn't see the mailman watching, just waiting for me to snap.*

When Chad arrived Saturday morning, Frank was outside waiting in the carport.

"Well, good morning, fella," Chad said. "Looks like you've been outside waiting."

Frank said he'd just been getting the paper as he jumped into Chad's convertible Corvair. He thought, *It's funny, he didn't look suspicious that there was no paper in my hand.*

They drove along for a while, and then Frank started talking about cars. "How do you like this rear-engine setup? Does she handle better with the weight being centered? What size engine do you have in this model anyway? I didn't see any markings..."

Chad quit the humdrum mediocrity. "*Frank*, excuse me, but I'm going to have to call BS on you. What's this coffee clutch really all about?"

Frank turned to face him. Chad was the one man he must come clean with right away. They'd been through too damned much in Vietnam to lie to him now.

He blurted, "Okay, this is it, Chad. I have a plan."

Immediately, Chad replied, "Oh hell, I was afraid of that. This isn't like the touch-and-go on that North Vietnamese Air Base, is it?"

Frank assured him. "No, it's nothing that hairy, at least not for you."

Chad heaved a visible sigh of relief, no doubt recalling what Frank was truly capable of.

Frank stated he would need a Pan Am flight engineer's uniform and a flight to Panama City, Panama. Chad sat in stunned silence for long moment, looking as if he could figure this one, and then turned in desperation. "How soon will you need this?"

Frank replied nonchalantly, "Oh, you know, as soon as possible."

Chad sat in silence, keeping his eyes on the road. In Frank's mind, things were going splendidly. With Chad, it was another matter. Frank took the time to explain. His plan was to enter the country as a Pan Am flight engineer. Then, dressed as a local, he would find Eduardo A. Torres at the Bonocante shipyards in Panama City. He had gleaned a tip from Det. Joe Chalmers that he worked there.

Chad remained speechless as he parked his car in front of Lois's Drug Store. Frank could see he wasn't about to go in until he got more answers, so he reluctantly obliged.

"Chad, it's this way," Frank began, "either you help me or you don't, but I think you know what I'm all about."

"Oh, sure. I think I got that part pretty well figured. The part that bothers me is my being an accomplice to a plot where you pose in my uniform. You're talking about jeopardizing a flight engineer's career here, buddy—perhaps his whole life."

Frank shot back coldly. "The bastard who took my family needs killing. Are you in or out? What would Peggy say if she knew what I'm about to do?"

There was dead silence between them again as his words sunk in. Chad turned away, biting his knuckle, and then spoke toward the window in a slow, deliberate tone. "You think you got me by the short and curlies 'cause Peggy loved Ramsay that much?"

Frank shrugged. "It's like that, isn't it, brother?"

"Well, just let me tell you somethin', mister. We both miss her. We miss her a lot, dammit, but taking someone's life won't bring her back. Will it?"

Frank conceded. "To me, it seems like a start."

"Frank, you've got to start seeing things clearly. You're just too close to it," Chad said. "You're blinded by your own pain and anger. I can see that from here. Now, if you don't find a better way to deal, it's gonna eat you inside out. By then, you may find you have no friends left. Now, you know what's on in my mind. As soon as you told me that man needs killing … hell, I know that about him and about another hundred thousand other pushers in this country. Sure, I know the tune, 'God Damn the Pusher Man,' but, Frank, you're an officer and a gentleman. You took an oath, remember? Duty, honor, country—have you forgotten all that?"

Frank defended himself. "I'm on leave."

Chad remonstrated, "Yeah, so does that mean you can just drop all responsibility and take leave of your senses? Maybe I'm chock full of Uncle Sam's blueberry muffins here, so correct me anytime where I'm wrong."

Frank could see Chad revving up like he always did whenever he knew a cause was just. He was just getting started.

"You want an honest, hard-working engineer to lay his job on the line so you can fly to Panama in search of a coke dealer who killed your wife and unborn child?"

Frank fixed his eyes upon him in earnest as never before, speaking coldly. "Roger that. Now, let's go inside. I'll give you the details."

As they sat in Lois's Drug Store, Chad brooded over his mug of coffee, while Frank detailed his plan. Frank could see the look of true amazement on Chad's face as he acquainted him with the intricacy of detail he had put into it, right down to the shipping schedules. He already knew his quarry would be in the right place at the right time. Thanks to Detective Sergeant Chalmers, he had all the information he needed. Fortunately, he unwittingly helped after posting bail for Frank's contempt charge. The detective had commiserated with Frank over coffee, providing him with information about Bonocante's operation in Panama and his hunch about Little Eddy's next stop. It was enough to inform Frank where Bonocante would most likely place Little Eddy after his debacle in Tampa until things cooled off.

Speaking quietly, Frank laid out the rest of his plan after ordering a couple of burgers. "I just need to pose as a nonflight status engineer on a weekend flight to Panama. The least you can do is get me a uniform, can't you? We *are* about the same size, right?"

"Well, yeah, I guess so. But what am I supposed to say?" Chad asked.

"Listen, it's easy. I'm just the new guy on the route, okay? I'm flying down to look over the operation there before I take on my new duties as flight engineer on one of the regularly scheduled runs between Miami and Panama; it happens all the time, right? I checked.... Am I right?"

Chad appeared uneasy but reluctantly admitted, "Sure, I guess you're right. It does."

"Well then, it should be no sweat. I'll just sit in the back minding my business until we arrive. Then, I'll tip my hat to the stew and deplane, never to be heard from again."

Chad said, "Sounds clean enough—perhaps too clean. Is that the way you figure to clear customs upon arrival?"

"You got it, buddy boy."

"Oh, I got it all right. I'm afraid I got a snoot full. In fact, I don't want to hear any more about what you're gonna do while you're there either, if you get *my* drift."

"Just leave that to me. You can trust in one thing. Justice will be done. You can count it."

Chad looked up from his cup with a thoughtful look. "That, my friend, is just what I'm afraid of. It seems to me there's something I read ... now, how did that go? Oh yeah, 'Vengeance is mine saith the Lord.'" Raising his eyebrows, Chad looked exasperated. "Heaven help us all, Frank."

12

On time and in spite of his reservations, Chad came through. The uniform was starched when he arrived on Frank's doorstep holding a flight engineer's ID badge.

Frank was completely blown away. "Chad, you're a jewel. How can I ever repay?"

"Just come back alive. And one more thing … when you arrive in Panama City, be sure you go through the line with the rest of the flight crew. They don't usually ask to see your passport; just the ID should be enough."

Frank was greatly relieved to hear that last bit of information, as he had no passport.

"Just look in on my place every couple of days 'til I call. Okay, Chad? You'll see my car in the drive. That way, you'll know I'm still gone."

Chad just spun on his heel at Frank's doorstep, waving in the air. "Adios, mis amigo, y via con Dios," he said.

Chad did not want to see Frank's face, possibly for the last time. The men both knew very well people who get themselves in deep trouble with the Omar Torrijos regime were usually never seen or heard from again.

Frank walked back into the house, contemplating what he had gone over a hundred times. Now, he recited in shorthand in his mind as he dressed before the mirror in his bedroom. Everything he did next would depend upon his observations of Little Eddy. To reduce unnecessary contact in country, he would already have the name and address of a reliable knife dealer in the city before leaving his home. Naturally, all his transactions would be in cash. It helped that the medium of exchange in Panama was also the US dollar; that simplified matters.

Language wasn't much of a barrier either. Frank spoke broken Spanish, and most educated Panamanians spoke a little English due to the long-term US presence in their country. Although his direct means of opportunity and execution were unclear at present, there was no doubt about his motive.

As he stood straight and looked in the mirror, he cinched the belt a little tighter. *Married life must agree with Chad,* Frank thought. *He's put on a few pounds. Back in Thailand, we used to wear garments interchangeably as the houseboys continually mixed up our laundry. Back then, it really didn't matter because we were both the same waist size.*

Frank shrugged his shoulders and stepped back to gaze at the handsome Pan Am flight engineer looking back. At least his appearance prepared him for his mission of vindication.

The next day's weather was predicted to be hot and dry. Frank awoke to a sunrise that resembled a dusky red fireball implanted on the horizon. This was the first day of his journey. Soon the day cooked into a typical sweltering late spring day in Tampa.

It was June 19, three weeks since Frank had laid Ramsay to rest. Her new granite marker stood by the smaller one of his unseen son's grave in Woodland Memorial Cemetery in South Tampa.

At the funeral, Ramsay's father told Frank he would look in on him occasionally, knowing he would have too much time on his hands during his furlough. So far, Frank had managed to stave him off, saying he would be with a buddy of his in Colorado in order to get away from the scene for a while. Frank told him they would be hiking and camping in a remote area where they could not be reached easily, so they need not worry.

Frank also knew Mike and Jena were preoccupied with Ramsay's civil wrongful death suit. Frank figured he and Jena would be sufficiently distracted to the point where they wouldn't be overly concerned with his whereabouts. With all they'd been put through, they deserved compensation for their grievous loss. At least that was Frank's understanding of wrongful death suits. After all, Little Eddy was in the employ of Bonocante at the time of the crime and serving as his courier/chauffer.

If justice were done, it might assuage their pain in some small way. Deep inside, that's what Frank hoped. He knew, of course, they'd never find closure out of such a senseless, horrendous tragedy. Secretly, he hoped they could drain the coffers of Bonocante mercilessly. Yet, his bitter judgment told him Santo's consigliore and battery of refined attorneys would prevail, proving might makes right—at least in their sorry-ass world it did. Frank vowed that he'd make sure that sick reality was about to change.

The day of his departure dawned rainy. Frank arose at six o'clock that morning and dressed in his Pan Am uniform. He was ready to cab it to the airport. It was Tuesday morning, and he was traveling light. He needed an overnight bag, two changes of casual tourist clothes, tennis shoes, socks, two black cotton T-shirts with pockets, three changes of underwear, and his all-purpose Swiss Army knife. Every toilet article was contained in disposable plastic bottles. Last, but not least, he carried Bausch & Lomb binoculars for bird watching—nothing to alert customs should they decide to search his bag.

When he stepped out of the cab, the departure area felt moist and damp. The thermometer registered ninety-three degrees. It was a typical June day in central Florida. His destination was one hundred degrees. He planned to be in and out of Panama in less than a week if humanly possible. On his return trip, he would be a tourist on a direct flight to Miami.

Tipping his driver, he shouldered his bag and walked through the automatic doors into the entrance lobby of departure. The entire terminal complex at Tampa International was almost overwhelming, having opened a year earlier. The multimillion-dollar terminal was the pride of Tampa. It boasted being *the* most innovative airport terminal in the nation.

Inside, works of modern art and sculpture abounded, decorating the interior tastefully. Displays and brightly decorated shops were everywhere. The floors were colorfully carpeted, and escalators conveyed passengers to and fro on every level of the seven-story, steel-and-glass-structured spacious terminal. It was truly a state-of-the-art international airport complete with monorail passenger shuttles to and from airside transfer lobbies.

To Frank's horror, Mike and Jena Davis were riding one of them! They appeared to be engaged in conversation with another couple he did not recognize. In seconds, they would be departing the shuttle that was on its way toward Frank and some others waiting to board it.

Frank agonized. *There's no time for this. I'm on a tight schedule with a one-way ticket to ride in less than twenty minutes. I've got to think of something fast.*

Frank abruptly turned his back to the shuttle and pushed through the crowd of passengers preparing to board the shuttle. Hustling into a newsstand, Frank grabbed up the nearest magazine and put it up to his face, pretending to be browsing when the shuttle off-loaded. Mike and Jena walked out ahead of their friends.

"Wait a second, y'all. I want to pick up a paper over there." Pointing at the same newsstand where Frank had taken cover, she explained that she wanted to check the weather where Frank and his friend were heading to in Colorado. "It can be quite changeable in the mountains," she noted.

"Oh, Jena, can't it wait 'til we get home and watch the news?" her husband asked.

Jena looked over toward the man with the magazine held in front of his face. She hesitated as a curious feeling came over her while looking at the man in the Pan Am uniform.

"That's funny," she said. "Oh, I suppose we can catch the weather at home. Let's get on to the ice cream shop."

The two couples turned to walk down the concourse.

Mike asked Jena, "What was funny?"

Jena replied, "You'll just laugh. I thought I saw Frank standing in that magazine store a second ago. He was wearing a Pan Am uniform."

Mike laughed. "Now, that would be funny, especially since he's an air force pilot camping in Colorado right now. I think you just have him on your mind lately."

Jena said, "Yes, you're right. Sometimes we see what we want to."

Frank watched their backs for a minute, making sure they didn't turn around. Then, he replaced his copy of *Redbook* on its stand and headed for his transfer shuttle.

Each airline had its own transfer lobby that terminated at the aircraft docking sites like spokes on a wheel with their hubs terminating at the center of the terminal.

Frank shuddered. *Of all the days … wow, that was close.*

Standing aboard the shuttle, he held on to the metal post and looked out as he viewed a sight never seen at any airport before. The one-of-a-kind marvel of modern engineering was called the overpass taxiway. Its design allowed airliners to taxi over passenger cars running underneath on a multilane highway. Engineers claimed it was a revolution in space saving as far as airports go. Soon, Frank exited his shuttle and turned at the blue-and-white Pan Am sign marked gates 25–35. He tried to shake off memories as he walked. *Ramsay and I sure had some good times here. It's funny we didn't have to spend much money doing it either.*

Soon, he was in the concourse, focusing on gate 31 where he would meet the pilot and his crew in their ready room. The pilot had already been notified he would have an extra engineer on board for the leg to Panama City. Frank took a seat in the back of coach, wanting to remain as unobtrusive as possible.

13

One hour after takeoff Frank was taking in the view from the window, watching the sparkling Gulf of Mexico slide beneath as he listened to Bobby Darin on his headphones. Bobby was singing something about sailing when a female voice caught Frank's attention.

"Would you like a drink?"

Frank turned, peering from under his aviators to see a blonde-haired, blue-eyed stewardess with all the features of a heartbreaker leaning over the empty seat next to him. Having served the other passengers in the cabin, Frank was her last. He thought, *I'm not flying; I could have a drink if I want.* Thinking better of it, he decided to act the professional and instead requested ginger ale.

While pouring his drink, the woman asked, "Will you lay over in Panama City, or do you have to turn around?"

He hadn't thought about that question. So he promptly made a response that wouldn't entail his being seen getting on another plane without the uniform later.

"Oh, I'll be laying over a few days," he said.

She returned a genuine smile. "Oh, really? Me too."

Frank offered a smile out of politeness.

She bent down closer, whispering, "I'm finished serving. Would you like some company after I stow my cart?"

Frank didn't know what to say. For an awkward moment, he thought, *Doesn't she see my wedding band? Or does she care?*

Reluctantly, Frank answered, "There's no one else sitting here, if you want to sit down." *What was I thinking?* he thought. *I don't need to talk to anyone, especially a single stewardess. The fewer people I come in contact with on this mission, the better. What would Ramsay think of me now? Would she want me to flirt or avenge her? My mission is clear. I must stay cool and relax. All of this will blow over soon.*

When she returned, Frank detected the scent of fresh perfume. Sitting next to him, she offered an out stretched hand. "Hi, I'm Toni."

He knew that much from her name badge.

"You're Frank, the flight engineer, right?"

So, she could read name badges, too, Frank thought.

"How long have you been with Pan Am?" Toni asked.

Now he realized that along with her unmistakable southern accent, there were about to come twenty questions. Frank closed his eyes briefly and then smiled. *How the hell did I get into this?*

Toni was obviously younger by at least five years. She was flattering sweet enough even in the non-figure-flattering uniform Pan Am provided. He guessed she was in her early twenties and hailed from the Deep South. She seemed rather forward for someone just introducing herself.

She started, "Have you ever been to Panama?"

"No. Actually, this is my first time," Frank answered.

"Oh, you simply must let me show you around. I know all the right places, honey. I can save you money, time, and trouble finding a place to stay too."

With that sort of offer, he thought, *Is it my imagination, or is she coming on to me?* Even if she wasn't, Frank couldn't think of a good excuse to refuse, and he had to maintain his cover, so he agreed.

"Where are you going to stay, Frank? I hope you didn't settle for one of those cheap dives near the airport."

He didn't want to tell her he'd already settled for a cheap dive near the docks. Of course, his choice favored a location nearest where Little Eddy worked. Frank could care less about breathtaking views or top-notch service. Besides, he would be traveling on a thin wallet. All he cared about was a clean room with a shower and a bed where he could lay his head for no more than a week.

To the contrary, Toni offered up a descriptive tour of the Intercontinental Miramar, a five-star hotel replete with twenty-five stories of breathtaking views over the Pacific shores of Panama City. Of course, she planned on being part of that scenery herself. She described it as a most elegant hotel with full amenities and a simply dazzling rooftop pool with a dance bar.

"I think professional travelers should always stay in the best rooms. You know it's better that way. We can set an example for our customers, too, and just have fun. Don't you agree?"

As intense as she was, it wouldn't matter whether he agreed or not. After several such unsuccessful passes, she began taking his wedding band a bit more seriously.

She looked demurely at the ring. "Y'all wouldn't be engaged now, would you?" she asked.

It would have been far too easy for Frank to lie right then, and that probably would have been the end of it. But, somehow, he felt it was just too soon after his grievous loss to dishonor Ramsay's memory that way.

Frank replied, "Actually, my wife died recently, and it's something that can't be put in the past easily."

"Oh, I am so sorry, Frank. I didn't mean to … ah, I mean that's just awful. Bless your heart. I must return this cart. Would you please excuse me? I do hope you can find some closure in your time of bereavement."

As he watched her walk away, for the first time in their conversation, he agreed completely. *Closure must come after revenge, right?* — or so he thought.

Frank didn't see her for the rest of the flight. How she managed that on the same plane he could not say. One thing he did recognize was the sound of the gear coming down for a landing at Tucumán International Airport. It was still morning, as Panama was on central time. Fortunately, a prearranged taxi was waiting for him. Hotel reservations were also confirmed ahead of time. Frank walked briskly from the terminal to the taxi stand. The ride to his hotel was more than thirteen miles. Fortunately, the fare was included in his hotel rate. For a week's stay at the Country Inn Suite in the Canal Zone, he laid out $200.

His room was centrally located in Panama City near the docks and fish market. The scent around the building reminded him of that. More importantly, it was within walking distance of the shipping terminal where Little Eddy worked.

The neighborhood was surprisingly clean and quiet, unlike his room, which was a bit on the spartan side. The mattress on his bed wasn't exactly orthopedically fitted for high thread count cotton sheets either.

Nevertheless, for as long as he planned on being there, it would suit his needs. At least it was air-conditioned, and he could grab breakfast and dinner in the diner downstairs. The ice maker down the hall was out of order, but Frank wasn't there to party. So far, Toni's globetrotting advice was useless, but it was of little consequence. He had no room in his plans for her anyway—at least not at that point. Instead, he was embarked on a journey that promised grievous consequences for one.

The manager at the front desk greeted Frank with a smile that might have melted silver, making him feel right at home. Speaking in English, he seemed anxious to please. The man told Frank that as his guest he would be supplied with fresh towels daily, and his room would be cleaned every other day provided he left the request on his door. Frank thanked him for the information and went into the diner to get a sandwich and a Coke. Then, he climbed back up two flights to his room at the end of the walkway. Turning the key to number nine, he reentered his stuffy little room at eleven thirty on the morning of Wednesday, June 20. He noted it was the last day of spring.

His first order of business was to crank up the air-conditioning. The lingering scent of stale tobacco was nearly overpowering. The next morning was ushered in with a deluge. He had arrived just in time for the rainy season.

When he stepped from his room, the steamy heat pressed in all around him just like in Ubon. The only thing missing was the stench of spent jet fuel and human feces. Another foul corruption that vitiated the nostrils of his imagination was the fact that Little Eddy was close. More so than ever, Frank resolved to kill the man in the worst sort of way. This was the day his plan would begin to unfold in his world.

He took to the streets, dodging puddles as he walked through morning steam rising through cracked asphalt. Vendors busily made their carts ready on side streets as he silently passed by on his way to the docks. He could hear heavy freighter whistles nearby as ships were approaching being piloted through the first locks of the great pathway between the seas known as the Panama Canal. Everything in this country revolved around it. It was the very lifeblood of this tiny isthmian part of the world. It was a narrow nation with a grandioso canal flowing through.

Frank was walking through the heart of a fascinating crossroad. This thin squiggle of land a hundred miles wide, at most, offered a rich history made up from seven indigenous peoples—a melting pot of cultures in which Frank sought one man. His prey was a bastardized American of Panamanian extraction. How he loved simplicity.

As Frank walked along, he was reminded that revenge is a plate best eaten cold.

Just then, an old palindrome he'd learned in school popped into his head. He visualized it on the blackboard in his history class: A MAN A PLAN A CANAL PANAMA. Backward or forward, it spelled the same. To him, it was both a sentence and a plan he had in mind for the man he was seeking. Frank had a plan, and he was in Panama nearing his prey on the canal.

To begin, he knew he had to visit the native Indian shop he researched in a Panama City travelogue. When he made his purchase there, the first step would be completed. The rest would come together in due time.

Following directions he'd copied out of the travelogue, he came upon the Indian Souvenir and Gift Shop. It was a squat structure made to appear like a trading post located deep in the Darien Province where indigenous Cuna Indian tribes thrived and practiced ancient native rites and rituals. In such hunter-gatherer civilizations, there was a need for extremely sharp cutting tools designed to deal with jungle hazards and game. That's why Frank was there.

When he ducked through the intentionally low door frame under a thatched roof, he could see hundreds of artifacts displayed in glass cases. Most of them were replicas painstakingly re-created by natives who retained their consummate skills. If not for hunting, at least they passed on these genuine artifacts in this modern city for profit.

Inside, Frank found exactly what he was looking for. It surprised him that there were so many knives to choose from. Before him were blades sharper than any manufactured cutlery in the world. These were flint knives chipped and fashioned by the Kuna Indians of Panama to the keenest edge known. Frank approached the glass display case to find his weapon of choice. He'd realized from the outset a handgun for a noncitizen in Panama was out of the question. Panamanian authorities made it strictly illegal for noncitizens to possess a firearm.

He chose a nine-inch drop point hunter's knife made from strawberry flint, which gleamed back at him. Its handle was fashioned from dolomite. The shop owner assured him it was a genuine Kuna knife. It was an exact replica, if nothing else. The shop owner knew, by the way his eyes fixed on his choice, he was ready to buy.

The shopkeeper made his move. "My price is three hundred dollars, but since you are a *Norte Americano*, I will let you have it for one hundred seventy-five. It is a good price, no?"

Frank held the precious blade in his hand, inspecting its glistening curves and feeling its perfect balance. He agreed, but bartered further, knowing it was customary.

"Do you have a sheath for it?" he asked. Frank upped the ante to the knife and a sheath for $150.

The shopkeeper grinned, accepting his bartered price. Leaving the shop, Frank began navigating the narrow streets of Panama City. He encountered numerous beggars along the way. It was something he had not expected. He wasn't prepared for old, broken men and women leaning on crippled children or lying about littering the sidewalks. They impeded pedestrians, lying on their mats and crying out piteous pleas, extending upraised, withered arms with lowing cries for help. Quickly, Frank learned how the local pedestrians dealt with them when they became burdensome.

Whenever they became an impediment to their locomotion, harried citizens would scold with a scurrilous tone as they simultaneously shook a little finger in their faces, spewing expressions like, *No te quiero ni te necesito.* "Roughly translated, it meant, "I don't want or need you!" Or worse, they would shout *vete*, meaning *get out*, as they would scold a dog. In some cases, it worked. Frank witnessed that even for a beggar this was enough. These expressions seemed to cow them.

Despite true empathy for those afflicted and the less fortunate, he, too, found himself employing this tactic to keep them at bay. It seemed heartless, but on the other hand, it was impractical to deal with every one of them. Clearly, this was not part of his plan. Frank thought he could traverse the distance on the map much sooner than he had. Now he was facing a dilemma. Dock workers in Panama City were unionized and would soon be on noon break. Panamanians take siesta breaks seriously and never come back early.

In fact, the opposite is usually true. Eventually, he would have to stop for a meal himself somewhere in order to wait them out. Then, something totally unforeseen occurred.

The Festival Corpus Christi, La Villa de Los Santos was spilling into the streets all around him. It was a religious festival that could last for two weeks. A wild and crazy festival, it was known for its elaborate dances with men in devil masks celebrating a plethora of arts and agricultural displays carried aloft. And the whole thing was color-fully erupting throughout the neighborhood around him. Frank was becoming engulfed in a parade of revelers churning through the narrow streets. He soon found himself being swept along with the throng of people. It was either that or risk being crushed in their overwhelming mass of humanity.

As he was pressed along, he became alarmed. Anyone pushing up against him might discover he had a concealed weapon. This was not good. If it was discovered, he could be reported to the *policia* as a *tourista* with a knife. He could be incarcerated. Former research told him it was strictly illegal for tourists to carry concealed weapons in Panama.

No sooner was he caught up in this situation than he found himself being pushed around the corner, further from the docks. Not only was he late, but now he was going in the opposite direction. He could see things were quickly getting out of hand. Frank didn't care for confu-sion, mayhem was not his style, and he definitely did not thrive on chaos. Clearly, he knew he would have to abandon his plans for the day and return to his humble abode.

14

"I don't have plans and schemes, and I don't have hopes and dreams. I don't have anything."

The words right out of that fifties tune by The Platters seemed apropos at the time. They were spot-on for the way he felt the next day. There he sat on a sagging, piss-stained mattress in his claustrophobic room that reeked of stale tobacco in the Canal Zone rethinking his entire plan. Then, it dawned on him. He didn't have to figure a damn thing.

He would just have to let things happen. All he had to do was be in the right place at the right time.

First, that meant bailing from that snuff-colored room. It was clear his objective was to move on. His purpose would be to make a new plan. Downstairs, Frank found the desk clerk vibrantly warm as usual.

"*Ola, Señor.* Are you enjoying your stay?"

Frank didn't seem to hear him; he had things on his mind.

Watching his back, the desk clerk curled up his lip smiling by himself. Then, he picked up the telephone. Outside, the heat of the morning hit him like a sledgehammer. It seemed a shame to waste soap. By the time he reached the end of the street, his shirt was clinging to his back. There was no sense pretending; anyone not wet with sweat by now on this street was asleep somewhere in the shade.

The Avenida Central in Panama Viejo confirmed this wisdom. This area of Panama City was close to Bonocante's shipping terminal. After a short walk, he drew close enough to glimpse the terminal itself. Here, homes began losing their previous charm of the French colonial, Spanish architecture he left in old Panama where homes were lovingly kept up by their owners. Now, the neighborhood degenerated into a checkered collection of abandoned homes. Squatters stared out from the darkness within, just sitting there in rundown hovels. Frank thought about such people existing in the shadows of squalor; through the ashes and the anguish, they just stayed on near the path he trod.

He remained on course, getting as close as he could. Quietly observing, he was deliberately dressed low key, Panamanian style in an attempt to blend in to his surroundings. Now he could see huge cranes rising out of the morning mist. Like prehistoric behemoths, they grasped cargo out of holds in ships within sight of the Bridge of the Americas majestically spanning the canal. Nervously, he grasped the sheath holding his sharp Kuna knife with his sweaty palm. It was his sole means of persuasion. He continued walking and soon came upon a cluster of vendors. He hoped they were unlike those he'd encountered before. Approaching him warily, some even hung back, not so eager to do business in this shifting nefarious world of the docks. Everything was transitory here, changing with the tide.

All around, men drifted in and out of view as they worked in the heavy morning fog, hefting, heaving hard, and grunting as they unloaded palletized cargo. Stevedores would halt suddenly, allowing an occasional heavily laden forklift to pass by into the mist. No one looked Frank's way. The stevedores worked in silence, too busy to give him the time of day. He stood still in the misty fog, trying to get his bearings.

Intermittently, the lonely sound of foghorns forewarned in the shrouded canal. He rocked silently to and fro as he strained to hear in the dampness. As he stood there on the dank timbers of the long dock, a light suddenly stabbed through the mist. It traced straight and level at the height of his shoulders. Remaining frozen, he anticipated being spotted. Then the light slowly crept on until it faded from sight. Heaving a sigh of relief, Frank realized it was probably some sleepy-eyed guard completing another stultifying round with his flashlight. Somehow the guard overlooked him among the others lumping cargo.

He had seen the elephant; now it was time to get out of sight. He arrived at the docks with a purpose, but his objective eluded him at present. He came to grips with the reality of the situation. It would take at least another day to exact revenge. He needed to see his prey for that deed.

First, he needed a place to hide and sleep till next daylight. Coming that far without a hope of even spotting his prey caused him to remain and seek him the next day. All he needed was a place secure from guard patrols. He soon found it under some tarps draped over cargo at the far end of the dock. Next, he needed drinking water. Again, the tarps provided. An unsavory trickle of condensation ran off the humid tarps. It was enough until it rained again; at least it would suffice for the night.

His last essential was sleep. Easier said than done on a huge dock where every creak and groan from men at work and ships at berth produced a cacophony of sounds that sent chills up his spine. Then there was the constant patrol of the armed guard.

Nevertheless, sleep finally came in fitful snatches throughout the humid day and night. He awoke warily at the intrusion of every sound emanating from the surrounding ships.

At last, daybreak revealed to him his true position. The dock came to life once again with racing forklifts and shouting men bent on loading and unloading cargo.

Again, he was not the subject of their interest, although he was peeking from beneath the tarp directly into their midst. He realized he must have finally succumbed to sleep, dozing off long enough to allow their clumsy approach. Clearly, they had no clue he was hidden under the tarps.

The day dawned with sunshine glaring off the canal. *Now what?* he thought.

Suddenly, he boldly stood up from beneath the tarp and began staggering down the dock for all to see. At first, some were shocked to see him there—a man clearly out of place. Others started pointing know-ingly, chuckling to themselves. Frank had managed to fool them into thinking he was some wayward drunk who had slept it off the night before on the docks. They allowed him to pass with little interest. The armed guard at the end of the dock would not be so easy on him. He only hoped his ruse would hold up under the guard's scrutiny.

As he approached the guard shack unsteadily, he unzipped his fly and pulled out his shirttail. Coming close enough for the guard to see, he shoved his little finger far up his nostril, as if he were seeking some obscure nose boulder, which, in turn, gratefully offended sufficient to provide his safe passage without further ado.

Once he left the sun-drenched docks, he reversed his course on the Avenida Central until he reached a small cantina. He was famished and thirsty after camping on the docks nearly twenty hours. Frank was about to allow himself a hearty breakfast. Taking a seat at a sidewalk café, he waited as he took in the sights and smells around him.

It was going to be another blistering, bustling day with a light morning breeze and the promise of another sweat-soaked scorcher.

Frank's view of the street in front of him included a policia walking his way. He seemed to be interested in him. All at once, another policia was walking toward him from the opposite direction. What he had been looking forward to was some steaming hot coffee and sustenance. Instead, he was suddenly a person of interest in a crowded street café.

The first policia stood before Frank and addressed him. *"Buenos dias, señor."*

Before Frank could answer, the waitress hurried to the table, ready to take Frank's order.

The policia said, *"Perdóname, señorita. Donde esta su modales. Soy habalamamos a es hombre."*

The waitress looked at Frank plaintively.

Frank remained seated, hoping the table would hide his knife.

He said, *"Por favor, no entiendo.* I speak little *Español.* Please, let's all speak in English, if that's possible."

The one policia who joined the other spoke to Frank in English. "This officer wants to speak with you, and the waitress interrupted."

The waitress intervened. "That is not true. He called me over. It is my *job* to take orders from customers."

Frank said, "I'm glad we can now speak in English. What is the problem, officer?"

He replied, "Are you Norte Americano?"

"Yes," Frank replied.

"May we see your passport?"

Frank said, "I still don't understand why we are having this conversation."

The English-speaking policia repeated the request. "May we see your passport, *por favor?*"

Finally, Frank said he did not have it with him.

The officer speaking in English turned to the other and began speaking in Spanish. Then, the second policia looked at Frank. He said, "It is not good to walk the streets here without a passport. The officer here thought you fit another Norte Americano's description. There has been a man in this area attempting to fill false prescriptions. He says he is sorry to have bothered you. However, you must show your passport at the local policia station. It is not far from here. So you must go and get it."

Frank remained seated. He asked the officers if he could eat first since he was very hungry and the waitress seemed to need his business. The second policia looked Frank over closely, gave the doting waitress a glance, and then decided they could provide him that courtesy. The two left as quickly as they came.

Frank watched them amble down the Avenida. "It's taken me this long to decide what I want, hasn't it?" he remarked.

The young waitress couldn't help but admire his aplomb. She smiled, saying, "I can make it the house special if you like, sir."

There in Spanish before him was a description he could make out with the aid of small photos beside each selection. In one picture there appeared a platter loaded with fried eggs and empanadas, along with what he took for toast.

After the waitress took his order, he found the *hombre's baños* and freshened up just in time for his steaming hot platter. Later, he learned what he thought was toast was actually *hoyaldras*, which were fattening but very tasty. The remainder of his platter was filled with fried plantains, giving off a sweet aroma. He dove in, polishing off the entire platter and washing it down with three cups of strong Panamanian coffee, while observing the street life in Panama Viejo.

Beggars were beginning to gather in their usual places, laying out colorful homespun blankets on the sidewalks where they would sit; lame or not, it made no difference. It was their way. They resumed their shabby existence with outstretched hands, imploring with piteous cries. Amid this cruel cultural chasm, the only thing that remained the same between them and Norte Americano was the currency.

Frank had to admit that Panama had one of the better socioeconomic structures in Central America. He dared not dream of conditions elsewhere.

Just then, the waitress interrupted, asking him, "*¿Es usted Norte Americano, verdad?*"

"Yes, really. Is it so obvious I'm from America?"

"I think it's your sunglasses," she noted. "Are they not the kind military pilots wear?"

Frank thought, *Thank goodness I wasn't wearing them on the dock this morning, it would have been a dead giveaway. Maybe that's what attracted the policia.*

The waitress commented, "I think the policia are always picking on you Americanos." She bent down and whispered, exposing her breasts in her low-cut blouse. "Our dictator, he is very interested in any Americanos. I think he is afraid some are spying on his regime. He is very—how do you say? He makes his people obey strict rules. Do you understand?"

Frank remained expressionless. "Yes, I understand," he said. "Would you please bring me my check now?"

"*Oh, si. No problema.*"

When she returned, Frank asked, "Would you know where a man might rent a small boat around here?"

"There is a marina about three blocks from here, along the Avenida."

"Thank you so much. I appreciate that."

"No problema, sir. I wish you happy sailing."

Yes indeed, he thought. *If she knew what I wanted the boat for, she'd scream.*

Frank paid his check, giving her an ample tip, and then stepped off the curb to join the throng headed toward the center of Viejo Panama.

The waitress said, "*Adiós, señor, y muchas gracias.*"

As he pressed his way back toward the marina on the avenue, Frank thought, *It's funny. I've walked right past this place twice and never even noticed.* He guessed it's true what they say: you never really notice a business until you have need of it.

Their service was growing grimly important to him, especially if he was to get around that dock guard. Frank made up his mind how he was going to get to Little Eddy. The very thought of his gold-toothed smile set his thoughts off on a new reverie of revenge. Quickening his pace, Frank rounded a bend and peered over the bobbing heads of the diminutive populace in front of him. He saw the familiar brightly painted sign with huge orange and blue letters on a yellow background.

En español, it read, *Puerta Hacia La Mar Marina*, Gateway to the Sea, Marina. He mused, *How could I have missed that?* It just shows what happens when the mind focuses too much on one objective. He reminded himself to avoid tunnel vision in his full-blown quest for retribution.

There it was, right in front of him—a fully equipped marina with rentals. It beckoned pros and amateurs alike to ply the waters of the Canal Zone. It was easy to see their mainstay were private vessels. They were moored in the brown water, tethered under corrugated metal sheds that hugged the seawall alongside the Avenida.

Frank approached the establishment and saw it advertised half-day and two-hour excursions. Finding the man in charge, he could see he was a fortyish looking gent wearing a weathered straw hat and equally worn denim jeans with diesel-soaked tennis shoes.

One thing Frank remembered about boats and diesel was diesel and tennis shoes don't mix. Judging from the smell of this gent, he seemed to be an old hand himself.

"Perdóname cuánto eres la pequeño el barcos por mitad a días."

The old man smiled. *"Esta bien, señor.* I speak English. The small boats, they are ten dollars for half a day with fuel."

Frank noticed the leaky old Mercury outboard hanging off the back of the fiberglass twelve-footer. Wondering how many cranks it had left in it, he reckoned it really didn't matter much. He didn't have far to go, and oars were available. So he said he'd take it. The old man insisted Frank take a life jacket, which was another dollar. Frank didn't argue. It was the rules, so he took it to humor the man and got in the boat.

He started the little outboard for Frank, and the familiar scent of burnt diesel wafted over him. It reminded him of life in Ubon; in those stifling hooches shared with diesel generators. The cloud of exhaust drifted away on the breeze as the little engine came to life.

According to plan, he would ply his way through the turbid brown waters of the canal, watching for buoy markers. He was careful to stay to the right of them so as not to interfere with shipping traffic constantly traversing the canal in both directions.

It was easy enough to stay out of trouble as long as it didn't rain. All he had was his Panama hat for protection from the elements. He took his black nylon parka and draped it across the boat seat. By now, he had already removed the hot faded orange life jacket, tossing it at his feet in the soggy bottom of the little boat. He certainly didn't need to be wearing anything that made him easier to spot.

Frank's plan was to get close to the dock where Eddy worked and then cut off his motor and drift to the nearest buoy. There he could latch on and observe awhile. Hopefully, no one would spot him. Up close, the buoy was larger than he expected. Fortunately, it concealed him and the boat. It was ten o'clock in the morning, and sunlight was reflecting off the water in his face. The canal traffic had picked up to full pace. Annoying waves rocked his boat continually against the buoy. At least his view of the dock was clear. With his binoculars. he could even spot the guard making his rounds along its five hundred-foot length. He wondered if the guard could spot him, or did he even care? So far, he didn't seem to be looking in Frank's direction.

Frank concentrated his attention on the dock office of Bonocante's Shipping Co., where he imagined Little Eddy would be. The shack was wooden, about fifteen-foot square, with windows across the top all around. They let in light, but not so much as to make it feel like a greenhouse. He could see it was air-conditioned, and the door rarely opened except for the occasional foreman delivering paperwork.

Frank reflected on his quarry sitting in air-conditioned comfort working in his little shipping shack. The very thought of him being so close made his skin crawl. Frank wanted to pluck him out, root and branch. Frank envisioned his face again with that gold-toothed leer. It helped him complete a mental picture of his eminent, slow death. Frank had something really special in mind for him.

Suddenly, he was standing there on the dock. Frank thought, *God doesn't give; he sends.* Pompous Little Eddy was outside the shack lighting a cigarette with that same gold lighter, the one he held in court that day. Frank's hands shook as his thoughts returned to the memory of his withered wife and the cruel words he spoke that day. Frank lingered, regaining his composure as he watched him take that last long drag. Exhaling slowly, Little Eddy suddenly looked up for a moment. Was it Frank's imagination? It seemed as if Little Eddy was staring right at him.

That's impossible, he thought. *How could he know I'm here watching through my Bausch and Lombs?* Frank eased down in the boat, collecting his thoughts, telling himself this must be done right. *I'll only have one chance. I can't blow it! I'll be back.* With that, Frank slowly rowed the small dinghy out and then started his motor, pushing out into the canal, knowing another day would see his plan finished.

The next day at the motel Frank walked downstairs early for a good breakfast, knowing the day ahead would be strenuous. Mr. Caruso, the desk clerk, waved to him. He greeted him with his best morning pleasantries, so Frank walked over to him.

He said, "Mr. Caruso, I've got to hand it to you. For a man in your station, you always manage to remain outgoing and cheerful. How do you do it?"

"Well, Frank, my mother always told me to put love in your heart, and the rest will be easy."

"That's a nice sentiment, Mr. Caruso. It's a shame more people can't claim that attitude." Just then, it crossed Frank's mind that the clerk knew his first name, yet he did not know the clerk's.

"By the way, what is your first name, Mr. Caruso?"

He demurred and then told him it was Rob.

Frank remarked, "That's a bit unusual for a Panamanian name, isn't it?"

He replied, "Yes, well, my father was in the US Army. He was stationed here for a while. Since he has gone now, I shortened my name to Rob."

Frank asked, "What was it before?"

The clerk replied, "My given name is Robinson."

Frank said, "Then, it's Robinson Caruso?"

"*Sí,* you are right that it is, Frank. You see why I shortened it, no?"

"Well, yes, when you put it together like that, I can see what you mean," Frank agreed.

Robinson said, "I can explain. You see, my mother was Panamanian and my father American. My mother always told me that if their first child was a girl they wanted to name her Robin. Since they had a son instead, well, I think you can figure out the rest. At least my father had a good sense of humor, no?"

Frank wiped away a growing smile underneath his mustachioed face. He said he had to get on to breakfast.

"Good-bye, Robinson."

Rob smiled sardonically behind Frank's back as he walked away. Pulling the letter addressed to Frank from its pigeon hole, he placed it under his end tray.

* * *

After breakfast, Frank had some last-minute shopping to do. Throwing the Bausch & Lomb case on the bed, he headed for the shower. He'd done enough planning. Now, he felt he could do this in his sleep.

After a clean sweep of scented soap from his body, he pulled on black jeans and a long-sleeved black cotton T-shirt with a pocket. Donning his Panama hat, he laced up his tennis shoes. Checking himself out in the mirror, he slid his knife in his right front pocket and then shoved leather gloves in his parka and tied it around his waist. He placed his binoculars and an extra pair of black socks in a bag.

Moving stealthily downstairs, he pushed cash in an envelope into the manager's mail slot with Caruso's name on it. Rob would never see Frank again. That also was part of his plan. He walked briskly down the Avenida, and rolled up his sweaty sleeves.

There was a taxi station ahead, one block from the marina, where he would meet Señor Ramos. Frank had prearranged for a cab to take him to the airport. Ramos was to pick him up in front in front of the Zócalo at precisely 8:00 p.m. It would be dark by then, and his work at the dock should be finished. That morning, he entered the Zócalo and purchased black steel-toed military jump boots, the kind the airborne Rangers wear. He also bought a New York Yankees ball cap. Later, he planned to ditch the boots and parka, buy a Hawaiian shirt and tennis shoes at the Zócalo, and rendezvous with Ramos. Appearing as a local *tourista*, he would board Pan Am flight 131 scheduled for departure at 9:30 p.m. for Miami. When he arrived in Miami, he planned to rent a car for his return trip home.

By the time he reached the marina, it was noon. From the rental agent in the straw hat, he purchased a ten-foot bamboo fishing pole, a reel of forty-pound test line, and forty feet of yellow nylon rope.

"Is this all the rope you have?" Frank complained. "Don't you have anything darker?"

The proprietor put up his arms and shrugged as he shook his head. Frank realized it was a take-it-or-leave-it deal. He then snatched up an Eveready waterproof flashlight and a one-foot hooked elastic bungee cord. He paid in cash and then loaded the equipment in the boat, making sure the flashlight was kept dry in the tool compartment under the rear seat of the boat. Looking in the tool kit, he confirmed only a Phillips screwdriver and an oily rag existed inside. The little man in rotten tennis shoes couldn't contain his curiosity.

"Will you be fishing for snook?"

"Yes, how did you guess?"

"Well, señor, usually they are caught in the canal much farther east in Lake Gatun."

"I have time to kill today, so I think I'll go ahead and give that a try," Frank said.

The old gentleman eyed Frank suspiciously as he shoved off. Then, he crooked his decrepit finger at him. "Your life jacket, señor! It is the law, you know. Do you want me to lose my license?"

Frank dutifully donned the filthy, hot jacket and then twisted the throttle. As he drove the little oil-seeping outboard through the greenish-brown wake of the canal, he stared up at a towering Japanese freighter headed west just exiting the canal. It would be a long afternoon, of that much he was certain.

15

It was all Frank could do to stand the afternoon heat on the canal. The buoy near the office shack was rocking gently when Frank reached it. He tethered up cautiously, closely watching the dock. Things were quiet. Siesta was in full swing. Even the flies seemed listless, droning about Frank's face at a notably slowed pace. He pulled his hat down over his eyes as he slid down in the uncomfortable wooden boat for a nap.

Surprisingly, he dozed off for three hours, only waking when a distant blast of a ship's horn jarred him to his senses. Apparently, a passing cargo ship's crew thought it great fun to watch a sleeping fisherman jump out of his skin. He arose and pushed up his ball cap to peek out from behind the buoy. *It's time to get busy*, he thought. He held his binoculars up to his eyes to get a close-up view of the shack on the dock. There was movement inside.

Frank was in luck; one of the shadowy figures he made out was Little Eddy. Frank spotted a tendril of smoke filtering out the door that remained ajar. Beyond that space, another figure paced back and forth. Apparently, the second person accosted Little Eddy, who remained seated as he leaned back in his chair continuing to smoke. The first man seemed angry, waving his arms in animated gestures. It seemed like he was trying to convince Eddy of something. Then suddenly, he pushed the door open wide, making a silhouette of himself in the doorway as he faced Little Eddy. Finally, the man shook his fist with emphasis, pointed his finger at Eddy, and then walked off in a huff.

Frank kept his glasses locked on the man until he disappeared around a tall stack of lumber at the end of a warehouse. Waiting patiently for thirty minutes, Frank determined to his satisfaction that the man wasn't coming back. Either way, he felt it was time to make his move. Frank didn't want to risk having Eddy slip away.

The reddened spring sun was sinking behind its own reflection on the darkening Pacific beyond the entrance to the canal. It appeared so huge on the horizon that he could not face it without shielding his eyes even with aviators on. Already, he took the precaution of extending his pole and pretending to fish for snook off the transom using shiners for bait. Nothing was biting. Of course, that didn't matter. In fact, he was glad. He only wanted to work his way closer to the shack before Eddy left.

With the final fleeting rays of sunlight filtering across the becalmed canal, he could just make out Little Eddy's figure hunching over his angled desk. With his binoculars shielded under his hat, Frank could see Eddy pouring over some paperwork.

He smiled, thinking derisively, *Who are you trying to kid? You probably barely know how to read.*

It was probably a stack of manifests he must finish checking before locking up and joining his cocaine amigos to get high in the heat of the night somewhere. *He's probably already jonesing for his nightly fix,* Frank thought. *His habit is probably full-blown now that he lived in Panama, the land of cheap cocaine. He's probably already succumbed to the drug's surreal grip like a dead man walking.*

Frank's binocs revealed the return of the man who'd previously had words with Little Eddy. Frank wished he could read lips. The two were having an animated conversation, with the big guy standing in the doorway doing most of the talking. Eddy just stared down at the floor and nodded affirmatively. Although sound carried well across water,

Frank could only make out a few words until the big man shouted to Eddy, "*Is that clear?!*"

It appeared to Frank that the big man was asking Little Eddy to sign something, and then he did. Then Frank could hear the office door slam shut, and at the top of his lungs, the big man shouted as he left, "*It'll be your balls, Eddy!*"

It was easy to see he was really angry with Eddy about something.

Meanwhile, Little Eddy sat in his office fuming and thinking. *That pig of a foreman—just wait till I call the boss in Tampa. He will not be pleased when he learns how his best courier is being treated. That stupid ass doesn't know half this dock comes to me for their stuff. Hell, that's one of the reasons I'm sittin' here in this stupid shack. That's so damn funny too, 'cause it's all here right under my feet. There's enough cocaine here to blow his freakin' mind permanently. He's such a donkey. One night he's gonna wind up dead in some gutter with a hotshot of heroin in his veins.*

"Oh, we're all so sorry," we'll say at the funeral. "We never knew he had such a serious drug problem."

That stupid pig doesn't know who he's messin' with. Santo will take me back in a heartbeat—I know it. Just as soon as the heat goes down in Tampa; I know he'll want me back on the street. That's right; I could probably get a hit fixed on this jackass who thinks he can take my manhood. You wait and see, big guy, 'cause somebody's comin' to rip you off, baby. Then we'll see who's cock of the walk on this dock.

Just as Little Eddy prepared to leave, he took one last snort of cocaine and laughed out loud. *Cock of the walk on the dock—now that's funny*, he thought.

* * *

Suddenly, Frank felt a sense of urgency. He didn't want to miss Little Eddy again. He knew he must act before this devil eluded his grasp. It was pure hell waiting in the boat and sweating out the minutes there, waiting for darkness to obscure his movements. His fingers continually ran over the smooth handle of the pink flint Kuna knife as beads of sweat ran down his spine collecting in his skivvies.

He pulled on leather gloves, and then quietly dipping his oars into the brown/black water beneath, he pulled hard, deep, and steady, forcing his oars to draw him silently to the dock.

There, he slipped the rope around the barnacled dock post, tying it fast with a crunching square knot. Just then, the light in the shack went out. *This is it!* he thought. *The time is now—do it!* Everything depended on stealth. Frank slid off the wet boat seat, leaning forward and cautiously pulling himself halfway onto the dock into the prone position with his legs dangling; he waited silently as he caught his breath.

Little Eddy came out of the shack and closed the door behind him, placing the padlock through its hasp on the door. With one more exertion, Frank pulled himself completely onto the dock. Then, in a split-second effort, he leapt to his feet in a squat position. His eyes nervously traversed the dock for any possible interference. He crept to the wall of the shack just around the corner from his pray. Pulling the knife from his pocket, he held it high in his right hand close to the side of the shack, coolly waiting, holding his breath, praying for Little Eddy to round that corner.

As he did, Frank struck! Thrusting with a gloved left hand, he clasped Little Eddy's mouth instantaneously, preventing his making a sound. Instinctively, Little Eddy struggled until he felt Frank's right hand pressing the cold Kuna knife point to his jugular. He stiffened at first and then stood perfectly still. Now, Frank knew Little Eddy was his. Frank was a head taller, forty pounds heavier, and completely in control. Eddy's eyes widened with fear, as he was pinned against the wall of the shack. His eyes searched Frank's for an answer.

From that point on, Frank was on automatic, and it was *entirely* personal. Quickly, he yanked the oily rag from his back pocket, unceremoniously stuffing it in Eddy's mouth.

Keeping the knife uncomfortably pressed to Eddy's jugular, it produced a slight trickle of blood with its razor edge. Next, Frank yanked his captive's hands behind his back. Then, with his free left hand, he unhooked the small bungee cord from around his waist. Wrapping it around Eddy's wrists several times, he hooked the ends to complete his bindings.

Now, Frank was ready to drag his pray backward around the corner to his boat only a few feet away. When they reached the boat, Frank needed him in quick. He kicked Little Eddy the rest of the way into the boat, not caring how he landed. He regretted making that last move as soon as he made it.

The clunking noise of Little Eddy's body landing in Frank's boat traveled well across water. Frank worried that the sound had traveled far enough for the guard to hear.

Frank knew he had to get back to the buoy as soon as possible. Gingerly, he climbed in, propping up Little Eddy to face him on the bow seat of the boat. He quickly secured Little Eddy's feet to the bottom of the seat with a length of yellow nylon rope, so there would be no man overboard before his time. Then, Frank started rowing hard and deep for the buoy with his prize. *Just one minute more, and we'll both be hidden*, he thought.

Unfortunately, Frank's supposition was spot-on. The guard had, indeed, heard Little Eddy's body clunk into the boat. Now, he was stabbing into the darkness with his flashlight, but to no avail. The guard picked up his pace, running the length of the dock as he waved his powerful light into the darkest spots, sweeping just over Frank's ducking head.

Finally, Frank was now safe, for the time being behind the buoy with wide-eyed Little Eddy. The look of sheer terror in his eyes revealed exactly what he saw and remembered about Frank. He knew who he was and no doubt guessed what he was there for. Of course, only Frank knew what was in store for Little Eddy.

Frank was in the moment. *Will I actually enjoy this, or will it be just premeditated, automatic action as it was up to this very moment?* Frank wondered. Did he even want to know the difference? He couldn't be sure.

Frank believed in his very soul that he could carry out exactly what he'd planned with the skill of a surgeon. Not only was he capable, but he was willing. That was the nature of the beast of vengeance within him. He let the demon in; it had been crouching at the door all along. Now, it controlled him completely.

When he was ready to leave him alone that night, Frank recalled seeing Eddy strapped helplessly low in the water with thirty-five feet of yellow cord strapping him to the buoy. Little Eddy faced the canal and high tide.

Feeling a twisted twinge of poetic justice, Frank likened him to Captain Ahab tied to the great white whale in Herman Melville's *Moby Dick*, pinned there by his own ship's harpoon ropes. *Which will come first?* Frank wondered. *Will the cuts to his lower parts attract enough crabs to finish him off, albeit slowly, or will some crewman on a passing freighter spot his mercifully drowned carcass at low tide in the morning?*

According to his calculations, the incoming tide would reach its high point within the hour. Of course, that was entirely up to the moon, not Frank. By then, he would be just another tourist taking a cab to the airport. Just before he shoved off, Frank heard one last muffled scream. It was shriller than the rest, so he decided to derive a little pleasure for his efforts. This would be the last chance he'd get, after all.

Leaning in close, not wanting Little Eddy to miss a word, Frank whispered in his ear. "Go ahead. Scream, and scream all you like." Frank fumed. "You've taught this man how to say he just doesn't care."

Finally, Frank whispered through his gritted his teeth. "You've caused enough pain and suffering and death to cost you a lifetime."

As Frank slowly dipped his oars into the dark waters, he looked upon Eddy's face. His eyes darted back and forth wildly with the rag in his mouth taking on water. Feeling numbly spent, Frank's work in Panama was nearly finished. He felt immensely satiated. Just then, he thought he caught a glimpse of Little Eddy's eyes widening.

Could it be? Frank thought. *Am I hearing yet another muffled scream? Maybe it was just the pinches of curious flesh-eating crabs already going about nature's work. Of course, first nibbles wouldn't be enough to satisfy; no, they're just tasting, making sure their pray is completely defenseless.*

Now, Frank rowed further, fantasying about crabs crawling over Little Eddy's sensitive parts and sensing his helplessness as they joined in the feeding frenzy.

Deep in his reverie of crustacean execution, a sudden horn blast from yet another passing freighter jolted him back to reality. Apparently, his visions of vengeance had caused him to row off course. He was too far out in the canal. Immediately, he corrected with back oaring. Then, he started cranking the oily little outboard. At first crank, there was no ignition. Then, he cranked the little diesel again. It coughed and then died. His mind raced, *Oh God, please not now! C'mon, you little bastard, start!* Once again, he tried, yet he remained adrift as he watched the ship pass on. Then, he started cranking his heart out. Finally, it sputtered and *started!*

A sailor on the fantail of the passing freighter waved as they passed, as if to say, "Okay, buddy. All right, I see you, just watch yourself out there." Frank had no more time to kill on the canal. Revving up his little Mercury, he cruised until he sighted the marina lights just after seven thirty. Everything seemed quiet, so he pulled in at the rental dock.

The old man in the straw hat was nowhere to be seen. Frank stowed his oars and tied off the boat. The old man would find a present on his return of a ten-foot bamboo fishing pole and a slightly used reel of forty-pound test line. Earlier, Frank had wrapped the flashlight, gloves and Kuna knife in his parka, along with his military steel toed jump boots, and dropped them in the canal. *Let them look,* he thought. *Good luck.* He paid in advance for the boat, so he wasn't concerned with the rest. His next stop was the marketplace right next door.

Soon, Frank was picking out a Yankees ball cap and a pair of Jack Purcell's tennis shoes. Coming out of the shop with his shoes in a bag, he accidently bumped into a policia, who eyed Frank suspiciously. Frank must have been a sight wearing all black with wet pants and no shoes. Perhaps Frank was departing sooner than the policia thought necessary. He was the same officer who accosted him earlier in the day. The sweat forming on his brow must have alerted the policia to something. Frank noticed him touching his sidearm as he moved closer.

"*¿Señor eso es Norte Americano?*"

"*Si,*" Frank replied nervously. Switching to English, he asked, "Is there a problem, officer?"

He immediately replied in broken English. "Did you report to the policia station to show your passport, señor?"

Frank said no and explained that he had been fishing. What did he have to lose? He had no passport anyway.

The Policia replied, "I thought so; your pants are still wet. Do you have license to fish the canal, señor?"

Frank's face flushed as he stammered. "Ah ... why no."

He continued to press, asking, "Did you catch anything?"

"Why no, nothing at all, señor."

"Well, that is fortunate for you, señor. If you had, I would have to report you to my cousin. He's with the fish and game commission. Since I am not, I will let it go. But, the passport matter, that's not good."

The sweat on Frank's brow was like that of a pig's. Suddenly, two other policia ran past them, heading into the market. One yelled back, "There's a thief in the market with a gun *darse presa!*"

Without saying another word, the policia with Frank turned and ran after them.

Gratefully, Frank stepped aside and walked quickly across the market square toward the driver he'd arranged for, who was waiting patiently. Barefooted, Frank greeted him and slipped into the steamy backseat. Frank consoled himself. *You got nothin' to worry about. In a few more hours, you'll be back in the good ole USA.*

The remainder of his ride to Tucumán Airport was uneventful. He sat back quietly watching the scenery whiz by as he doted on the day's events, feeling both lucky and vindicated. Ramsay's soul was avenged, and retribution was his. So where were the fireworks? What? No twenty-one gun salute? He guessed it was true what they say about revenge being a dish best eaten cold. Frank came around to the realization that there would never be any fanfare if all went according to plan.

16

The taxi stopped abruptly, jolting him out of his thoughts. He had arrived at the Pan Am departure gate. Frank generously slipped the cabby a twenty for the short ride. After all, he was alone now with no one else in the world to support. It was raining again. The warm, steady rain soaked his tennis shoes as he jogged into the terminal. Entering the men's room, he dried his face and arms with paper towels and then reached in the bag he had stowed in the cab. He was traveling light. He only had one stop left. Once he rented a car in Miami, it would be six hours home to a world he understood.

What then? he thought while standing in the men's room. He wondered what the future held. It seemed strange to him that somehow the man in the mirror looked no different than before. What was he expecting to see? Some sort of monster looking back at him? Not him; he told himself he had no regrets, none whatsoever.

With all his being, Frank pulled it together, focusing all his energies on new plans and schemes. At this point, he was beginning to feel a little spooked by his own sense of self-awareness. He really knew who he was and what he had just done. Frank was stubbornly realizing the true nature of his overwhelming obsession. It was then and there he started coming to grips with the powerlessness over the evil force that drove him. He was seeing clearly what it really was. It had become an insidious creeping, gut-wrenching, animalistic, evil thing that was still growing inside. Yet, he reasoned that delaying his departure wouldn't be prudent. In fact, he convinced himself that it would be dangerous, even reckless.

What he didn't realize was revenge was like a dangerous drug that already had its hooks in him. So, before he left the men's room, he resolved that getting on that plane meant the beginning of a new plan. Because he could hear that little voice deep within him saying, *Keep your promise to Ramsay; make your life worthwhile.* He wanted to listen to that voice, but something else was tugging at him, drawing him in a different direction. Something more remained on his path of revenge.

Outside, he heard the boarding call for his gate number. He left the men's room in a rush. A large blue-and-white sign farther down the concourse posted departure flights. Ticket in hand, he was ready to complete the boarding process; this time, he would be returning as a civilian. The Pan Am ruse was over. It had served its purpose. All he had to do now was get on that plane.

As Frank approached the counter for Flight 424 nonstop to Miami, he saw Toni Richards, the southern blonde stewardess, standing in the doorway of his flight.

Frank began to stew. *Of all the damn luck, and after everything was going so smoothly. How could he catch the same flight with this chick back to Miami?*

Pulling the bill of his cap lower, he sidled up to the ticket counter, hoping she wouldn't spot him. On the slim hope she may not even recognize him in plain clothes, he sat in the last row of the boarding area and held up a discarded newspaper. He had eluded her so far. Then, he realized as long as she stood in that doorway he had to pass her.

* * *

Not everything back at the canal was going according to plan. The same rain falling outside Tucumán Terminal was drenching Pablo, the security guard, as he diligently searched the Bonocante shipping dock for the source of the suspicious clunking sound he'd heard an hour earlier. When his search led him to the shipping office, he discovered the lock was on the door.

Little Eddy is gone, but he did not check out with me at the gate, Pablo thought.

Passing him was the only way of getting off the dock unless he took a boat or swam. Now, Pablo was doubly suspicious. Little Eddy didn't like boats. He couldn't swim. Little Eddy confided that fact to Pablo in one of his higher moments.

By nine fifteen in the morning, Pablo's search of the dock area remained fruitless. He even looked into the warehouses. Knowing it would not bode well with Santo Bonocante if every measure wasn't taken to find Little Eddy, he made his decision. Pablo decided that he'd take out the motor boat and search around the dock. *I hope I don't find Little Eddy drowned*, he thought.

Pablo was a dedicated guard and needed to keep his job, even if it meant pulling Eddy's drowned body out of the canal. Countless times, he observed Eddy weaving down the dock after leaving his shack at the end of the day. Usually, he would be drugged, drunk, or both. Twice, Pablo had to pour him into a cab just to get him home.

So far, his boat search for Eddy revealed nothing around the dock. A few minutes later, Pablo sat still in the boat. He listened to an unusual, nearly imperceptible but unmistakable, repetitive thudding sound. As the sound traveled well across water, he soon identified its source. It was coming from the channel buoy about thirty yards straight out from Eddy's office. Rowing toward it, he followed the sound, scanning with his flashlight across the dull brown water through the rain that glistened off the buoy. Then, he spotted bands of shiny yellow rope stretched across the buoy several times. *That was never there before*, he thought.

As he headed over toward the buoy, the thudding grew louder. On the opposite side, he was shocked as he shone his flashlight on the top of Eddy's head. His big nose barely broke water as gentle waves rocked the buoy. Little Eddy's eyes darted rapidly back and forth, reflecting his extreme agony. If the scene beneath the murky waters were revealed, one would have seen his lower body being ravaged by mud crabs in a feeding frenzy as he slowly slid under the ropes.

Eddy's lower torso was covered in mud crabs feasting on his flesh, picking him apart with their pincers in some places already to the bone. The bloodied water on the surface mixed with loose particles of his flesh that, at times, escaped the crab's claws. They floated toward the surface or into the hungry mouths of swirling shiners with alarming regularity as Eddy convulsed at the sight in horror.

His blood loss was rapidly drawing him closer to hypovolemic shock, staved off only temporarily by the tourniquet effect of the nylon ropes binding him to the buoy. By this time, Eddy had already oozed too much blood into the canal. He was slowly slipping into a coma.

Pablo hurriedly reached out of the boat and held Eddy's head up out of the water, immediately recognizing the rest of his face. His lower torso could have been anybody's guess. His own mother would find it repugnant to look upon the remainder of his body.

Pablo cried out. "Oh, Eddy, what have they done to you?"

Speaking rapidly and nearly in shock himself, Pablo tried to concentrate, thinking about what to do next for the ravaged man.

"*Oh no! Ah no, Señor Eddy. Tu necesidad la hospital, lo mas pronto posible.*"

Pablo quickly snatched the radio from his belt and called for an ambulance. Yanking his Ka-Bar knife from his boot scabbard, he feverishly began cutting the nylon ropes binding Eddy to the buoy. Then, as Eddy's body started slipping beneath reddened waters, Pablo put his strong arms gingerly under Eddy's ragged, bloody armpits and carefully tugged his shredded body into the boat.

* * *

At the airport, Frank found himself wrestling with his conscience. Why did Toni have to complicate things by reentering his life in such an awkward, unwelcome way?

Toni said sarcastically, "I see you're flying a bit casual today, Flight Officer Grin. Is there anything I can get for you, perhaps a pillow after your exhausting layover?"

Taken aback at first, Frank quickly recovered. He managed a sheepish smile. "Thank you, Toni, but no. I'll just take my seat. Thanks again, though."

She was not amused, but she had to let it go for the time being. Other passengers were coming aboard. Soon, she was busy helping others find their seats and overhead space. She planned to grill him about his new attire and abrupt departure after their arrival in Panama. Obviously, she knew something wasn't quite right.

Toni was not put off easily. The daughter of a U.S. Air Force general, she was used to getting her way in life. Her earlier disappointment in Frank had not set well. Thirty minutes into the flight, she spoke to another stewardess in the galley.

"Hey, sweetie, can I take this drink cart back for you?" Toni asked.

The younger stew obliged. "Be my guest. It's all coffee or tea to me, you know."

Toni smiled curtly as she wheeled the cart slowly working her way down the aisle as she waited on passengers. Mixing drinks and passing out peanuts, she worked her way toward Frank. He sat near the back of the plane with the shade pulled down and the bill of his Yankees hat tipped forward, trying for some much needed rest. When Toni finished, she turned her full attention on him.

"Now, tell me, sir, what was all that about in Panama? I thought you were interested in finding a decent place to lie over." Then Toni whispered. "Don't pretend to be sleeping, mister. I know better."

Frank slowly raised his cap while thinking of a good excuse. "Toni, your offer was generous, perhaps too generous. You see, I've just been through a nasty divorce that left me with a rather thin wallet, if you know what I mean. The kinds of places you described—well, I knew I just couldn't afford it right then." Frank looked up pleadingly, hoping she'd buy his story and leave him alone. No such luck.

"You mean to tell me you got divorced from the wife who you couldn't get over losing earlier? What gives really? The minute we hit the tarmac, you were out of that terminal like your hair was afire. You know, you really make a gal feel like her flaps have been dumped."

Frank cringed. "Please, Toni, keep your voice down. Look, I'm awful sorry, but it's embarrassing to be so low on cash that you have to take stand-in flights for your friends."

Toni's expression changed to one of genuine concern as she leaned in closer. She whispered, "Oh, my God, is that what you've been doin', darlin'?" Toni continued, "So, why all the sad stories? When I checked the roster, there was no Frank Barrett scheduled out of Miami on that flight, standby or otherwise."

Frank was pinned on the horns of a dilemma. If he revealed his subterfuge in Panama, it might arouse her suspicion further. Yet, telling her the truth was becoming very important.

He said, "Listen, when we get down in Miami, we can get out from under this grind and have some fun. What do you say to that?"

The next few seconds meant yes or no and a change in his immediate future. Admittedly, he was desperate. He had to make things right with her in order to make the rest of his plan work.

Toni said, "You know you're damn lucky I see something in you I wanna like. Have you done any time in the service?"

Frank thought, *Thank God no lies there.*

Frank replied, "Yes, as a captain in the U.S. Air Force." Frank went on to tell her about how he was now training F-4 pilots. He also told her that he did, in fact, lose his pregnant wife and unborn son.

Frank's eyes plead in an effort to win her confidence. She waited a moment and then looked about the cabin, taking on an air of frustration.

Finally, she spoke. "All right, mystery pilot, you better come up legit this time. Because, right now, you're flying by the seat of your pants with all flaps and no throttle. You're telling me your poor pregnant wife and child died. This better be the truth, fly boy, or I'll call the real captain in a heartbeat. Do you get my meaning?"

Frank looked up soberly. He said, "It is the truth, the whole truth, and nothing but the truth, so help me God. Now what are your plans after this flight?"

There was a ten-second pause before she started in again. "Not so fast, Sky King. What do you take me for anyway? Do you see any wet marks behind these ears? If I had a quarter for every line I've heard in this business, I'd be passing gas through silk by now."

Frank interrupted her speech before she embarrassed any sailors on board. "Listen, Toni, it's for real, on the level." Frank made her an offer. He said, "I'll spring for lunch when we get down, and I'll explain everything." Then, he added the proviso, "If you don't like what you're hearing, you can go your own way."

However, Frank decided, if she did want to spend some time together, he was going to Tampa, and perhaps she'd like to join him. He even offered to pay her way back to Miami.

Toni allowed a slight grin to form on her luscious lips. What she now decided to keep from Frank was the fact that she was planning on going to Tampa anyway to see her parents.

She replied, "Well, I will be laid over for five days; it's the end of my cycle. What do you think about that, captain?"

Frank replied, "Well, then how would you like to spend some time with an U.S. Air Force captain who's trying to make things up to you?"

"I guess that could be arranged. I need to get my car out of Pan Am parking. We're only allowed to keep them there while were working."

Frank's thoughts whizzed ahead. *If she has her own car, maybe a rental would be unnecessary. That way, there would be no paper trail of me being in Miami whatsoever. How bad can that be?*

Just then Toni straightened up as she caught sight of another stewardess in her peripheral vision. She was standing in the galley waving, trying to get her attention. Toni turned, quickly pushing her cart back up the aisle. As she reached the galley, her crewmate chided her.

"You've been down there too long. The captain wants coffee."

Toni winked. "I'll bet he wants cream with it, too. Either way, he'll get what he likes."

"You wouldn't dare, would you?"

The Boeing 727 banked slowly northward, righting itself from its former easterly heading. Now, traveling at thirty-two thousand feet, the Caribbean below was totally obscured beneath a midstrata cloud layer. Nevertheless, it was clear blue skies on top for the rest of the flight.

By the time they touched down, Frank had everything arranged with Toni for a ride in her car to Tampa. Toni was arranging for a quick start on her departure. Everything she had on board was just overhead. When they touched down in Miami, she was ready.

Obviously, Frank had little on the plane. Hastily, they made their way through the abbreviated customs procedure. This is what Frank was truly counting on. As her traveling companion, customs agents figured him as another a pilot out of uniform. When he flashed his name tag with Chad Grin's name on it, he pretty much had a dream ticket back into the country, especially since he didn't fit the profile of any known bad guys.

Before Frank knew it, they were standing in front of the Pan Am employee parking lot. *This is great*, he thought.

It was all beginning to make perfect sense. Before he could even collect his thoughts, he could hear Toni's lilting voice calling to him from what seemed like another world.

"What about that lunch, Frank? I know a great little Cuban place right off the highway here."

Frank had hardly had time to admire her beautiful little '56 gunmetal gray convertible Thunderbird. He kept thinking, *What a classic. How lucky can one guy get?*

Toni came back. "They have great deviled crab rolls. Do you like those?"

"Yes," he said, "but I don't care for the hot sauce."

"Me neither. I don't care for those fried potato things they make either. They're way too fattening. Most of their food is fattening, but I do enjoy a good Cuban now and then, especially when they're toasted."

He replied, "Yeah, there was a Cuban like that once leaning on a lamppost. Boy, was he toasted."

Toni laughed at his joke. The best part of her laugh was that it was soft and sweet, like music. Frank found himself staring until she noticed.

He asked, "Where are we headed?"

"It's called Hurrara's, just a few miles from here."

Frank nodded. They put their things in the trunk, slammed it shut, and left in a hurry. Later, Frank watched her speedometer creeping upward. On the next bridge they crossed, he saw posts blurring as they accelerated past eighty. He could tell from its sound, the 292 V-8 engine was performing beautifully.

Frank warned, "Say, we don't need a ticket, do we?"

Toni turned, lifting her aviators and giving him an impassive gaze. "What's this 'we' stuff? Suh, you gotta mouse in y'all's pocket? There's only one wheel I see in this here car."

Leaning over, she spoke in a measured tone. "When y'all start driving this here car, then you can do the thinking. So, just sit back and enjoy the view, captain." Toni loved putting pilots in their place. She resented their authority and the way some pilots often flaunted it.

Frank sat back and enjoyed the view as he was told. It was a gorgeous, bright sunny day. He didn't want to make waves at present, so he started taking in the sights as they sped across another series of bridges that led them over the heart of sparkling Biscayne Bay. They were eastbound on the JFK Causeway heading for the village of North Island. The bay was filled with colorful sunlit sails sliding the yachts across the bay as they tilted ahead of the wind. Frank felt a pang of guilt as he thought how Ramsay would have laughed and enjoyed the sun-splashed view.

Soon, churning dust around them as they came to a halt in the parking lot of Herrera's. Frank felt a huge sense of relief, swearing to himself he would never let Toni drive once they reached US 27 North headed for Tampa.

Inside, the Cuban cuisine was familiar; it reminded him of Falgies back home in Tampa. As he waited at their table, some thoughts of Ramsay and him together came rushing back. He wanted to push them away over the dock or somewhere out back where they wouldn't intrude on the present. He was about to chide himself for feeling that way when the waiter arrived. Composing himself, he ordered something Toni found surprising.

Frank asked the waiter, "Do you serve smoked mullet?"

"Of course, sir, that is one of our specialties. Would you like some salad with that? Perhaps a caesar?"

"Yes, that would be fine. The young lady would like one of your famous Cubano sandwiches."

Toni concurred, "Yes, please. Make it the very best. I would also like a bottle of sparkling Madura wine for my friend and me if you please."

Frank raised his hand in protest. "If you're drinking this afternoon, I'm definitely driving. It's over three hundred miles to Tampa, and that's more than six hours of driving time."

"I'm well aware of time distance equations, Captain Barrett. They're one of the first things a stew learns in training. Besides, I wasn't aware you were on the driving team, suh."

Frank took a break from his thoughts, realizing what was actually taking place right before his eyes. Obviously, there was a transformation taking place in Toni's normally outgoing personality. Now, it dawned on him. Toni, the stalwart stew, raided the little cart she'd been pushing. By now, she was feeling the effects of several vodka miniatures, compliments à la Pan Am Airlines. By the time their sandwiches arrived, it was quite obvious the stew was nearly stewed.

At least she was quite cordial and did not embarrass herself or others around. Apparently, she could hold her liquor pretty well. Her present condition served to make Frank recall his coming home and finding Ramsay rip-roaring drunk. Even then, he could not stop loving her. The old heartaches he'd been experiencing since she'd been gone were coming back. Toni was beginning to notice he was lost in thought.

"What's the matter, Frank?" she asked.

Frank replied, "Nothing. Just a little chill, that's all."

"Thash funny; I feel warm. We're two funny birds, aren't we?"

When they finished their meal, Frank offered to drive. She was in no condition anyway, and so it went for the next six hours. Just before pulling into Tampa, Toni awoke and asked Frank to stop. Of course, she had to pee. He obliged her since he could use a break and they needed gas.

They entered the bay area around six o'clock that evening. Frank drove directly to the house. Newspapers stacked by the front door told him no one was paying much attention to his whereabouts. That was fine with him. He handed Toni the key and asked her to let herself in while he checked the mail. Noticing mostly junk mail, he tucked it all under his arm and headed toward his car. Then, he heard Toni calling from the front door.

"Frank, how do you turn the air-conditioning on? It's stifling in here."

His mind returned to the day he left. He'd switched off the breakers in case of a power surge. Now, it would take another half hour to get the house cool enough for some much-needed sleep. He still had visions of Ramsay's love squarely fixed in his brain. Unshakeable as her image was, he needed sleep. He told Toni he would sleep on the couch and went off to get some sheets. When he finished making his makeshift bed, he called out to her in his bedroom. "Good night, Toni."

She did not reply. He waited a few minutes longer and then figured he better check in on her. He found her face down on the bed with all her clothes on. Shaking his head, he could see she needed sleep, too. So, he slipped off her shoes. Being the gentleman he was, he rolled her to one side of the bed and then pulled the sheet over her. That night, Frank prayed as he did when he flew over North Vietnam.

"God, make of me an instrument of thy will. Thy will be done."

17

One thing Frank was certain of was getting sleep that night. He really needed it. Toni awoke instinctively at seven o'clock the next morning. She headed for the bathroom, while Frank made coffee. As he did, he reflected on the past week's events and thought it was time he reported back to base. He felt disjointed even though he'd only been out of the cockpit a few weeks. It seemed more like a year. He wondered how his squadron was getting along. As he watched the brown-black elixir of life dribbling slowly into his Mr. Coffee coffee pot, he figured that they must be getting along just fine without him.

In fact, he was starting to feel a bit sorry for himself when Toni entered the kitchen.

"Mmm, that smells good. Where are the cups?" she cooed.

"Second cabinet on the right," Frank I said absentmindedly. "Maybe you'd like some eggs."

"That sounds terrific. Have you got any bread? I can make some toast if you like," Toni offered.

Frank said, "That sounds like a deal." He also told her he was going to the base to report to his commander.

"Take me with you, please. I haven't been there since Daddy was active."

"That reminds me. What is it you said your daddy did anyway?" Frank asked.

She hesitated a moment, and then she confided, "He was a two-star general when he retired. If I told you where he is now, I'd have to kill you."

Frank replied, "Very funny. You know the old adage: everybody likes a little ass, but nobody likes a smart-ass."

"Well, why don't you ask him yourself? My parents live right here in town. Actually, I was going to ask you if you wouldn't mind going over there so I can visit them."

Frank asked, "Is that supposed to be the fun part of your trip to Tampa? Why don't you get dressed, and I'll fix us up some eggs and toast, okay?"

"Sounds great, but I don't want to wait too long."

By nine o'clock, Frank was driving toward the base. His house was two miles from the Bay Shore gate. After driving a few blocks east down Napoleon Street, he made a right turn toward the base, which was situated on a peninsula jutting out into Old Tampa Bay.

The bay itself was first discovered by Spanish explorer Hernando Desoto in the sixteenth century. He was there for God, gold, and glory in the name of the king of Spain. Frank sought neither of these; instead, he found himself being drawn back to the path of revenge.

He was enraged at the thought of living in the same town with Judge Harry Lee Cowen. He couldn't stop thinking about the man who freed Little Eddy. Allowing Little Eddy to return to Panama, Judge Cowen committed a most grievous miscarriage of justice from Frank's point of view. *That paid judge of Bonocante's will not escape justice*, Frank thought.

Frank approached the guard gate and slowed to enter. He held out his military ID card. The guard saluted, saying, "Good morning, captain."

Frank returned the salute. "Good morning, Sergeant." Frank drove along the flight line, looking at all the different types of aircraft painted in their spinach and sand camouflage paint scheme. A blind man could see it, or at least feel it. There was a buildup in airpower slated for Nam.

When Frank reached Colonel Perry's office, he asked his adjutant if the colonel was busy.

The adjutant touched the button on his speakerphone.

"Captain Barrett is here to see you, Colonel Perry."

"Send him in," Perry replied curtly. "What do you have on your mind, captain?"

Frank told Colonel Perry his bereavement leave was half over, and he wanted to be reassigned to his cycle of advanced combat training.

"Well, Frank, that meets with my approval. Just be sure they schedule you for a complete flight physical prior to your return to flight status."

Frank replied, "Affirmative, sir, and thank you."

Colonel Perry said, "That's all right, Frank. You've earned it. How's your leave going anyway?"

He replied, "Fine, sir. No worries, just interested in getting back in the ol' saddle, you know."

"Well, Frank, I can understand that. Do you also feel you might be ready to consider another go-around in Ubon? You know, there's a lot you could teach those new guys over there. Heck, before you know it, this whole thing will be over. Pretty soon none of us will be taking combat hazardous duty pay."

Perry stood up from behind his desk, placing his hands behind his back as he ambled over to his office window and faced the flight line. He watched the increased activity outside. He lowered his voice as he turned back to face Frank. "You know, there's one big push on before all this ends."

Raising his finger to his lips, the colonel almost whispered. "It's designated Linebacker II. Maybe you'd like to get in on it. Just say the word. I'm sure I can fix it for you, Frank."

"Thank you, sir, for the opportunity. It's certainly worth thinking about."

The colonel replied, "Well, anybody who's earned the DFC in my wing has the right to go. Just remember that, Frank."

"Yes, sir. It sure would be great to go with the rest of my squadron. Thank you for your confidence in me, Colonel. Good-bye."

Frank snapped off a salute and turned to leave. When he stepped out of the colonel's office, he stopped to take a deep breath. His head felt warm, and his knees felt weak. He wondered if he was getting a cold or had cold feet. Colonel Perry's offer took him by surprise. Up until then, he thought remaining in the states as flight instructor was the thing to do. Now, another possibility loomed in Frank's not-too-distant future. He thought, *I've got another matter to take care of first.*

Leaving Colonel Perry's office, Frank felt he needed a drink and a quick decision. Driving to the Officers' Club, he spotted a flight of F-4 Phantoms climbing out over the bay. He thought, *I know just where you're headed, men. Yes, as a matter of fact, I do.*

When Frank entered the bar, he felt as though he was the only one there. Only two majors sat at the far end of the bar. Quickly, he glanced at his watch. It was only eleven o'clock in the morning.

Huh, Frank thought, *my visit with the colonel just seemed longer.*

Frank sat at the other end of the bar facing toward the majors who were in the midst of an animated conversation. When the bartender arrived, Frank ordered a double Jack Daniels on the rocks.

"Sorry, sir, we can't serve hard liquor here until noon. But, I *can* serve you a cold beer."

Frank said, "No thanks." As he turned to leave, one of the majors called after him loudly. "Hey, you must be one of those Linebackers. Are you too busy to come down here and drink with us?"

Frank turned and slowly walked back toward them. He had sized them up as high-time jet jockeys with graying hair. From the looks of them, they had just come off duty. They still wore their flight suits. They appeared old enough to know better.

When Frank reached the two, he asked the major who had spoken, "What did you just say?"

The first major replied, "I was just saying maybe you were too busy to come down and drink with us."

Frank replied, "No, no, before that. It seems the major doesn't remember all he said."

The major squinted, and then it came to him. "I asked you if you were one of those Linebackers."

"That's right, major," Frank said. "You shouldn't be bandying that word about. Someone might get the wrong idea."

The major shot back derisively. "How the hell would you know what I'm talking about, captain?"

Frank was ready to engage the major further when the bartender came between them. "Listen, fellas, you're getting a little loud. If you wanna argue, take it outside, please."

Frank was leaving anyway, so he started for the door, thinking discretion the better part of valor. The major got Frank all wrong. He started following him outside. Then the major called out to Frank from the front steps of the Officers' Club. "Is this where you wanna do it, captain, 'cause I'm ready anytime."

Frank responded, "Look, I can see you've had a long day and a few beers." Frank noted the name on his flight suit. "You, above all, major, should know the word you used involves sensitive information. Even on base, we can't be too careful."

Major Boyle stared back at Frank. His darkened eyes proved he was tired. In fact, he'd been up all night training. He was helping pilots to prepare for Operation Linebacker.

Now, he spoke apologetically. "You're right, captain; I was a bit out of line back there in the bar. Can I buy you one for the road?"

Frank smiled. "Nah, thanks anyway. I gotta few things to take care of. I'll take a rain check on it, okay?"

Major Boyle replied, "Sure, Captain Barrett. I'll see ya when I see ya."

Frank waved, saying, "Don't take off downwind."

Major Boyle just chuckled and walked up the steps to reenter the club. Frank was glad he got his point across without entering into a scrap. He had more-important matters to tend to, like dealing with a crooked, retired, bought-off judge.

Passing through the Dale Mabry Highway gate, he continued to head north. Dale Mabry Highway was one of the main highways in town. It was originally built as an emergency evacuation route for the base in 1942. By now, its sectioned slabs of concrete settled in places due to the sandy sediment of Florida. That gave the impression of riding on a washboard. The resultant popping sound of tires on disjointed pavement created a rhythmic beat when driving on it. Frank drove north on Dale Mabry for eleven miles. He then turned west on Highway 580 for another four miles. This brought him to the entrance of the Bay Crest Retirement Community.

Most of the homes were built in the mid-sixties, representing one of the more exclusive communities in northern Tampa. Many of the larger homes were built next to the intercoastal waterway. This arrangement provided residents access to Old Tampa Bay. As he passed through the neighborhood, he was impressed. Having seen enough, Frank turned his Mustang around using someone's driveway. He had done his homework. He held in his hand the address of one Honorable Harry Lee Cowen—or, as Frank put it, 'his slimy ass is goin'.

Now, Frank approached the main clubhouse of Bay Crest. Frank parked in the portico and walked into the clubhouse.

At the front desk, there sat a pretty, elderly female receptionist.

"Hello, I'm Frank. How are you today?"

"I'm just fine," she responded. "What may I do for you?"

Frank replied, "Is your schedule of activities posted somewhere around here? My dad would like to know what sort of recreation facilities you provide."

"Oh, yes, we offer a wide variety of activities here. In addition, we offer the latest in amenities. Perhaps your father would be interested in our most recent flyer that updates our residents here with a calendar of our upcoming events."

Frank smiled. "Yes, that would be a good start. Thank you very much. That will be helpful."

When the receptionist returned, she held the clubhouse calendar in her hand along with some promotional material about the community. Frank thanked her again for the information. Back in his Mustang, he gripped the steering wheel tightly as he drove back down Dale Mabry with plans of vengeance wheeling in his mind. When he reached his home, Toni was watching TV.

* * *

Toni looked up. "Well. When you go out, you stay out. I've been bored stiff hanging around someone else's house half the day."

Frank said, "Things took a little longer than I thought. What can I do to make it up to you?"

Toni smiled mischievously. "Well, for starters, you could take me out to lunch. Then, I'd like to visit my parents."

Frank said, "Where would you like to eat?"

"Well, let's see. Oh, I know. There was an ad on TV. They told of a place called Wright's Gourmet. The ad made the place seem very appealing. There were pictures of highly stacked sandwiches, salads, and a wide variety of other delicatessen delights. What do you say?"

Frank replied, "It sounds great as long as you know the way. Let's go."

"I think I can find it easily," Toni said. "It's right off South Dale Mabry."

Frank said, "Good. That sounds pretty close by."

Just as they were leaving Frank's next door neighbor showed up in front of them. "Oh dear," Trudy said. "I didn't realize you were entertaining, Frank."

Frank was not in the mood for Trudy at the moment and was inclined to give her the brush-off. Instead, he tolerated her presence, speaking kindly to the neighbor who helped him through the trauma after Ramsay was hit. He recalled she even buried little Barkley for him.

"Trudy, we were just leaving to get lunch."

"Oh, that's all right. I just came over to pick up my casserole dish. It can wait. You won't be gone long will you?"

Frank said, "Well now, that all depends. Oh, I'm sorry. This is Miss Toni—"

"Rogers," Toni broke in. "It's Toni Rogers. Nice to meet you, Trudy. Would you like to join us for lunch?"

Frank's ears started turning red like they did whenever he was upset. He was standing right in front of Trudy, so there was no way he could communicate with Toni without Trudy knowing.

Trudy replied, "Oh, heavens no. I appreciate the invite, but I must put lunch on the table for my husband." Trudy took one long last look at Toni, and then she excused herself and headed back home.

Frank heaved a sigh of relief. Once in the car, Frank confided to Toni. "You just missed going to lunch with the most talkative woman in my neighborhood," he quipped. "Some say she once detained children on Halloween to tell them about the dangers of accepting gifts from strangers. She can talk the bark off of a tree."

Toni just laughed. "Oh my, bless her heart."

Lunch was sumptuous at Wright's Gourmet Sandwich Shop.

Frank said, "I m glad you were watching TV while I was out, or we might have missed this pleasant dining experience."

Toni smiled. "I declare, I've never seen such a huge club sandwich in all my born days. Do you suppose you would mind going over to see my parents for a while?"

Frank had been working on a dodge for that experience, but with her providing transportation all the way from Miami, he felt he couldn't refuse. "All right, but I must reserve the right to leave should your father become pretentious as some generals want to do."

Toni apparently took no offense to Frank's request. Instead, she explained, "Oh, I'm just certain you will enjoy his company. He was a pilot, too, once, and he surely can regale you with his war stories if you let him."

Frank explained that he may not have that much time, because he still had some things to take care of.

Toni smiled. "I'm thinkin' you'll get along just fine with the both of them. We're what you might call a flying family. My daddy met my mother in Sweetwater, Texas, where he was training the WASPs to fly."

Frank recalled, "Oh yes, my dad told me all about the Women's Air Service Pilots. They were instrumental in freeing up our pilots in World War II by transporting bomber aircraft over to England."

Toni enthused, "Yes, that's it. Y'all got that right. Some of the other pilots used to laugh at my daddy for teaching women to fly, but he proved in many cases they actually made better pilots. For instance, they had a lighter touch on the controls than some of those ham-handed pilots comin' out of basic flight training. But, I'll let Daddy tell you all that stuff, if you give him the chance."

Leaving Wright's Gourmet, Frank asked Toni which way to go.

Toni replied, "Just turn right and go north on Dale Mabry. It's about ten miles from here. They live in a retirement community called Bay Crest."

Frank swallowed hard, gripping the steering wheel of his Mustang hard as he turned northward on Dale Mabry for the second time that day. When they drove through the entrance to Bay Crest, Toni gave him directions to her parents' home. Soon, Toni was pointing ahead.

"There it is," she said. "Just ahead—2213 West Douglas Street."

Frank said, "Douglas was the name of an aircraft manufacturer in World War II."

Toni replied, "It's no surprise. Dad had a hand in helping the community association name the streets around here."

Frank asked, "Does he go by general, or would you like to tell me his first name?"

"Oh, I'm sorry. He goes by Harold now. He's not too stuffy either."

Frank maintained, "That's a bit unusual for a general, retired or not."

Toni encouraged, "Come now, Frank. You'll see. He's very down to earth—for a pilot, that is."

Frank thought, *Touché, Toni. Here I am going to meet her old folks at home, and I just can't get Ramsay's words out of my mind. What the hell am I doing here anyway?*

Frank resigned himself to the meeting, thinking it might help him know the area better. "What's your mother's name?" he asked.

"It's Dorothy," Toni answered. "They've been married ... let's see now ... it's been thirty years already. I'll have to remember to buy them a little old anniversary gift soon."

Frank asked, "By the way, Toni, are you an only child? I haven't heard you speak of any siblings."

"You got it, suh. I'm the one and only in this family. Come on in and meet the folks."

General Richards answered the door. His appearance didn't surprise Frank. Dressed in Bermuda shorts, an Izod Lacoste polo shirt, and Dockers, his thinning sandy hair topped an ample six two frame.

His outstretched hand belied the fact he was still giving Frank the once-over. "Well, hello, Mister ...?"

"Daddy, this is Capt. Frank Barrett. He is an F-4 flight instructor over at the base."

"Well, it's good to meet a fellow pilot. Come right on in, captain."

"You can call me Frank if you like, general."

"All right then. I see Toni's been talking about me. This lovely lady behind me is Dorothy; she's my wife of thirty years. I hope you caught that hint, little girl."

"Yes, Daddy. We just got in from Miami, and I haven't had time to shop for a card."

"A card? Why I expect your momma will be lookin' for something a heap sight better than that."

Dorothy was five ten with a remarkably good, sturdy figure for her age. She reached out and gave Frank a handshake with a steady grip. She wore her silver hair short. It was the only feature that belied her true age. Otherwise, her complexion was as tanned and youthful as she appeared vibrant.

She said, "Harold, you hush now. It's enough that she's safe and right here with us, and you know it."

Listening to Harold and Dorothy, Frank knew just where Toni's Southern accent came from. That made perfect sense.

Harold asked, "Well now, captain, what brings you over here with our little girl?"

Toni said, "Oh, Daddy, I'm not your little girl anymore."

Frank suggested, "You can just call me Frank if you like, sir."

Harold replied, "All right, then you can just call me general. I think you'll find I'm not such a stuffy old SOB after all."

Dorothy said, "Why don't you show Frank around the place, Daddy?"

"Sure, no problem; follow me, Frank. I'll show you my new boat."

Frank followed Harold's lead, passing through the back sliding-glass doors into the lanai. The screened-in lanai was spacious, covering the width of his two-story home. It was appointed with the usual patio furniture and colorful plants indigenous to Florida.

Frank observed, "A fella could entertain quite a few guests out here."

Harold replied, "Well, Dorothy and I don't have much else to do now that we're retired. For me, it's either a get-together or fishing. I've made a lot of fishing buddies since I moved in here. It's tough choosing who goes out with me anymore."

They walked back across the lawn to the channel behind the house. It was clear the community was designed for access to the intercoastal waterway, which led to Old Tampa Bay. There, before Frank, was a dock fitted with twin launch booms supporting an ivory-colored fiber-glass-hulled 36"3' Corsair hardtop. Harold must have taken notice of Frank's admiring eyes.

"She's powered by twin Mercury 380 HP inboards. This ol' gal can get up and dance if she wants to."

No doubt about it, she was a trim, sporty-looking craft aptly christened *General Endeavor*. The custom designed Biminis hardtop really gave her a touch of class and the look of speed. Frank truly did admire his boat. Already, it crossed his mind about asking if they could take her out for a spin. He had Judge Cowen's place in mind. Harold must have read his mind.

"We could take her out, if you like," Harold said.

Frank replied, "Oh, hell yes!"

18

"Yes, I'll tell you, Frank, it's truly hard to choose which of my fishing buddies will join me on my next outing," Harold noted.

"Certainly, we could all have worse problems," Frank replied.

He seemed to ignore Frank's comment and moved right along.

"Why, just last Saturday I got a call from Bill Pilkinton over on de Havilland Drive. The weather was nice, so he called to see if I was going out fishing. Not ten minutes later, old Harry Cowen over on East Vultee Street wanted to do the same thing. I said, 'Harry, old buddy, what's the matter with your boat?'"

Judge Cowen's name spoken aloud made Frank's blood begin to boil. He squeezed the taught lines together on the boom where he was standing. As he tried regaining composure, he got the funniest look from Harold.

"What's the matter, Frank? You look sort of flushed. Is it too hot out here for ya?"

Frank struggled to keep his emotions under control as he turned and walked farther out onto the dock. "I'll be fine." Frank assured him. "It's just sometimes I just get a little whiff of Thailand in the wind."

In that moment, Harold confided in Frank. "Ah yes, I do understand. My time in World War II wasn't always a picnic. Let's go back in and let the girls know we're going to take the *General Endeavor* out for a spin."

As they walked back to the house, Frank thought about the Judge. *Now I'll have a shot at seeing the jaded old bastard.* He was already dreaming up a plan of how he could get a closer look at his digs. Knowing any self-respecting fisherman would keep a pair of binoculars on board, he was planning on getting a hold of Harold's.

Back in the house, Harold announced his intentions to Dorothy and Toni.

"Where should we go?" Frank asked.

Harold replied, "Oh, just out for a spin. We don't need a destination, do we?"

Frank thought, *No, I suppose not.*

Toni said, "I'm ready to go. Frank and I will meet you at the dock, Mom."

Harold said, "Well, crew, let's get this excursion underway, shall we?"

Frank snapped off a mock salute and took hold of the boom crank. "Aye, aye, sir. We're ready to lower away, sir."

Harold replied, "Good, you may lower away, mates."

Toni had a mixed look of excitement and curiosity in her sparkling green eyes. It was a beautiful day for a cruise. She was particularly happy her father was taking her out on his boat for the very first time. He'd only had time for his friends and fishing before. She was thrilled to be joining in this part of her father's life. Dorothy exited the lanai and made her way toward the boat. She looked very stylish in her bright pink shorts and sandals. Her Hawaiian top shouted a profusion of colors that made her look festive for such an occasion. They nearly had the boat lowered on the water as she stepped on to the dock. Her sunglasses perched upon a cute little color-splashed ball cap made her appear the consummate boater's wife.

Harold said, "You look absolutely smashing, my dear. Your captain welcomes you aboard."

"Why thank you, kind sir."

Harold donned his captain's cap as he stood by the gangplank to offer his hand to Dorothy. After she boarded, Toni and Frank followed. Once the ladies were seated comfortably in the wide, curvy couch seats at the stern, Captain Richards and Frank took their places at the helm. Harold gave the orders as they prepared to get underway. Soon, the engines roared to life. Frank could feel the power of this trim craft pulsing underfoot.

"Prepare to cast off, mate," Harold called out.

"Aye, aye, sir. Prepared to cast off all lines," Frank responded.

"Cast off all lines."

In a matter of seconds, Harold powered the *General Endeavor* into the intercoastal waterway, which ran behind the homes in his neighborhood. Once they were lined up in the middle of the channel, he applied full power. It gave everyone on board a thrill feeling the acceleration driving the bow up while pushing the waters aside with a powerful surge.

They were underway, feeling the wind in their faces. Frank looked back and caught a glimpse of the gals hanging onto the railing alongside their seats. At first, they put up sporting smiles and tried to appear game for the ride. It wasn't long, however, before Dorothy shouted to her husband. "Harold, can't we slow down a bit?"

"Why sure we can, honey darlin', that's no problem."

Harold chopped the throttle. The *General* responded instantly, its nose slipping gracefully back into the channel. Now, they chugged along at about ten knots. Frank watched carefully, noting address numbers painted on the seawall of each home. This thoughtful touch allowed seaborne visitors to find neighbors easily from their boats.

Frank plied Harold with a chance question, hoping it wouldn't garner much attention. "Harold, didn't you say Judge Cowen lived on your street?"

"Yes," he said, pointing. "That's it coming up now, 2033 East Vultee. Why do you ask?"

"Oh, I knew someone who had dealings with him once."

"Well, I hope all went well. I hear he was pretty tough on the bench. He's retired now."

Frank asked no more questions; he just carefully noted the location as they passed, while making a plan for the return trip. Of course, he never told Toni of his dealings in court with the judge. The very thought of that day of travesty made him boil with rage in his heart. Harold must have noticed something was amiss.

"What ho, mate? It seems you're preoccupied. Just now you looked as though you were a thousand miles away."

Frank managed a smile as he made an excuse about daydreaming about what it would be like to own a boat like his.

"Well, if you play your cards right, I might let you handle her on the way back."

Frank replied, "That would be excellent. Yes, indeed." Frank turned his head for one last look as they left the judge's place behind. *I'll be seeing you soon, you greedy ol' bastard*, Frank thought.

Just then, Dorothy called forward to Harold. "Now that we're out of the channel, you could go a bit faster, you know."

"Sure, honey, we're on our way," Harold agreed.

Dorothy turned to Toni. "I do declare retirement has made such an old fart out of him. He agrees with everything I say. I tell you it's boring, you know. In the old days, he was such a firebrand. He wouldn't listen to a thing I said unless he was in favor of it in the first place."

"Oh, Momma, he's just being respectful of you."

"Well, he could sure do it with a little more pizzazz."

Just then, Harold called back to Dorothy. "What do you say we head across the bay to Safety Harbor at Philippe Park? I'll bet they'd enjoy the view there."

Dorothy shouted over the twin Mercury engines. "Sure, that's a good idea."

At that, Harold opened the throttles and made a beeline across Old Tampa Bay headed west for the farthest point jutting out into Safety

Harbor. "Now, you'll see what this baby can really do. Hold on to your hats, girls!" he called out.

Frank shouted over the engine noise, "*Philippe Park?*"

Harold shouted back over the roar of the twin power plants. "*It's a county park. I'll explain later.*"

Harold drove on for fifteen minutes until they reached shallow water in the harbor. Harold cut his engines, and they slowly drifted into a quiet little picturesque piece of heaven known as Safety Harbor. Dead ahead was a three hundred foot promontory that loomed above the bay.

Harold regaled us. "This is the oldest park in Pinellas County. It bears the name of Count Odette Philippe, known for introducing citrus to this area. The park was originally a plantation where original bitterroot stock was delivered from Spain. Some of the original citrus trees still survive. Incidentally, Count Philippe was also the personal surgeon of Napoleon Bonaparte. The mound you see jutting out in the harbor is a Calusa Indian burial mound created over the years from discarded oyster and clam shells. This property is listed on the National Register of Historical Landmarks. And, that's the end of my tour guide speech."

The jutting spit of land they were looking at was nestled in one of the calmest harbors Frank had ever seen. The surface truly looked like glass, shattered only occasionally by the determined dives of cormorant fishing birds.

Harold went on. "As you can see, the bluff ahead is part of the Indian mound overlooking the harbor." The rise at the top of the mound fell sharply from that point to a narrow white-sand beach at the edge of the harbor. Everything seemed to flow gracefully with old palm trees swaying invitingly in the onshore breeze.

Frank turned to Toni. "You know, we should visit this park someday, don't you think?"

Harold broke in with a suggestion. "Say, I know a little seafood market at the dock here. Maybe we should pick up some fresh blue crabs for our dinner."

"That's a great idea, Dad," Toni said. "I haven't had a crab cookout in ages. What do you think, Frank? Do enjoy boiled blue crab?"

"Sure, but only if it's prepared with Old Bay Seasoning."

"Oh man, now you're talking. I can hear those juicy crabs cracking right now," Harold enthused.

Dorothy ventured. "Well, why don't we pick up a bushel and point this craft homeward? I can whip up some potato salad to go with the crab, if you like."

"That settles it. I'm the captain, and I say, be reasonable; do it my way."

On the way back, Frank asked Harold, "Say, do you have a pair of binoculars on board?"

Harold replied, "I sure do. I never cruise without them. Just look over there in that front compartment to your right."

Sure enough, Frank found his prize. They were a nice rubberized pair of Bausch & Lomb 7x35 9-degree glasses. He removed them from their case and stabilized his arms on the outer railing. He had a look all around, getting acquainted with them. Then, he sighted in on a buoy and adjusted them for up close viewing. Frank stood by Harold's side as the girls opted for the cushioned couch on the stern. As soon as they got near the judge's home, Frank lifted his binoculars, trying to get an idea of his layout.

Suddenly filling Frank's lenses, the judge appeared. He was walking through his living room with a scantily clad blonde in tow. She was quite a looker, or hooker; either way, she was clearly half his age.

Harold interrupted. "Say, fella, are you spying on my neighbor?"

"Oh, hell no, Harold," Frank said

Frank took one last glimpse, which revealed the judge and the blonde lying down on his couch. Then, he broke off quickly and stowed the glasses in the front compartment. The gals stayed in their seats as they prepared to dock. After tying down *General Endeavor*, Frank walked toward the house with the rest of the group.

Frank said, "Well, that was quite an experience. You've got a trim craft there, Harold."

Harold replied, "Thank you, Frank. It's the first and best boat I've ever had. If you'll excuse me and Dorothy, we're going to start preparing our crab feast."

Toni's parents disappeared into the house, leaving Toni and Frank outside. Frank walked back through the lawn to the dock and watched the sun just touching the bay. It was a beautiful sunset, which made their day.

However, Toni sensed something was amiss with Frank. He seemed withdrawn and lost in thought. Toni approached him from behind as he stood on the dock. "Did you enjoy the boat ride?" she asked.

Frank turned to face her. "Yes, it was very nice."

Toni saw something more in his face. She was inquisitive enough to try to find out. "What's the matter, Frank? You seem out of it. Is there something troubling you?"

Frank heaved a heavy sigh and spoke directly to Toni. "Yes, there is something troubling me. A thing that happened not long ago, keeps coming up."

"Do you mean the loss of your wife?"

"Yes, of course, that troubles me too, but there is so much more to deal with," Frank answered.

Toni urged Frank to share more. "What do you mean? Maybe its best y'all got it off your chest."

Frank decided to tell her the whole story of the defendant and the way Ramsay's case was settled in court. Frank began. "You see, Toni, after my wife was struck and suffered, the way her case was handled in court turned my life upside down. The defendant really had no defense. Everything he did was witnessed by the police. Tests proved he was a coke addict. Surely, the evidence in the case clearly showed he should have been put behind bars for at least twenty years. Yet the judge ruled that because he was an illegal alien, he should be deported back to the

Panamanian authorities. Nothing more was done. It was a total miscarriage of justice."

Toni sympathized. "Oh, my God, Frank. You must have been devastated."

Frank continued. "That's not all. The defendant was proven to be an employee of the local mafia. They put up his defense, and according to the detective on the case, they most likely bought off the judge."

"Oh my. What happened then?"

"Later, I learned the defendant was deported to his native country and went back to work for the mafia and its interests in Panama. Listen, Toni, I want satisfaction from that judge, and he's right here."

Toni said, "What are you talking about, Frank?"

Frank finished telling his story. "It's true. He's right here in your dad's neighborhood. His name is Judge Harry Lee Cowan, and justice will be done."

Frank began telling Toni how he planned to get enough on him to ruin him for the rest of his miserable crooked life. He told her his plan was to get a private eye on to the lying philanderer.

Suddenly, Toni backed away from Frank. Immersed in his vengeful thoughts, he continued suggesting Toni could help him.

Toni's eyes glared. "Hold it right there, dammit! Sure, I'm sorry as hell for your loss. Yeah, I feel for you, buddy; you got messed over all right. But, I'll not be part of anything you do that's illegal or immoral. That's where I draw the line, buddy boy. I don't know what you did in Panama. I'm thinking right now I don't wanna know either. But, this tears it with us, Frank. I'm not helping you frame anybody. I don't care if he's rotten to the core. In fact, if this is where you're coming from, I don't want any part of *you*. Vengeance accomplishes nothing—it's hollow. You should know that. You should be man enough to realize that. Don't give up your life for something as cheap and unsatisfactory as revenge, Frank."

Suddenly, Toni fell silent. Her eyes filled with tears. Her body was trembling. She was struggling to maintain some semblance of control.

Frank just stood there, knowing she was determined now to have nothing whatsoever to do with him. Frank knew no matter how he felt deep inside, ultimately she was right. For a while, it seemed the air was charged between them. Then, Frank chose to break the silence.

He said, "Some people deserve retribution. It balances the world. No doubt you'll see that someday."

There was nothing left to say. Frank walked away.

19

Frank and Toni's relationship was shot. In hindsight, Frank realized he should never have tried involving Toni in his misguided quest for revenge. Thus, he began his quest for justice alone. Only Judge Harry Lee Cowen remained on Frank's mind. His world centered on planning for the deed to be done.

First, Frank would need the services of a private detective. Not knowing where to start, he went to the yellow pages and picked a number to call.

"Hello, this is Fales Detective Agency," the voice on the other end of the phone said.

Frank asked, "Do you investigate spouses suspected of being unfaithful?"

Burt Fales replied, "If I didn't, I'd be home in bed right now myself."

Frank was unaccustomed to such a crass response and dwelled a moment, reconsidering his making the call. But, the urge to feed his vengeful soul bid him to continue. "I'd like to know what that sort of investigating would cost."

"Well, sir, my flat rate is fifty dollars a day. If I have to work around the clock, it's more depending on the conditions of my surveillance. In some cases, I've contracted for twice as much. My services are not guaranteed, but my former clients have managed to keep me in this business for fifteen years."

Frank digested that last remark and concluded he was straightforward enough. His main concern was getting someone who kept his word and got results.

"How soon can you start, Mr. Fales?" Frank asked.

"Call me Burt, and it all depends. Why don't you come down to my office, and we can discuss it."

Frank's hand fidgeted with the telephone cord. Then, it came to him. "I prefer to act anonymously. Can you do that?"

"I have in the past. Usually, a PO box will suffice for necessary exchanges. That arrangement will require a deposit of one hundred dollars. If you decide you don't require my services the next day, I keep the check, and you're finished with me. Otherwise, I'll go to work and notify you in a week of my progress. Then, the balance is due, in cash, if you decide to retain me."

Frank assured that he understood and told Burt he would start right away. He promised to call later with the address of his P.O. Box at the post office. Then, he would place the cash deposit and Judge Cowen's address in the box. If his plan worked, he figured to be in the air flying toward Southeast Asia when all hell broke loose in the judge's world. He had to act fast, though, if he were to depart the following week with his squadron.

Three anxious days past before Burt left evidence in Frank's box on Wednesday. It was a shocker to say the least. Pulling the glossy eight-by-tens out of the envelope, Frank discovered one young blonde was not enough for the old Judge. One photo explicitly revealed his honor naked on the floor in his living room with three female partners.

Jackpot! Frank thought. *This is a real eye-opener. Now, the rest of my plan can begin.*

Immediately, Frank pushed the photographic evidence back in the envelope and included a brief printed note at the post office counter. Then, he mailed the contents by certified mail with a signature request from Mrs. Cowen. Of course, there was no return address on the envelope. Frank knew he was taking a chance that the judge might try to sign for it himself, but he counted on the postal service to do its duty diligently.

The next step now fell neatly into place. Frank's prior observation of the Bay Crest Clubhouse revealed that the judge was a regular for Thursday night bingo at the clubhouse. If the sequence of events went as planned, the photos sent to his wife should arrive after the bingo numbers reader received her reprints. Either way, the social fallout would appear insurmountable. In addition, a short printed letter of explanation marked URGENT should appear on the desk of the editor of the *Tampa Tribune* around about the same time with more reprints of the judge's dalliances.

At any rate, by the time Frank arrived overseas, the crooked judge's goose should have been thoroughly cooked. Time would tell, and so would Chad, who promised he'd write.

The only thing left for Frank to do was get some rest and prepare to join his squadron. Frank was ready to throw himself into his work. At least he found it the most gratifying part of his life at the time.

Frank was put in charge of a replacement squadron for the Eighth Tactical Fighter Wing preparing for a tour of duty in Southeast Asia. He found solace in getting his squadron of new McDonnell Douglas F-4D II Phantom pilots ready for their baptism of fire in the air war. They say be careful what you wish for.

The air force had finally upgraded their aircraft. The package included improved ordinance, including radar and laser-guided bombs. Most of all, the improvement in air-to-air missiles was dramatic. Frank's old squadron suffered a 14 percent rate of success with the AIM-7s and not much better with the heat-seeking 9s. This caused missed opportunities when the enemy was right in their sights. The missiles were locking on more efficiently now due to the improvements in the weapon's guidance system, making them more reliable.

The basic armament configuration of four AIM-7 sparrow missiles and four AIM-9 sidewinders mounted on wing pylons was augmented by the new twenty-millimeter cannon pod.

Another improvement was the deployment of Wild Weasels. These specially equipped F-4s and F-105s held an array of counteroffensive radar suppression systems. These aircraft could fly ahead of formations and provide interference on sorties with countermeasures needed to fly interdiction missions. They held the antiaircraft batteries and SAMs at bay. The Weasels also served to bait enemy aircraft defenses. They could trick AAA sites into targeting them with their radars. Then, when enemy radar waves bounced back to their source, Weasels could target *them* for destruction. It was like playing a game of flashlight tag in the dark. The drawback of radar suppression missions with their so-called flashlights, was their visibility to the enemy. Later on, Frank would learn just how dangerous that game of cat and mouse became. At present, there came a change in Captain Barrett's schedule.

After an exhausting training flight, Frank received a call in the locker room. He was to report to HQ. When Frank arrived, he was told to go in; the colonel was ready to see him.

Frank wondered if he had been found out somehow. He thought, *Maybe the detective squealed.* Standing before Colonel Perry, he snapped off a salute. "Captain Barrett reporting for duty as ordered, sir."

Colonel Perry said, "At ease and sit down, Frank. I've got a bit of news for you."

Frank felt beads of sweat forming on his brow. He was worried. *Did they somehow discover his movements in Panama, or was it the judge right there in Tampa?* The tension built as he awaited the colonel's news. He wished he were not dressed in a flight suit right then. It only made him sweat more.

Colonel Perry finally got to the subject. "Frank, the powers that be want you to hold over for another cycle of training."

Frank couldn't contain his disappointment. "Why?" he blurted.

Perry shot back. "Because they think you're needed here."

Frank looked from side to side as if he could reveal someone else in the room responsible for his outrage. Then, he quickly brought himself under control. "Colonel," he pled, "you know this is the big push; you told me so yourself. I've prepared myself mentally for this tour. It's just not right; it's not—"

Frank caught himself short of saying it wasn't fair, knowing fairness was never a promise in his world. Standing up straight, he asked the colonel what his assignment was to be.

The colonel said, "Frank, we only want to hold you back for one cycle. We need combat-experienced command pilots in the worst way. If we're to pull off Operation Fullback, we are going to need men like you to teach replacement pilots every trick in the book that you learned over Nam. I think you can understand that, major."

The new rank escaped Frank for just a second; then it dawned on him.

Frank asked, "Did you just say major?"

"Yes. Effective immediately, you are promoted to the rank of major. Congratulations, Frank. You might say it's the way the brass operates. Consider it their way of saying thanks for the job you're doing and will do. Frank, you're fast becoming what you soon shall be. Just keep that in mind."

Frank answered, "Well, thank you, Colonel. What about seeing action before the big push is over?"

Colonel Perry said, "Just hold your horses, Frank. I'm sure there will be plenty of combat left after the next cycle."

"Does that mean a second tour in Thailand?"

"Yes, Frank. If I have to go to the commanding general myself, I'll see to it. I admire your zeal and aggressiveness. It's what we need in pilots today."

Frank quickly came to terms with his new responsibility, reconciling himself to the new set of circumstances.

Colonel Perry said, "That will be all, Major Barrett. Carry on."

Frank saluted and left with a whole new wedge of life facing him.

* * *

The following day, as Frank's old flight of thundering phantoms climbed out roaring over the bay, beneath them everything was running on schedule for Santo Bonocante. Another ship destined for Buena Ventura was slipping out of Port Tampa. By now, even the mayor of Tampa, Nick C. Nicero, was in on the take from the local mafia. He helped make sure there were lax customs inspections, if any, at Port Tampa.

For Bonocante, it was business as usual. The mafia shipped phosphate out, and cocaine came back from Columbia through the Panama Canal hidden in fertilizer bags. Also, employees like Little Eddy were allotted a small portion of coke to sell locally under the noses of union bosses on the docks. Once the lion's share was delivered to Tampa, distribution on the street was controlled by the local mafioso.

Months later, Bonocante sat in his office listening to his accountant, Herman Hanson, going through the figures. His boredom factor was at its peak.

Herman said, "Now, we come to Jack's Cookies. Your profits there have been soaring. Perhaps we should open another conduit for those monies. It could become an IRS target if we show the increased flow of legitimate monies so soon."

Bonocante said, "Yeah, whatever you guys come up with, so long as my hands are clean, all right? Don't forget, though, we have to plow enough back in to keep up our scheduled deliveries."

Herman replied, "Yes, sir, we're keeping track of that, too. So far, everything is on schedule."

"Good. Now, let me talk to Tony; he's waitin' outside."

Herman made his exit politely as Tony passed him in the doorway. The door was barely shut behind him when he approached Santo Bonocante at his desk.

"Boss, we've got a problem," Tony said.

"What is it now?" Bonocante asked.

Tony Scaglione always made sure he was right before he approached his boss. That way, he gained trust and respect from him. Once again, he was dead right.

"Little Eddy flew the coop. He's left the hospital in Panama City, and ain't nobody knows where he's at."

"What the hell kind of gratitude is that after I covered all his hospital bills? We gotta get him back, Tony. There's no tellin' what he'll do if he gets strung out like before. We don't need no loose cannons in this outfit. Find him before he finds his way to the DA. Now get out there and find his ass!"

Loose cannons like Little Eddy couldn't be tolerated in any organization, especially if he showed up in the wrong place. He possessed enough information to sink them, if he ever turned state's witness. He needed to be found.

When Little Eddy left the hospital in Panama City, he limped using a cane. After three months of physical rehabilitation, his skin grafts were healed, but often painful. Doctors told him he could no longer have sex. That much was obvious whenever he looked in a mirror at where his genitals used to be. They told him he would require a complete sexual makeover, which required several more operations—not something covered by the mafia's health plan, this much he knew. Making his way to a side door, he escaped the hospital in a cab.

In spite of the hardships, Eddy fomented a plan. He would sell the coke he had set aside from several shipments to fund his return to Tampa. He had one man in mind he desperately wanted to find. For him, there was an overwhelming, all-consuming desire to take out Capt. Frank Barrett—the hard way. First, Little Eddy needed to meet the security guard on Bonocante's dock. Sitting in the cab that navigated the crowed narrow streets, Eddy schemed how he would approach the man who had saved his life six months earlier.

Eddy left the cab at the docks, stiffing the driver. Until he sold his stash, he had little to spare. Fortunately, it was nearly midday when he found Pablo in his guard shack alone eating lunch. He limped up to the shack, taking care not to catch his cane between the heavy wooden planks of the dock.

"*Pablo, mis amigo. ¿Como esta usted?*"

Pablo spun around quickly when he heard the ragged voice of Little Eddy behind him. Eddy's golden grill was gleaming back at him.

"Well, I see you are recovering, mis amigo. I was worried about you."

"Oh, I see. Is that why you never visited me in the hospital? Perhaps you were afraid I might be too shocked over your well wishes."

"Now, Eddy, you know I must stay here. It is my duty. Then my wife, she gets nervous when I don't come home right away. You know there are a lot of desperate characters hanging around our neighborhood at night."

"Don't concern yourself, amigo. I forgive you," Little Eddy said. "So are they treating you okay?"

"Oh yes. You know the company is very good to me."

"What about you? Will you be returning to work soon?" Pablo asked.

"No, I don't think so, not right away. I'll need more time to recover, you know. By the way, I would appreciate your not telling anybody I was here. Okay?"

"Is something wrong, Eddy?"

"No, Pablo." Little Eddy assured him. "It's just that I don't want them to think I can work yet. I'm enjoying my vacation, you know?"

"Oh sure, Eddy. I get it."

"Let me ask you something, Pablo. Are you still living in the barrios near the marina?"

"Yes, although my wife wishes we could get a better place."

"Yes, I understand. It's a shame you could not move up to a better neighborhood," Eddy said.

"Well, you know, mis amigo, it all takes money," Pablo noted.

"Maybe I can be of some help to you and your wife."

"What do you mean?"

Little Eddy looked both ways, making sure they were alone, and then he spoke quietly. "I wonder if you could do me a favor, Pablo?"

"What is it, Eddy?"

"Well, I have some things in my shipping shack here on the dock. I would like to pick them up, but as you know, I don't want anybody to know I'm here."

Pablo volunteered. "I could get them for you. Just tell me where they are."

"Well, that is where I think I can help you, my friend. After all, if it were not for you finding me when you did, I wouldn't be here today."

"What are you saying, Eddy?" Pablo questioned.

"I think we could make a deal that would help you a lot, especially since I feel I owe you."

"What are you talking about?"

Eddy leaned in closer. "I need you to open the shack for me tonight, so I can get my things without anybody seeing me, you know?" Eddy explained.

"Oh, Eddy, what you ask is risky. After all, you are not working here now. Only authorized personnel are allowed on the dock. You wouldn't want me to lose my job, would you?"

"Of course not, Pablo. You are my friend. That is why I am willing to make it worth your while. I will give you five hundred dollars just to open the door tonight and look the other way. I will only be there ten minutes. That is all—I promise."

Pablo wrinkled his brow and then answered cautiously. "That is a lot of money." Then he looked very serious. "Are you sure you will only be ten minutes? No more?"

"Yes, I promise, and I have cash. What do you say?"

Pablo scanned the dock, looking for any sign they were being observed. The siesta had begun. As Eddy planned, all workers were inside the cavernous warehouses lining the dock, resting in the shade. He looked back at Eddy. "Show me the dollars, amigo."

Immediately Eddy opened his wallet, displaying several hundred dollars.

Pablo's eyes widened. "What time will you be here?" he asked.

"At nine o'clock sharp," Eddy said. "Is it a deal?"

"All right, as long as you pay me first, and only you can go in the shack. I will stay outside to cover you."

"Fine. Nine o'clock sharp. Be ready, amigo." Little Eddy directed.

"Si, I'll be here."

That evening Little Eddy appeared on time, which was surprising because he was coked up. It was a habit he had little trouble resuming following his hazy, morphine-laden days of recuperation. Now, he was full-blown on the track of getting his secret stash. It was a sultry night in late January. The seasons made little difference in this equatorial clime. He was drenched in sweat anyway due to his anxious, drugged state. When he reached the dock shack where Pablo spent his shift, it was empty. The lights were out there, as well as the rest of the dock. This was not normal. Eddy's drug-charged state of mind only increased his sense of paranoia.

Where is Pablo? he wondered. Then, as if on cue, he saw a flashlight illuminate several yards down the dock. His pounding heart eased a bit. *It can only be Pablo stationed near the manifest shack*, he thought. Immediately, Little Eddy turned toward the beam and moved forward. As he drew nearer, the outline of Pablo's figure remained hazy.

Little Eddy called out in a hoarse voice. "Pablo, is it you, my friend?"

"Yes, of course. Be quiet."

Eddy warily made his way along the dock joining his companion. "Why did you leave the lights out, amigo?" he asked.

"I felt it would be safer. Here, take my flashlight and find the things you must have. I will stay on guard by the railing until you are finished. Go quickly now."

Eddy took the flashlight and held it beside his leg to illuminate his way to the unlocked shed. He staggered to the door and entered clumsily. He then went to his knees and felt along the floor until he located a small square of carpet, which he pulled aside. Underneath he revealed loose boards on the wooden floor. This was where he had cut a square foot in the flooring.

He slid his fingernails into the small grooved cut and removed the floorboard. Underneath was a burlap bundle of pure Columbian cocaine. As he reached for the bundle, his light disturbed a wharf rat sleeping among the burlap. Its beady eyes reflected the glare of light. The intruder's hand caused it to scurry. Eddy tugged the bundle out of its dusty resting place. Holding his light to it, he noticed the ends of the bundle were gnawed thoroughly by rats. Shaking his head, he couldn't help wondering what a high that must have been for unsuspecting rats. He managed a small chuckle.

20

The flight from Panama was remarkable for Little Eddy. He found flight fascinating. He had never been on a plane in his life. He had been on big boats, but never on a commercial aircraft. Now, thrill reminded him of getting high. He missed his usual snort of coke ingested with lunch. His personal pleasure would have to wait even though he felt jittery being deprived of his sense of well-being. The thought of getting high constantly crept back into his consciousness, robbing him of essential sleep. He could not set his monkey free. His sleep formed a brief passage of escape—that, and alcohol of course. He decided to order a double from the stewardess. Afterward, he managed to dream on fitfully, while murder remained his destination.

When Little Eddy was hospitalized, so-called friends infiltrated his hospital room, supplying him with coke, compliments of the mafia—for a time, it was enough to keep him happy and compliant.

When the bump and rumble of the landing gear shocked Eddy awake, he began trying to clear his head. The plans he'd made were simplistic. The less complex, the better; Eddy wasn't a complex man. For the time being, he only had to thoroughly vilify Frank as his sole adversary in Tampa.

After landing, Little Eddy headed off to the car rental booth with his only bag. Later, he was determined to steal a nondescript car on the day of his deed. Before that, he would use a rental while getting acquainted with Frank's schedule and movements. He figured he would be in the bay area no more than a week, and then he would use his one-way ticket to Belize. There he could live off the remainder of his cocaine sales to wealthy touristas. So far, his thinking went no further. Until then, his cocaine would remain in the trunk of whatever car he was driving.

One thing constantly weighed on his mind—the possibility of being spotted by his fellow workers. He knew full well the organization considered him a walking death knell. One call from him could bring down a world of heat on the mafioso. Alive, Little Eddy was a curse to them all. Once his whereabouts were confirmed, a contract would be put out.

Ironically, as dangerous as it was having a mafioso spot him, he completely overlooked another figure in his past. That was Detective Sergeant Joe Chalmers of the Tampa Police Department. His involvement with Eddy began with his trial when he recognized certain figures seated in the courtroom that day. He later learned they were there to report back to Bonocante that everything was well in hand in Judge Cowen's court.

Presently, Joe happened to be working a car theft ring. The perpetrators *modus operandi* was to use rental cars taken out with false IDs. They used them for delivering the booster. In other words, his accomplices took the thief to the car to be heisted, and then loitered nearby in case he needed a quick getaway. Normally, the heist would go smoothly under the experts touch, and then the rental would be returned to the agency.

Eddy headed toward the rental agency after retrieving his bag. He approached Avis, initiating his paper trail. In order to reduce his profile, he decided to sleep in the car during his stay. He addressed the clerk.

"Yes, Miss, I would like to rent a midsized car, please," Little Eddy said.

"Yes, sir. Welcome to Tampa. May I ask, do you have a preference in models?"

"No, I want something economical. I will be traveling alone."

"I can get you a Mercury Comet if you like," the woman noted. "It comes in a two-door. We offer unlimited mileage for eighteen dollars per day. Will that be satisfactory, sir?"

"Yes, thank you," Eddy agreed. He filled out the necessary papers using his real name and address, knowing he would be switching cars later. The rental clerk tried to sell him insurance, which he naturally refused. He paid in cash, and the clerk handed him a packet explaining rental conditions along with the keys.

"You'll find your car located on level one; it's a light green, custom Mercury Comet. Do you have any questions, sir?"

"No, that will be all."

"Enjoy your stay with us, sir, and thank you for choosing Avis. You know, when you're number two, you try harder."

Eddy turned from the counter and spotted the sign marked elevators. He was impressed with the ultramodern design of the terminal. Limping toward the elevators, he truly admired the architecture and interior design of Tampa's avant-garde air terminal.

Eddy never really considered the after effect of killing Frank. If his plan for vengeance was successful, he would simply slip away into a life of obscurity. Those left behind to mourn would wonder why a seemingly innocent U.S. Air Force officer was gunned down by an unknown assailant.

True revenge takes no prisoners, thought Eddy.

Detective Sergeant Joe Chalmers was making a routine check at the Avis rental counter at the airport. Flashing his badge, he requested the clerk show him the roster of rentals for the past few days. So far, he had not turned up a single name he could use in his investigation. Joe thanked the clerk when she handed over the roster.

"This won't take long, miss."

"Whatever I can do to help. Just let me know, detective."

Joe ran his finger up the list of the past few days' rentals. Working backward on the list, suddenly his finger stopped at the latest rental. He couldn't believe it. There was Eddy's real name and signature. A surge of excitement coursed through his veins as his heartbeat quickened.

"Miss, could you show me the copy of his driver's license?" he asked.

"Sure, but I think you'll be disappointed. There's no picture on it."

"What?"

"Yes, I thought you knew. Panamanian driver's licenses don't require photos," the woman explained.

Joe was incredulous. Apparently, Panama hadn't caught up with the United States. It didn't matter. Fortunately, Joe knew his man on sight. Joe automatically ruled out any possibility of Eddy's connection with the car theft ring.

"Was the man you rented this car to carrying baggage?"

"No. As a matter of fact, I thought it a bit unusual that a man traveling from Panama would have only one bag."

Frank asked, "Where do you park the rentals?"

The clerk said, "They're on level one."

Joe spun on his heel and headed for the elevator. Punching the level-one button, he decided not to wait for backup. His mind raced ahead on the ride down. *What is it I can do to detain him? I can't hold him for renting a car. He's passed through customs, so he's here legally and most likely not armed.*

This all added up to zip for Joe. Yet, he knew damned well Little Eddy wasn't there to sightsee. There had to be some connection. His thoughts turned to Bonocante. *Whatever he's here for, it must be financed by him.*

The doors opened on the level one. Joe trotted toward the rental booth situated in the center of the multilevel parking lot. There was one Avis man on duty.

"Say, mister, did you see a man who just rented a green Comet?"

"Sure, he just left ... oh, about two minutes ago."

Joe's arms dropped to his side with a look of desperation clouding his reddened face. He was gone. Joe could only look down the exit ramp and wonder where his quarry might be headed.

In a few minutes, Joe's car appeared on the exit ramp. He had a hunch where Eddy might go. Taking Memorial Drive from the airport, Joe drove to Dale Mabry Highway and then went south. When he reached Interbay Boulevard, he turned right. He was headed for Port Tampa. Parking in front of the guard's gate, Joe approached him.

Joe flipped out his badge for the guard. "I need to go to the shipping office," said Joe

The guard stepped aside. He was used to police coming and going. The Bonocante dock was a rough place, and stevedores were tough guys who often got into scrapes with the law.

As Joe entered the office, heads turned. Obviously, he was not a dock worker. One of the clerks rose from his desk to intercept the interloper. He was a frail Barney Fife–like man wearing suspenders and steel-rim glasses.

"May I help you, sir? Do you realize you are in a restricted area?" the clerk asked.

Flashing his badge again, Joe announced, "I'm Detective Chalmers. I have a few questions for you."

"Are you searching for something or someone? Do you have a search warrant?"

The clerk was used to law enforcement personnel sniffing around the docks and trying to talk to stevedores. Usually police called ahead, knowing it was private property. Under the circumstances, this clerk contested his presence. He was in no mood to answer questions. He stood at the counter separating visitors from employees in the office.

"What is it you had in mind?" the clerk questioned.

Joe could see by the sour look of contempt on the little man's face that he wasn't going to get very far. Nevertheless, he had to start somewhere. It was a cinch he wasn't going to see anyone in management, so he started asking questions.

"Have you an employee by the name of Eduardo Alfonso Torres?" Joe asked.

"I don't know. I'd have to check."

"I'll wait. I've got time."

The clerk sneered. "Well, I've got better things to do, but since you're already here, I'll cooperate. How did you get in here anyway?"

Joe replied, "Don't worry. I checked with the guard first."

The clerk turned away to check his files. Walking away, he muttered, "You know, there are laws against trespassing on private property."

He took his sweet time looking up Mr. Torres's records, leaving Joe to sit and cool his heels. Finally, the clerk returned with a file in hand.

"He's listed as an employee at our Panama City terminal."

"Is he currently employed?"

"It says he's on medical leave."

"Does the company know he's left the country?"

"I wouldn't know. Will there be anything else, Officer?"

Joe stood up, silently looking around himself, making the clerk wait for a change. "I guess that will be all," he finally said. "Thanks for your cooperation."

"Anytime, Officer. Only, just call ahead first. Maybe we can have some doughnuts waiting for you."

As soon as the door closed behind Joe, the clerk picked up the phone.

"Yes, operator, connect me with the head office, please."

After a brief pause, the secretary for Bonocante's Shipping came on. "How may I direct your call?"

"Yes, miss, transfer me to the personal department, please."

"Yes, sir, one moment, please."

A moment later another voice was on the other end of the phone. "Personnel, how may I help you?"

"Yes, this is Mr. Collins in shipping. May I speak to the supervisor, please?"

"One moment, please. I'll try that extension."

Robert Collins held the line, waiting for what seemed an eternity. He was contemplating hanging up when a female voice came on.

"This is Miss Rossi how may I help you?"

"Yes, Miss Rossi. This is Mr. Collins down at the shipping office. How are you today?"

"Well, I'm fine, thank you, just a little busy right now. What is it I can do for you, Mr. Collins?"

"Miss Rossi, I was thinking perhaps I can be of assistance to your department. I just learned one of our dock personnel on sick leave is wanted by the police. The detective I just spoke with has reason to believe Eduardo A. Torres is here in Tampa. I thought you might want to confirm his whereabouts since he hasn't checked in with our office here."

"Yes, Mr. Collins. Thank you. I'll check into that right away. I appreciate your interest. Good-bye."

Robert spoke to the phone in his hand. "Well, she's a cool bird. I'd have thought she would show more interest in a tip like that."

He put down the phone and returned to his desk. *Those supervisors upstairs never appreciate us dock personnel*, he thought.

Robert didn't realize it, but his little tip would start the clock ticking for Little Eddy. When Santo learned of Little Eddy's arrival in Tampa, he decided to call a meeting with his capos.

"We have a problem," Santo began. "For days now, I have engaged our people in Panama in a search for Eduardo Torres."

The mention of his name caused a stir in the room. All of the men shifted nervously in their plush, overstuffed chairs.

"As you may recall, we covered all expenses for his specialized treatment in Panama. Then, he snuck out of the hospital. Now, I have good information that he is here in Tampa."

An audible gasp went up around the huge mahogany table. No one there ever wanted to hear his name again, much less hear of his returning to Tampa. Little Eddy never divulged who his assailant was on that fateful night for obvious reasons. He just claimed he didn't know his attacker. Now Santo felt even more threatened by what he might say about his work as a courier for their drug trade.

Santo spoke for everyone there. "Gentlemen, I propose we take a contract out on Little Eddy."

There was a cold silence in the conference room. Not a man disagreed with Santo Bonocante, but no one wanted to say the final word. Finally, Santo cut the stillness with an announcement typical of his leadership style. "We take a vote. All in favor of taking out Little Eddy say aye; all opposed say nay."

At first, there was a chilly silence in the room. Inevitably, it broke with a unanimous vote of aye. Nothing more needed to be said. It was understood. Santo, acting as capo de capo would assign responsibility to the one selected to make the necessary arrangements. Santo gave the sign, and the meeting room cleared. Ten minutes later, Santo placed a call to an associate named Hunco.

Hunco asked, "Do you have any preference as to how he goes?"

"No, I don't care if you stuff him full of lettuce and feed him to the pigs," Santo said.

Hunco sighed. "All right then, this is gonna cost a lot money, you know."

Santo tensed up visibly, asking, "How much is a lot, Hunco?"

"I tell you what; I'll give you professional courtesy. I'll take him out for a two hundred grand guaranteed done deal, okay?"

Santo swallowed hard, hiding his disgust for having to pay so much for removing a weasel like Little Eddy. If he weren't so enamored of his own life, he would pull the trigger himself. Yet, as a legitimate businessman, he had to deal with the element of risk. If he were ever tied to a murder, his life would be all but over. On the other hand, with Hunco making the hit, he possessed credible deniability.

Santo said, "Then it's final. I'll arrange payment in cash."

Hunco smiled. "It's a shame I can't stay where I am right now. The weather's beautiful. I'll be seeing Mr. Torres soon; give your capos my best."

An audible click on the line signaled the heat was on. One vengeful predator would also be the prey.

21

Once Eddy left the airport, he drove the Comet to Dale Mabry Highway. He knew Frank lived just a quarter mile from Santo's villa. In spite of his coke-ravaged mind, he even remembered that Frank lived near the bay. As soon as he reached the area, he would check the phone book for the exact address.

Stopping at a convenience store, he limped up to a public phone booth. He quickly found Frank's listing: Barrett, Frank Capt., 3113 Napoleon Avenue, Tampa, 33241, 813-836-2841. A thrill coursed through his body as he ripped the page from the book. Soon, he would make his first drive-by, but first he had another stop to make. His craving for a fix was getting to him.

Despite relatively cool winter temperatures in Tampa, Little Eddy was burning up. He was sweating bullets. Wiping his brow with his sleeve, he heaved himself behind the wheel of his Comet. With grim determination, he punched the gas pedal and squealed out of the lot.

"Now, I have to find you, old partner," he said to himself.

Driving down the angling two-lane brick road known as Interbay Boulevard, Eddy headed for Port Tampa. It seemed an eternity before he reached the docks. He knew it was risky to be seen so close to the Bonocante shipping dock, but he was desperate.

He parked alongside the *Corrina* and stared up at the deserted cargo ship. Approaching the gangplank, he was anxious to meet Captain Diaz again.

The AK-47 guard was on duty as usual. Addressing him casually, he said, "*Buenos dias, señor ¿y como estás?*"

The Panamanian guard was not impressed with his familiarity. Widening his stance, he pointed his weapon directly at Eddy's head.

In perfect English, Eddy asked, "Is my old friend Captain Diaz here?"

The guard replied, "He is not on board now."

Eddy did not disguise his disappointment. "Do you know where he is?"

"He is where the captain always is this time of day—at a bar."

"Gracias. Do you know which one he favors?"

"No," the guard responded. "The captain, he likes them all."

Eddy turned away as he thanked the guard absentmindedly; the guard spat his thanks in return as Little Eddy returned to his Comet.

A search of joints lining the Port Tampa dock ensued. Time was thinning for the strung out addict. He cursed himself for locking up his supply at the bus station. He was so afraid of being nabbed by customs that he settled for a foray in the sleaziest bars of Tampa.

He chose the largest in a row of half a dozen juke joints on one side of Interbay Avenue. Entering the smoke-filled bar, he searched every face in the crowd to no avail. On his third bar, he won the prize. In a dark corner, with his back to the wall, Captain Diaz sat nursing his draft beer. Eddy decided to grab a brew himself to settle his nerves before plying the dear old captain. He gulped it down in several long swallows. Then, he bumped through the smelly afternoon crowd while trying not to spill his second draft.

When Captain Diaz caught sight of him, he took a gulp and then shook his head trying to clear his vision. At first, he thought Eddy was an apparition. Lately, he'd seen a few. Then, his vision came clear. It was truly Little Eddy limping toward him. Eddy got to the table and gave the captain his old salute.

"My captain, how do you fare, my old amigo?"

The old besotted cargo captain regained his composure long enough, sure as the wind, just in time to say something fitting. "Well, there you are, Little Eddy—in the flesh returned from the Panamanian straights."

Eddy replied, "Well, considering what I've been through, there's less flesh. May I join you and regale you with my tales of woe?"

"Certainly, this is woe's safe harbor."

Eddy drug up a chair while Captain Diaz took a long draught from his beer before uttering another word. "Tell me, what's been keeping you from my dock so long?"

"Many things have happened, captain," Eddy said. "Some not so pleasant. I've been working in Panama City for Bonocante. While I was employed on the docks, there I was attacked by a mad man who tried to kill me. Fortunately, a fellow employee saved my life in the nick of time. Now, that's in the past. The important thing is I have found you. Let me buy you a drink, my old friend."

Captain Diaz agreed, saying, "Rum would be nice."

"Coming right up, but only answer me one question in return, Captain Diaz."

Diaz cast a wary look on Little Eddy, recalling how he was never happy to see him unless it was in his own best interest. Eddy leered back at him, and then turned to buy them rum. When he returned, he toasted his ship.

"Here's to the *Corrina*." They each drank down their rum in a gulp. The wary Diaz allowed Eddy to buy another before renewing his search for the truth, no matter how unsavory it might be. Conversely, Eddy wasn't satisfied until Diaz had his fill. Only then would he inquire. He studied the watery-eyed captain's face until he thought he saw his opening.

"Do you still keep a stash on board the *Corrina*?"

The captain's face suddenly darkened with suspicion. Looking both ways for prying eyes, he asked Eddy the all-important question on his mind.

"Have you come to buy?"

"Yes."

"Well, then let's drink to that. Then I will walk with you to my boat."

"That's a good idea, captain." Eddy agreed.

The captain chuckled and then downed the rest of his rum as if Eddy had just told him something humorous. The two of them would have made a sight leaving the bar together. Diaz swayed, trying to find his balance point by leaning on gimpy Little Eddy.

They navigated the gangplank the same way, barely passing the guard with his doubtful assent. It wasn't the first time his captain had returned under the weather, although it was usually with someone of the opposite sex.

Once in his cabin, Captain Diaz sobered up considerably. Suddenly, he was all business. Eddy, on the other hand, was beginning to feel the liquor mixing with the beers in his stomach. It reminded him he hadn't yet eaten since he left Panama.

Little Eddy asked, "Captain Diaz, you do believe in the hereafter, don't you?"

"Yes, I do," he said solemnly.

Eddy flashed his golden smile at him. "Well, captain, then you ought to know what I'm here after."

The captain frowned at his sacrilegious remark but managed to stay on task. "What quantity do you seek?"

"How much do you have on hand?"

The captain scratched his unshaven face and straightened his suspenders. "That's something only I know," he slurred.

"What is your price?" asked Eddy.

"I'm moving my product in port for three hundred an ounce."

Incredulously, Eddy replied, "Why don't you just put a cartouche in my head? It's robbery. I sold high grade in Panama for half as much!"

For a brief moment, Captain Diaz appeared deep in thought, and then he stared Little Eddy straight in the eye from across the table. With his lips curling into a brief smile, he spoke in a low, steady voice.

"Ah yes, mis amigo, Panama, but these are the Ustados Unidos; take it or leave it, mis amigo."

Eddy relented. "Of course I'll take it. Where else would I buy on such short notice? I'll take three ounces."

Moments later, Eddy plopped in his car, pulled out his coke spoon, and snorted. Then he started the little Comet. Flooring it, he squealed his tires leaving the docks, attracting undo attention, especially from Carmine Hunco, who remained in the shadows watching.

Early that evening, Little Eddy cruised down Napoleon Avenue. He was watching the house numbers closely. Some details were seeping back into his memory from that fateful day.

Only snippets flashed through his consciousness as he stopped opposite Frank's home. It seemed to him that it all happened so long ago. It was four-thirty in the afternoon. He thought, *How long must I wait before that jerk flyboy gets home?*

It was Thursday. Frank had stopped by the Officers' Club for a few drinks with his buddies, knowing he was not on the schedule to fly Friday. Fridays were normally taken up with office duties.

Little Eddy drove down Napoleon Avenue about a block and found a vacant house for sale. He parked his Comet up on its steep driveway and waited in the shade of an old oak tree. He spent hours observing the comings and goings of Frank's neighbors—but no Frank. Disappointed, he drove his Comet out of the driveway at six thirty in search of a McDonald's on Dale Mabry. Once he was satiated with food, he could not get in Panama, he decided it was time to purchase a gun.

Little Eddy pulled behind a strip mall and stopped. He got out, lifted his front seat, and reached into the back of the rear seat crease and to pull out his reserve cash. Peeling off three Benjamins from his roll, he thought, *This should be enough to buy a gun. Frank's not worth any more, that's for sure.*

Eddy pulled back out on Dale Mabry and headed north in search of a pawn shop. A mile up the road, he found a two-story one. He thought, *Geez, this highway's got it all.*

Armed with a nickel-plated snub-nosed .38-caliber revolver, Little Eddy left the place with a slight grin on his face. *What do you know; I just bought a former policeman's gun. Wouldn't it be sweet if they tried pinning the murder on him?* Next, he drove up and down Dale Mabry, proving to himself that Dale Mabry offered up anything a man could want after dark. Hours later, the cocaine crash was hitting him hard, so he parked in an all-night gentlemen's club and slept till dawn.

It was time for Little Eddy to check out the situation on Napoleon Avenue again. As he drove down Frank's street, he could see the little wire-wheeled sky blue mustang in the driveway. *Pretty sporty, mister pilot man,* he thought. Eddy continued to the end of the avenue and then turned around using someone's driveway. He passed Frank's house very slowly this time, noting the layout of his carport and side entrance to the house. He was thinking, *That carport door must be the way he enters the house after work each day. I could nail him easily across the street from my car.*

Just then, the front door opened. It was Frank dressed in his flight suit. He didn't head for his car, so Eddy watched in his rearview mirror as Frank bent down to reach for the newspaper lying on his front walk. He stopped down the street and watched him with glowering eyes. Frank looked back with a sideways glance. The green car didn't register in his mind, so he gave it another glance as it sped away.

Pulling away, Eddy, felt his rage growing as he recalled the months of agony spent in the hospital after his multiple skin grafts and plastic surgeries. Even now, his lingering pain and suffering reminded him of Frank's exquisite form of torture. He thought, *It will be so easy to drop you right in your carport, flyboy.*

The memory of those days in the hospital suggested he take a couple of snorts. After that, Eddy's mind drifted. *Pain is an interesting thing; it can't be experienced again—only the memory of it lives,* he thought. He was feeling no pain now. By sundown, he was really blasted as he drove down Interbay Boulevard. It was raining hard, and Eddy couldn't make out the white dashed lines separating the lanes. He was on his way to renew his supply just like any addict would who had miscalculated his rate of consumption.

Speeding down Interbay near Port Tampa, with heavy rain spattering on his windshield, he suddenly caught sight of a large, gold Buick careening straight into his lane! Instinctively, he yanked his wheel to the right, causing him to leave the road. Leaping the curb, he suddenly found himself driving on what appeared to be the road.

Instead, it was a shuffleboard court slickened with rain. He was driving in a park! His knee-jerk response was to hit his brakes. They locked, causing his car to slide off the remainder of the shuffleboard court and into a cement block barbeque grill, blasting its blocks in the air. One landed on his roof, creating a dent deep enough to slice his scalp.

Glancing off the grill, his car decelerated to zero as it slammed into an oak tree. The steaming car pinned its driver, who was slumped over the wheel.

Little Eddy's scalp was lacerated and bleeding profusely. The impact of his chest on the steering wheel vacated breath from his lungs. Mercifully, he lost consciousness. The gold car never stopped. The next car stopped and made an ambulance call.

That call was truly a lifesaver for Eddy. By the time police could question him, it was ten o'clock the following morning. Noting the damage done in the city park, the police bought his story about being run off the road. There were no charges filed, but his decision to not take out insurance came back to bite him.

Little Eddy could not remember being rescued by the fire department that used cut-off saws and the Jaws of Life to extract him from the vehicle. He only experienced an incredibly intense headache. Two days later, the hospital released him as indigent. Avis came by and allowed him to get his personal items from the wreck left in the junkyard. He was able to get the back door pried open and retrieved his stash of rolled up Benjamins from the crease in the backseat. Next, he grabbed the gun box, which held enough cartridges to start a gang war, from the floor. His stash of cash would never be enough to pay for the damages on the car, but Little Eddy never intended to anyway. He just signed everything they placed in front of him and kept the carbon copies until he was out of sight.

All that was left to show for his tango with a tree were thirteen stitches on the top of his head and a crazy haircut. Now, the pain in his head and chest forced him to the nearest bus stop. On the way to Port Tampa, he downed the remainder of his pain pills from the hospital. Soon after he self-medicated with prescription pain killers, the bus arrived. On the dock, he discovered the *Corrina* was gone. Eddy plopped down on a huge turnbuckle in despair as he tried to make sense of his world. *Through the haze,* he reasoned, *at least I can steal a car.*

It was Monday afternoon, and Little Eddy was high on Demerol when he broke into a white Dodge Dart behind a bar on the dock. Again, he was on the path of revenge.

An hour later, he sat in the Dodge parked down the street from Frank's home. Past surveillance told him Frank was very punctual, arriving home at 4:30 p.m. on weekdays, except on Thursdays.

Someone else was punctual too. It was Carmine Hunco, the man hired to take out Little Eddy. Mr. Hunco was a former cigar factory owner before his business was nationalized by Fidel Castro, after the Cuban Revolution. He had been tailing Little Eddy ever since he received a tip from someone at the Port Tampa docks.

He noticed Little Eddy waiting down the street. He had no clue about Eddy's vendetta with Frank. All he knew was he was getting tetchier by the minute waiting to take action. Hence, he screwed his suppressor onto the barrel of his .45-caliber model 1911 Savage automatic pistol, thus adding one more length of cold professionalism to his preparation for a hit.

His weapon of choice had a history. It was one of two hundred pistols tested by the US Army in competition with the .45 Colt model 1911 semiautomatic pistol. The Army requested a few minor changes in the Savage model before final testing. Since the model was not as yet accepted, no serial numbers were stamped on the bottom of the breach block (the official position for all serial numbers). Out of the original two hundred pistols sent for refurbishing, seventy-two were never accounted for. Hunco's blue-finished pistol had no markings except for the Savage Indian Head logo stamped on the butt of the pistol. When handled with gloves, the weapon was completely untraceable.

Eddy still waited at the house for sale six homes up from Frank's. He watched, nervously glancing at his watch, before filling his coke spoon for one last blast. Shaking his head after the snort, he felt the cold, hard rush hitting his heart as he pulled his sweat-soaked shirt away from the vinyl seat. Just then, Frank rounded the corner in his Mustang. Eddy cranked his engine alive. When Frank drove past, Eddy slipped slowly out of the drive behind him. Frank paid little attention to the car behind as he pulled into his driveway.

Little Eddy came to a stop across the street from Frank's house. He snapped the cylinder out of his .38 with a flick of his wrist. He double-checked that all six rounds were loaded. When Little Eddy looked up ahead, he noticed a black sedan facing him on the same side of the street. A man sat behind the wheel with a weapon held outside the window pointed his way. Reacting with surprising speed, Eddy threw himself down on the seat while simultaneously jamming his right foot on the gas pedal and steering with his left hand. When Carmine saw the Dodge coming like a battering ram, he unloaded a full clip from his weapon. The riddled car drove on at an alarming speed.

Hearing gunshots close by, Frank dived for the carport floor. A second later, he heard a car crash. Lying there on the cool cement, Frank held his breath as he waited for the other shoe to drop. Next he heard the sound of a car squealing its tires.

Carmine backed away from the crash scene. In one move, he swung the back end of his car around ninety degrees to the opposite curb. Then, he turned hard and gunned it. With tires squealing, he beat it back the way he came. Frank was ready to get up, thinking the shooting had ended. He went to the edge of his carport and peered out in time to see a white Dodge spewing steam as it drove away, leaving a streaming trail of radiator fluid on the brick pavement. Trudy peeked out of her front door cautiously.

"Get back," Frank yelled. "There may be more of them."

Not knowing who "them" might be, Frank watched the slow white Dodge until it turned left and went out of sight. The thought crossed his mind to give chase, but he thought better of it when he stopped to think, *Somebody in that crash had a gun. What were they doing in my neighborhood?*

Just then, Trudy shouted out of her doorway to Frank. "I've called the police, Frank. Is it safe to come out?"

"Yeah—that is, I think so, Trudy," said Frank.

Around the block from Frank's house, Little Eddy limped the old Dodge over to the side of the road. He pulled himself out of the steaming car and struck out on foot, in search of the nearest car he could steal. Hobbling along the sidewalk without his cane, he found a yellow Chevy Camaro up on wheel stands in front of a garage two houses down.

It's a risk I'll have to take, he thought. *I hope there's nothing too bad wrong with it. If it starts, it's mine. Whoever was working on it must be waiting for the motor to cool.*

Suddenly, the Camaro's engine roared to life under Little Eddy's gifted hands. He dropped the hammer on its throttle and drove right off the wheel stands. Leaving a burnt rubber streak and two bent up stands in the driveway, Eddy disappeared in a cloud of blue smoke. The car's owner was seated in the bathroom when he heard the squealing tires outside and wondered what the hell could be happening. Meanwhile, both Little Eddy and Frank had a lot left on their minds.

22

Frank told Trudy to speak with the police. He changed his mind about possible gunplay and jumped into his Mustang to follow the trail of radiator fluid. The Dodge hadn't gotten too far. Frank found it abandoned near a house where a man was standing in his lawn talking to his neighbor.

Frank inquired, "Excuse me, do either of you guys know whose car that is sitting by the curb?"

The man who owned the Camaro spoke first. "It must belong to the guy who stole my damned car."

The neighbor added, "All I know is some guy raced out of here with John's car."

Frank asked, "What did he look like?"

"Well, like I told John, I didn't get much of a look at him. It all happened so fast. I was trimming my hedge when all of a sudden John's car went flying out of his driveway. The driver looked like he was a Mexican or somethin' like that."

John said, "I called the police. They told me a squad car was already on its way, which is strange because it was the first time I called."

Frank said, "They probably thought you were talking about the incident on my street. There were multiple gunshots and a car crash in front of my house over on Napoleon."

John said, "That damned thief sure got one of the hottest Camaros around, that's for sure."

Frank asked, "You didn't leave the keys in it, did you?"

John replied, "Oh no, I was just getting ready to change the oil in her. The keys are still in my pocket."

Meanwhile, Eddy was driving a hot car in a hell of a jam. Somebody was after him, and it didn't take a genius to figure who. His dilemma was clear. Should he stay and finish the job on Frank? Or should he head for the airport, ditch the car, and board the next flight out of Tampa for Costa Rica? Only Little Eddy could explain the logic that led him to his decision.

Eddy sat still in a supermarket parking lot to think. *I'm so close to Frank now. I'll never get this close again. The goon Bonocante hired, whoever he is, doesn't know what I'm driving, so I'll be that much harder to find. He'll never get to me before I'm on a plane. I can afford two, maybe three more days. That's all I need to nail that son of a bitch.*

Little Eddy started his new Camaro with the touch of a wire. Revving up the engine, he thought, *I'd like to see that hit man in the black sedan catch me in this.*

* * *

After the police arrived, Detective Chalmers also appeared on the scene. Based upon Trudy's testimony, he wasn't sure who the man in the white car was. As for the second car, he knew nothing. In an attempt to connect the two incidents, Joe interviewed John and his neighbor. The description of the driver in the Camaro was sketchy, at best, because he'd come into view so quickly. Next, he came over to talk to Frank.

Joe said, "I remember the day you were in court for Eddy's sentencing. How have you been handling things since then?"

Frank listened to the clock ticking on his kitchen wall, for what seemed an eternity, while Chalmers waited for an answer. Frank just sat still at his kitchen table. Finally, Joe started his line of questioning.

"Is there anyone in your life who might want to harm you?"

Frank replied, "No one I can think of, in particular."

Frank offered Joe something to drink, but he refused. Once Joe sat down, he began questioning Frank again.

"Why don't you start at the beginning? Did you use that information I gave you about Eddy being employed by Bonocante Shipping to find him in Panama?"

Frank shifted nervously in his seat before saying anything.

"Go on, Frank, I'm ready to get this down."

Knowing he had nothing to lose, reluctantly, Frank went on telling Joe how he developed a plan and flew to Panama to find him. He described how he left him in Panama. He gave Joe everything right down to the boat rental. It felt good to get it off his chest, yet he wasn't certain of the consequences of telling him.

Joe let out a low whistle. "Man, that's some story, and I'm terribly sorry about the loss of your wife. I can understand what made you do it at the time. What more did you do, Frank? Have you harmed anyone else lately?"

Cautiously, Frank said, "Where is this heading, Joe?"

Joe came back instantly. "I mean, did you do anything to someone in this country? Like a certain judge, for instance?"

Frank felt the pressure building. *There's that damn ticking clock again*, he thought. Suddenly, Frank realized he felt right about the whole thing. Leaning over the table, he looked Joe dead in the eye. What came next was not a confession; it was a statement. "That old judge got what he deserved."

Joe mentioned, "Maybe you're right; either way, now the whole town knows about him. His wife left him, and he's been brought down in public disgrace over this whole extramarital sex scandal. I'd say you're right on the money there. Did you have anything to do with the photos that showed up at his community bingo night last Thursday?"

"Never mind what you did in Panama. What you did or didn't do to Eddy there is irrelevant here. That will be a matter for the Panamanian police. I'm not gonna report it. Let them investigate; they can knock themselves out, for all I care. What I'm interested in is who your enemies are here and now. You see, our boys are busy pulling slugs out of that Dodge's radiator, and when the lab gets a hold of them, I'll bet you dollars to donuts they're all gonna match. You told me you heard one volley of shots, right? So, then, what were the two cars here for?"

Frank sat in silence for another long moment, contemplating Joe's question. Then he spoke slowly. "It's still a mystery to me."

Joe stood up. "Well, I'm finished for now, Frank, but if you wanna know my hunch, somebody was here to harm you. You know anybody in the mob, Frank?"

"No."

Joe cocked his head to one side. What he said next perfectly chilled Frank.

"I think you do and don't know it.… Little Eddy's back in town." Detective Chalmers closed his little black book.

"You wanna know what I think, Frank?" Joe didn't wait for an answer before speaking. "You tried to kill Eddy in Panama, but you didn't. Now, he's damned sure trying to nail you."

Joe handed Frank his card again on the way out.

"If you see or hear anything, just give me a call, okay? Don't bother showing me out. I know the way."

Right then, Frank couldn't show Joe out. He was too stunned. Joe's left hook news flash had really floored him.

The following day, Little Eddy sat in his car in the parking lot of Falgies Restaurant on Bay Shore Boulevard watching early morning traffic. Boring, dull, and tedious as it was, Eddy felt he was in the right spot. He figured Frank traveled Bay Shore every day to and from work. If Frank was going to work, he reasoned, he must drive by Falgies.

By the same token, Frank figured he had to follow the old dictum learned in Vietnam by jungle patrols. Never come back the way you went out. That seemingly small bit of wisdom saved countless men from ambush. Frank reasoned, *It should work for me. Better to be the hunter than the hunted.*

However, Frank's duty necessarily called him to report on base. Hence, that day, Frank took MacDill Avenue to work and entered the base through that gate. There were only two ways to enter MacDill AFB; the other was the Dale Mabry Highway gate. On that particular day, Little Eddy happened to be watching the wrong one.

23

After one o'clock that afternoon, Little Eddy gave up on waiting and took the Camaro out on Bay Shore Boulevard. It was a convertible with a black convertible top. As he rode along, Little Eddy felt the 396-cubic-inch engine straining at the hood, just waiting to be cut loose. Eddy had the top up, trying to keep a low profile, if such a thing were possible in such a show car. The thought crossed his mind that he should get another car. He could swap cars like changing shoes. Still, his sporting side clung to the muscle car.

His immediate objective was to cruise Dale Mabry and find a pusher for a fix. He knew he could never go back to the docks of Port Tampa. He suspected that was where he picked up his tail.

"Where are they? Is it too early? Where did all the players go?" Little Eddy muttered to himself as he restlessly cruised the strip. Then, he spotted something of interest.

A pretty young blonde was standing in front of a motel called the Mason Rouge. Little Eddy pulled up to the curb and beckoned her. She sashayed over to him and bent over with one hand on his door. She looked around the car quickly, trying to spot any sign of weapons. Then, she spoke. "What's your sport, darlin'?"

Little Eddy flashed his golden smile. "I'm looking for something special."

She replied, "Well, I'm right here, darlin', in the flesh."

Eddy said, "No, I mean I'm looking to score some coke. Do you know anyone whose dealing?"

She stood up straight away from him, staring with disdain. Looking up the road, she sniffed. "Try the 2001 Space Odyssey up the street, honey. There's always some action up there. By the way, I like your ride. Wanna come back this way and give me one?"

"Sure. Later, baby. I gotta get fixed up first. Then, you and me, we can go all night. You know?"

She replied, "Sure, baby, I'm into it. Check me out when you get back, sweetie."

Little Eddy pulled out with a slight squeal of his tires showing off his hot ride. As soon as Eddy was gone, the woman in the blonde wig stepped across the street to a white van sitting in a parking lot. She talked to the two undercover cops inside. "That was no good. I saw a chromed snub nose lying on the seat beside him." She stood up from the van's window and stretched her back.

"Fellas, I got to get a better beat. These damn heels are killing me. How much longer do I have to flaunt my wears around this joint?"

A voice from the dark interior of the van consoled her. "Just one more hour, hon. Don't complain; we collared three johns so far. We may not break any records, but we're doing all right in this zone. Just strut your stuff a little longer, baby. Don't worry; we got your back. Besides, we'll be good to go off shift soon."

Up the road Little Eddy scored at the Purple Lounge. He invested in an adequate supply for his stay in the states, even though he wasn't used to paying street prices. Where he came from, he *was* the pusher man. It sure felt different with the shoe on the other foot.

* * *

Flying near MacDill AFB, Frank was reaching the end of a busy day of training. His flight of four Phantoms had just finished skip-bombing practice over Avon Park, Florida bombing range. Flying toward Mac-Dill, Frank called the tower.

"This is Rhino Flight 4, coming in over the stacks at US Phosphoric requesting landing instructions."

"Roger that, Rhino Flight, you may approach runway 18, the altimeter is 29.73, winds are one zero at 160 degrees, report on left base for runway 18. Over."

"Roger, that's affirmative, tower."

Frank looked to his right at his wingman, giving him thumbs-up, which meant he could lead the flight in since his wingman had scored the most hits that day. As he rolled in for a forty-five-degree intercept to the left base leg in the flight pattern, the others followed suit. Frank's would be the last plane down, making sure all the rest landed safely. Just as Frank started rolling on to final approach, he spotted a bright yellow Camaro with black speed stripes sitting in the Falgies Restaurant parking lot. Not many cars were in the lot. It was an off hour for restaurant business. He thought, *Could that car possibly be Eddy's? If so, maybe I can get the drop on him.*

After landing, instead of going straight to the locker room, he went to the armory where all personnel firearms were kept locked up.

"Hello, Major Barrett. What can I do for you?" the desk sergeant asked.

"I'd like to check out my sidearm. I'm going to do a bit of practicing at the gunnery range tomorrow. Sure thing, major; just sign here, and I'll get you fixed up right away."

Frank signed the list and put down gunnery practice as the reason for his request. In turn, the sergeant inside the weapons cage handed over Frank's standard-issue .45-caliber 1911 Colt semiautomatic pistol.

The sergeant reminded, "The gunnery range will provide all the ammunition you'll need, sir."

As soon as Frank was out of sight, he rushed down the hallway and entered the locker room. Dashing to his locker, he took out his personal items and stuffed them into his pockets. He spun around and headed for the door. As he pushed the door, it flew right back from the other side in his face. In his rush, Frank had run into Lieutenant Baker, one of his students, spilling his soda all over him.

Baker shouted, "Hey, what gives here?" When he saw it was Frank, he apologized. "Oh, I'm sorry, major. I didn't see it was you."

Hurriedly, Frank said, "As you were, lieutenant. Sorry about that; I'm in a bit of a hurry."

The lieutenant watched him rush down the hallway, turning the corner in seconds flat. As he did, he ran into a flight sergeant coming up the hallway.

"Oh, sorry," Frank said. "I'm late for an appointment."

The old sarge said, "Easy does it, major. What's your hurry?"

Frank didn't answer; he just bolted out the hangar door into the bright sunlight. Shielding his eyes, he quickly made the visual adjustment to the parking lot outside. Once in his car, he pulled out his sunglasses. Starting the car, he peeled out of the parking lot. On the fly, he grabbed a clip full of .45-caliber ammunition from his glove compartment. He'd kept it there since the shooting business had started with Little Eddy.

He thought, *Must get to him before he gets to me.* He knew Eddy was stalking him, just waiting for the opportunity to nail him. Apparently, Little Eddy thought he could pull off his hit by covering Frank's exit routes from the base. This time, Frank had the upper hand. If it really was Little Eddy, this was a real break. Then, he stopped to consider what he would do even if he did get the drop on him. Thinking fast, he envisioned a course of action

I'll call Detective Chalmers, he thought. *All I gotta do is just hold him so Joe can ID him. At least, he can arrest him for car theft.*

Frank sped down Bay Shore Drive where the limit was forty miles an hour, passing cars and weaving in and out, hell-bent for Falgies. However, instead of turning right into the restaurant lot, he turned left a block before on to Gandy Boulevard and sped west two blocks. He turned south on MacDill and then right down Napoleon back onto Bay Shore again. He approached Falgies from the opposite direction. Because Bay Shore was a divided boulevard, he could arrive at the restaurant parking lot and drive in without Eddy seeing him from the other side of the building. He pulled into the lot on the opposite side where he'd seen what he thought was Little Eddy's car.

Frank got out of his car with his .45 and started creeping cautiously alongside the back side of the restaurant. He stopped at the outer edge of the building, peeking out carefully. He slowly pulled his weapon from the right hip pocket of his flight suit. From behind the Camaro, there was no way of telling for sure the driver was Eddy, but the odds were in his favor. Frank decided he would take the chance. Just as he started to round the corner with his gun drawn, a kitchen helper came out to dump trash in the dumpster. Shocked when he saw a man in a dark green military-style suit with a gun in his hand sneaking around the corner, he dropped his trashcan with a clatter and ran for the back door.

Little Eddy heard the clanging commotion. In his rearview mirror, he saw Frank with a gun ducking back behind the corner. He quickly reached for the wires dangling beneath the dash. Touching them together, he fired up the engine and put the Camaro in reverse as soon as he could. Pushing down on the accelerator, he backed the rear end of the Camaro straight toward where he saw Frank last. The car slammed into Falgies' wall, creating a further disturbance inside. The owner was already calling the police. Now, all the kitchen help huddled around the owner in the back hallway fearing the worst.

Beating a hasty retreat to his car, Frank pulled out of the lot just before the first police car arrived. However, the second responding unit spotted him easily speeding away from Falgies Restaurant and pulled him over. Meanwhile, Little Eddy was speeding westbound down Gandy Boulevard bound for Dale Mabry. The long day for Frank wasn't over; it began to end in ignominy as he stood spread-eagled against his Mustang while a policeman frisked him.

"I'll get that little bastard if it's the last thing I do," Frank swore under his breath.

When Frank was finally released after his ordeal with the police, it was eleven o'clock. It took Detective Chalmers and a wake-up call to Colonel Perry just to get Frank exonerated from the suspicion surrounding him and his concealed weapon. When Frank was released, Joe was still struggling with one last detail that kept niggling in the back of his mind. *Why were there shots fired and an auto collision just outside Frank's house? Was the man who stole the car a street over, in fact, Eddy?*

Frank knew it was. He'd arrived conclusively at that point. What he couldn't conclude was why the collision was in front of his home. Clearly, it was not part of Little Eddy's plan. So, it begged the question: who else might be standing in his way?

Once back at home, Frank recalled his last conversation with Detective Chalmers at the station. Chalmers put forth his theory about the other driver in the collision. Joe thought the person who interrupted Eddy's taking a shot was someone trying to take out Little Eddy.

Frank looked at the piece of paper he'd been doodling on. He had written Little Eddy's name and circled it with a line that led to the word *me*. He had drawn another circle with a question mark, representing the other automobile. Suddenly, it became clear.

Frank whispered, "Joe's right; there has to be someone trying to hit Little Eddy. The mafia makes hits." He dropped the pen and sat back. Whispering again under his breath, he said, "The mafia wants Little Eddy dead."

He thought, *Never mind for what reason, it doesn't matter so long as it fits.* Now Frank could sleep, that is, with a loaded .45 semiautomatic under his pillow. The next day Frank called the base and got a week's leave arranged. He figured he'd need at least that much time undistracted from his duties.

The first part of Frank's strategy was to lie in wait for Little Eddy. While Eddy continued to watch the base exits, Frank would watch for him. All he would need were binoculars and his weapon. Nothing would be left to chance. He would keep his car parked within walking distance and out of Little Eddy's sight. Which base gates he covered would be left to chance. Figuring the Bay Shore gate had its share of action, Frank would concentrate on the other two. The time frames in which Little Eddy expected him were Frank's morning and afternoon transit times to and from those gates. If Frank could be there at even one of those gates, the trap could be sprung. Frank felt he could intercept Little Eddy that way.

Near the Dale Mabry gate, there was a brush-covered area where Frank could conceal himself. Frank mused, *There's another problem. If Little Eddy gets shot first, it will be murder.*

The next day Frank jumped into his Mustang and drove away. He was convinced it was between him and Eddy. In Frank's mind, it had to be. That afternoon, Frank entered the Dale Mabry gate at four o'clock. He had his binoculars on the front seat and his weapon in the glove compartment. After spending some time at the gas station on base, he drove toward the Dale Mabry gate. At 4:35 p.m., he purposely went slowly while driving off base. Even though his sweaty hands slid on the leather steering wheel cover, he remained calm. Then, he spotted a police cruiser in his rearview mirror. The cruiser followed until he intersected Interbay Boulevard, and then the policeman turned right.

On his way to the MacDill Avenue gate, Frank turned the radio on. He almost laughed when he heard a pop singer stridently vocalizing, "I fought the law, and the law won." As he approached the gate, he couldn't believe his eyes. An empty yellow Camaro was parked in plain sight at a 7-Eleven store across the street from the stop sign where he sat. Frank eased out and then pulled in back of the convenience store.

Frank thought *"What am I doing? If I see him coming out of the store, what will I do? I'm not close enough to the gate for police protection. What's my next move?"*

Just then, Little Eddy appeared standing outside the door with a pack of cigarettes in his hand. Frank fingered the safety on his .45. Only twenty feet from the corner of the building, there he was in front of God and everybody pulling out his golden lighter. Cupping his hand to his cigarette, he lit up. Frank took one step forward from around the building and raised his gun. His finger threw the safety, and he slowly leveled the barrel and drew down on his target just as he was trained.

Frank said to himself, *He's got to go. So long, Little—*

Suddenly, Little Eddy's back arched, going entirely rigid, as if he'd received a bolt of high-voltage electricity. The telltale sign of the bullet was a red dot left in the middle of Eddy's forehead. Carmine's .45-caliber Savage round bored into his brain, taking most of it out the back of his skull. Hunco then slipped behind the flower shop across the street. His work was done.

Frank felt as though time had stopped; it seemed as if everything was moving in slow motion now as he watched haplessly. Little Eddy's slight frame crumpled to the pavement in front of Frank outside the 7-Eleven. His body slapped the pavement, leaving one last puff of smoke curling from his lips.

Frank stood with his gun aimed at the space between him and Little Eddy. It seemed an eternity passed until some woman parked at the curb started screaming from her car. Only then, did Frank come to his senses, retreating behind the building to his car. There he sat, gun in hand, trying to comprehend the last seconds of Little Eddy's miserable existence.

At first, Frank felt an enormous rush of relief come over him. But then, there came the agony of being cheated. He knew in his heart of hearts he should be elated; instead, he was feeling double-crossed. He was avenged, yet he never fired a shot. He couldn't help but feel cheated. Yet, there was no time to sort things out.

The police sirens made him start his car and go. As he drove, he sensed the irony that Little Eddy had met his demise just blocks away from where he took down Frank's only family. Now, Ramsay's words began to haunt him again. He could hear her sweet voice urging him to live out his promise, "Be a person of value." Now, the onus was upon him.

24

In the weeks to come, on-base training was stepped up twofold, and newly equipped F-4C Wild Weasels were arriving daily. It didn't take a crystal ball to figure out there was something big coming. Something was in the works, and Frank was smack in the middle of it. One more week of intensive training convinced Frank his squadron was fully trained and ready to go.

It was May 1972. The current Republican administration was anxious to bring the North Vietnamese to the peace table in Paris. It was within the realm of possibility that this might be the last gasp of aerial combat in the war. That's when something fortuitous took place.

As luck would have it, Frank was called to Colonel Perry's office at 0830 hours sharp. His aide greeted him, asking if he would like a cup of coffee. Frank just asked to see the colonel. His aide entered Colonel Perry's office and then quickly returned.

"The colonel asks that you wait a few more minutes."

Frank complied, taking a seat near a pile of tattered *National Geographic* and *Air Force Military Life* journals. He was convinced there was nothing he wanted more than a return to duty in Southeast Asia before the war ended. Frank felt he was destined to return to the skies over Nam; besides, he had a score to settle.

When Colonel Perry did receive him in his office, Frank was completely taken aback. The colonel appeared at once relaxed yet drawn, like a man who had just won a great victory after wrestling a giant.

"Come in, major. Do you know why I sent for you?"

Frank knew it was best to wait for it.

"It's active combat duty, Frank. That's the crux of the matter. You'd have to have your head up a mole's ass not to see what's happening here on base. I'm confident I speak for the rest of your squadron, when I say you're the man to take them into the fray."

Colonel Perry looked over the aviation pictures adorning his office. They documented his personal role in aviation history. Many photos preserved exploits in aircraft he flew. He would have given his right leg to be leaving right now with Frank's squadron to Southeast Asia.

"You have probably already heard about the North Vietnamese spring offensive," Colonel Perry said. "Well, I'm authorized to tell you we are prepared with our own offensive designed to bring the North Vietnamese government back to the peace table. You remember, I mentioned Operation Linebacker? Well, we're prepared to activate and your squadron will deploy within forty-eight hours. Is that understood, major?"

Frank stepped back and pumped out a salute. "Yes, sir, that's understood, Colonel. Will there be anything else, sir?"

"No, major, that's all. Carry on."

A true sense of yearning pulsed through Colonel Perry's body as he watched Frank leaving his office. Frank could tell he wished he were going with them into harm's way.

Two days later, it was official. Frank received his orders. The entire wing, including the C-141 refueling aircraft backup crews and mechanics, were departing. Frank had time to pack, but contacted no one. He stopped in front of the closet mirror and silently reflected, *Who would I contact, anyway?* Frank understood he was alone.

Things were really heating up on the flight line at MacDill. Frank liked the smell of it. Phantoms were everywhere, steaming around the ramp as they prepared for real missions. The training phase was over. He was entirely proud of his men. He knew they were as ready as they'd ever be. It was a real thrill when Frank heard the con tower officer speaking over his headset as his squadron taxied out to the runway in their Phantom F-4 IICs. His was the lead plane when the tower spoke to him over his headphones.

"You're approved for tactical flight operations. Major, you are cleared for a straight out departure. Go get 'em, Bee Sting."

Next, Frank heard the colonel's voice from the tower. "Major Barrett, I expect you to carry out your mission in the finest tradition of the U.S. Air Force. When you arrive at Ubon, you will officially assume command of the Eighth Tactical Fighter Wing. Your orders precede you. God's speed, Frank."

Frank flipped his visor down. "Thank you, sir. Thanks from the squadron for putting your trust in us."

"No sweat, Frank. I'll see you all after one hundred fine missions. I'll be buying the drinks at the Officers' Club."

With that, Frank pushed the throttles forward. He felt that familiar surge of power from 17,500 pounds of thrust per engine spooling up behind him in the twin General Electric J79-GE-15 turbojets. He was pushed back into his seat as his craft raced down the 11,500-foot strip. Way before he reached midfield, he was already airborne and retracting his gear and flaps passing through 1,000 feet. Increasing their angle of attack, he and his squadron climbed out of sight at 40,000 feet per minute. It was a good day to be flying.

For the long flight over the Pacific, they flew without armament, which normally consisted of four AIM-7 Sparrow and four AIM-9 Sidewinder missiles and a twenty-millimeter cannon pod. Without a normal bomb load of 750 pounds, two drop tanks were the only things holding them back from maximum performance. Frank's flight formed the lead in a finger four formation. With four flights, sixteen planes in all were on their way to join Operation Linebacker. Frank felt better, already seeing the peninsula of Florida and its problems slipping away. Ahead lay many stress-filled hours of flight, but the end was in sight. It was what he trained for. Clark AFB in the Philippines was his distant goal.

25

When Frank popped his canopy, the hot, steamy air brought back a flood of memories on rollout at Clark. The air seemed so thick it was like breathing through wet cloth. His arrival coincided with the hottest month of the year, with daytime highs averaging ninety-three degrees.

Frank's squadron was to layover three days to receive rest and minor repairs before pressing westward for Ubon, Thailand. Clark AFB was the largest, most urbanized American base overseas. It covered 14.3 square miles with a military reserve flight training area another 230 square miles.

Clearly, some recreation would accompany their brief stay before engaging the enemy over Southeast Asia. The four flights, composed of the sixteen men, decided to stick together. So, once they got cleaned up and dressed in their civvies, they descended upon the Officers' Club, namely, The Caboom Club. When several taxis converged at the curb later that evening, the men were already primed for a celebration.

As the evening progressed or digressed, some chose to join in maudlin drinking affairs, bidding farewell to the world as they knew it. At least for the uninitiated in the world of aerial combat, it seemed altogether fitting and proper.

As for Frank, he parted company with the main body of men, preferring to maintain a sense of decorum. After all, he was their commander. He chose to explore the gargantuan base with his wingman's crew. Acting on a tip about a movie theater, they took a cab as the driver entertained their mood.

He warned, "If you are new to base, I suggest you travel with caution and beware of the Filipino Lady in White."

My buddy, sitting in the cramped backseat, leaned forward to converse with the driver. He slurred, "What are you talkin' aboush, my good man."

The driver was only too happy to entertain his question. With an air of authority, he assured him. "She is our local ghostly legend. She will hail a cab, not unlike ours, late at night. Once the lady dressed in white enters, she will stay awhile, asking questions of our new visitors. Then, she will suddenly vanish from the cab."

My buddy, Earl, impolitely burst out laughing, destroying the air of mystique by suggesting the driver was trying to increase his tip. "Well, if that's the case, then one of us might have to get out with her 'cause this cab is crowded enough already," he said.

The driver seemed a bit annoyed with Earl's remark. "Oh no, señor, many say they have seen her. It is our local legend."

Earl finished. "Then, maybe we can get her to spring for your tip, okay?"

The driver was not amused. He spoke no more of the apparition. When we rolled up to the theater, the movie *MASH* appeared on the marquee in lights.

Frank suggested, "There are good reviews on that movie. Why don't we give it a try? It's about three Army surgeons assigned to a medical field hospital in the Korea. It's supposed to be a hilarious, yet dark comedy."

Earl said, "Oh, I don't know. I feel more like a flat-out comedy myself. I don't want to watch one of those films where you have to think."

The others laughed, agreeing that might be a bit of a challenge for Earl in his present condition. Nevertheless, after some prodding, Earl reluctantly agreed, and the group piled out of the cab to see the show.

Frank urged, "You see. Look, it has Donald Sutherland, Elliot Gould, Sally Kellerman, and Robert Duvall in it, too. Let's go."

Earl turned back to the cabby. "I'll keep an eye out for your lady in white. I'll put in a good word for you."

Frank went back and handed a generous tip to the driver. Then, he was placated in spite of Earl's smart-assed remarks. The movie was good, overall, with humorous situations foreseeable on the front in times of war. There was an underlying subtext of the movie indicating what war was really like. As they left the theater, Frank wondered if that ever dawned on Earl.

As with all carefree good times, the men's time on Clark proved woefully inadequate and brutally short. All too soon, they were transported back to the flight line. Their aircraft passed inspection, and they were ready for the last leg of their journey. It was impressive to see how the largest logistical support team came to fruition at Clark AFB. Now, it was time to do their part, once they reached the Royal Thai Air Force Base at Ubon.

Approaching Ubon's airspace, Frank radioed the tower twenty-five miles out. "Ubon tower, this is US Air Force Eighth Tactical Fighter Wing entering your airspace on westbound radial 270. How do you read? Over."

"Inbound Eighth TFW, I'm reading you loud and clear. You are cleared for a straight in approach on runway twenty-seven. The winds are easterly at five knots, altimeter is 29.90. Be advised of a local haze at one thousand feet on the north side of the field due to brush burning."

"Roger that, Ubon, will report on runway heading 270 on final five miles out."

Frank throttled back, allowing the formation to take the lead, and planning to watch them all land safely before him. As the last plane of sixteen, Frank reported five miles out with gear down and locked. The old trickle of a black unnamed river east of the field still served as the outer marker.

From his vantage point, the eight hundred-foot trees on the horizon took on a bluish-green hue as the sun took on the hue of a dull orange meatball through the haze on the horizon. Like clockwork, their birds slipped on to the runway one after the other to join their comrades of the fighting Eighth Tactical Fighter Wing.

As soon as Frank popped his canopy, he inhaled the heated atmosphere of Thailand's busiest air base. Following his bevy of fighters, he joined them, lining up precisely on the painted line. When the ground crew slipped the chocks beneath his mains, he let loose a sigh of relief. As they say, the flight's not over till the tires are chocked.

Frank felt a great deal of pride making that arduous Pacific crossing twice. All planes and crews were delivered safe and sound. The next challenge would be engaging them in the air war. Orders came sooner than expected. As soon as Frank's men were bedded down, he fell into his own bunk for some deep sleep.

The next morning came too quickly. At 0500 hours, Frank was greeted by the hooch attendant. His round face was right up in Frank's, as he was trying to convey a sense of urgency. He was a sun-bronzed Thai in his early thirties urging Frank to get up. He rose and looked around himself. Everyone else was asleep. Frank thought, *This man is making a mistake. Perhaps, he mistook him for someone else.*

Frank identified himself. "Major Barrett. Are you sure you have the right guy?"

The sinewy muscles around his neck grew tenser. "No mistake. You Major Barrett. Come now, see Colonel Dennis, your commander."

Frank was up and began pulling on his flight boots, recognizing the name he read in his orders. The wiry, half-clothed Thai now stood watching Frank dress, smiling all the while.

"You want coffee, major?" he asked.

At last, something encouraging came from the little man. "Yes," said Frank, "very much so, please."

When he returned with the elixir of life, Frank was almost ready for conversation.

"What does the commander want?" Frank asked. Frank thought surely they would receive a proper orientation to base before taking on actual missions. Yet, the only way he could confirm this was to get over to the CO's office.

His hooch attendant said, "I will wake others. You must go see Commander Dennis now. Okay? My name is Canman."

"Oh, yes," I replied out of politeness. "Mine's Maj. Frank Barrett."

It was not until later that Frank learned other pilots had dubbed him Canman as a joke. He came by an airman's fatigue shirt with the name Cameron on it, so pilots started calling him Canman as a play on words, because he was the man who cleaned the can. What's more, every time he tried pronouncing the name stenciled on his shirt, it came out Canman. After a few vain attempts to correct him, it stuck. Presently, Frank didn't know which way to tread. Canman must have read his mind.

"You follow wooden tracks to sign post. It shows way to go, okay?"

Frank just wanted to finish his coffee. Sitting on the edge of his bunk, he began to sense that oddly familiar ambience of Thailand at war. There was the pungent smell of raw sewage from the surrounding klongs ingloriously mixed with the odor of spent jet fuel.

The lingering scent of cooking oil managed to suffuse with the rest, creating that odd combination one never forgets. As he sat on the edge of his bunk finishing his mug, others started rousing around him. The men started questioning each other.

One of the squadron's pilots from Alabama was the first to vocalize his perception of their new surroundings. "Whewee, smells like somebody's cookin' up barbeque in the shit house! I sure hope I ain't invited."

Frank smiled knowingly and allowed the awful truth to sink in that this would be their home away from home. Making his way down the track of wooden pallets, Frank found the sign post Canman spoke of. Frank followed the arrow pointing toward HQ. It was still dark, so that might account for his difficulty in reaching the CO's office.

It had changed. The front steps were now smoothly cemented. A teakwood sign hanging above the front porch announced: "The Mighty Eighth Tactical Fighter Wing, Cmd. Col. Darryl Dennis." Beside his front door a wooden plaque read: "We don't keep the peace. We make it." Frank mounted the stairs thinking that worked for him.

26

Half a world away, FBI agents hid in their cars inside an empty potash warehouse at the Tampa Bay docks. Their vehicles were parked in a pinwheel fashion, facing outward, concealed in the cavernous warehouse. The agents were awaiting the signal from their superiors to pounce.

On the docks, a huge drug deal was about to go down. Other agents waited nearby, lying under tarps on the dock and wearing headsets. They were in constant touch with the bureau's command center blocks away in the Federal Building. Acting on a reliable source of an inside informant, this bust promised to be a record breaker. According to the informant, approximately two metric tons of pure Columbian cocaine would be delivered aboard a Panamanian registered ship named the *Corrina*. Presently, it was moored next to the potash terminal.

Three weeks earlier, Captain Diaz, who had been employed by Bonocante Shipping, was informed his services would no longer be required. He was to turn back and put in at the port of Cartagena, Columbia. There, a man would meet him with his final payment. Diaz was an old hand at smuggling. Immediately, he smelled a rat. Unaware of Bonocante's plan to foil the FBI, he remained at the helm with different intentions.

Captain Alex Diaz shouted orders through the ship's communication system. "Engine room all forward, full-speed ahead. Maintain present course."

"Aye, aye, sir."

The rest was history. On February 1, 1972, the *Corrina* lay docked at Port Tampa with its cargo intact. Captain Diaz would make a plea bargain agreement through his attorney with Hillsborough County's district attorney, thus handing over his entire cargo of Columbian cocaine to FBI agents. The rewards for Captain Diaz and crew were certainly more favorable than dealing with Columbian law enforcement. As for Bonocante Shipping, things were about to get worse.

Captain Diaz was to appear before special agents at their request.

The agent in charge waited now in his office, looking forward to meeting with the wily, old smuggler Diaz. This meeting would be informal; special agents would stop at nothing using Diaz as a way to get at the mafia and their trade. Fortunately, the FBI now had Diaz just where they wanted him. After a brief handshake and obligatory eyeball-to-eyeball stare, the lead agent at HQ relaxed a bit

"Captain Diaz, I know the position you are in now can only get worse. From where I'm sitting, it looks like you and your crew are going down for delivery of cocaine in massive quantities. In addition, we have you on illegal shipment of these drugs from a foreign nation. I'm sure your attorney will break it on down to your being a mere accessory to the fact. However, I've got you on enough federally attached charges to keep your attorney tied up for the next couple of years."

The head agent sat back in his swivel chair blowing smoke in the air from his Cuban cigar. He let his words linger in a swirling pall of spent tobacco. Then, he leaned forward with soothing in his voice. "Captain, how would you and your crew like to see that all that go away?"

The room was as quiet as the smoke hanging in the air. Finally, Captain Alex Diaz allowed a wide grin to form. "Mind if I have one of those fine cigars?" he asked. "They're Cohibas, right? I always like to weigh things carefully before delving into dangerous propositions."

"Sure, help yourself. There's a lighter there on my desk."

Alex took a seat without asking and lit up his fat, lengthy cigar. His gray eyes widened with satisfaction as the tip glowed. His first drag was strong. Then, he relaxed and sat back in his chair, as if he were experiencing a state of ecstasy. "Yes, indeed.... Ah, that unmistakable aroma."

The head agent sat stiffening in his chair and assumed his I'm-in-charge-here posture. "What makes you think my proposition will be dangerous, Alex? After all, I think you and your brothers might find my offer attractive considering your alternatives. By the way, can you speak for your crew?"

Alex returned a nod in the affirmative and then spoke assertively. "Unless I missed my guess, all you want us to do is help you get to the mafia trade, right?"

"That's putting it bluntly, but yes."

"I'm sure you understand any move against Bonocante would mean a death sentence for those making it. If me and my crewmen have to go down, why should we increase the risk by taking your offer? At least between my attorney and your DA, we stand a better chance of living out our sentences in some nice prison like Atlanta."

FBI Special Agent Wellsford sneered. "On the other hand, I might be able to get you hard time if I talk to the warden real nice. How long do you think you and crew would last in there? I'm sure you'd meet plenty of amigos you gave the bump to on your way up. I'm sure they'd love to return the favor on your way down. I hope you get my meaning, because I can personally guarantee it won't be pretty."

Alex rolled his eyes as he took another long draw on his cigar. He exhaled, letting his words mix with smoke rolling off his tongue. "You intrigue me. Why don't you spell out your offer?"

"All right, let's say I get you into the witness protection plan. In exchange, you can let us know dates and times of any future drug deliveries."

"There are two things about your plan I just don't think my first mate and I could deal with. Number one, after this last bust, it's going to be a strain regaining the family's trust. They're going to think I disobeyed orders to save my own neck. Number two, your witness protection plan seems to me like a witness in prison plan. Besides, where do you think you could hide a man like me in a style that would come close to what I've become accustomed to?"

"Well, with regard to number one, I must say that I agree. It will be tough to stay close to the family with all that's gone down. The way I got it figured, though, is they're just greedy enough to stay in the game. So, what if I could fix it so my people look the other way if they come across any future shipments that are in the works? That should go a long way toward restoring confidence, don't you think?"

"Yeah, it probably would—unless they smell a rat."

The agent assured. "We'll be careful. As for number two, I think you'd be pleasantly surprised at the accommodations we've provided our, let's just say, important guests in the program. Protocol doesn't permit me to divulge, but I think you'd be quite surprised with our list of individuals thought to be missing who really aren't. That is, if you get my drift."

Alex considered his last statement. He appeared visibly impressed. "I would like some time for my first mate and I to consider your generous proposal."

"Sure, but just be aware that timing is everything in this business."

"*Intiendo.* I'll get back to you before the end of this week. *¿esta bien?*"

"Okay, that should be fine," the agent agreed. "In the meantime, I'll arrange a safer meeting place for us as soon as I hear back from you."

Alex rose from his comfortable chair and snubbed out his cigar in the agent's ash tray. "Thanks for the cigar; it's been a pleasure."

Agent Wellford didn't bother to rise as Alex exited his office. As far as he was concerned, the time for formalities had passed. The majority of his time would now be spent in finding chinks in the armor of the local mafia that would eventually lead them to their trap.

Although playing the game was tedious and tiring, the thought of its rewards kept Agent Wellford going. He took solace in remembering nobody ever said dancing with the devil was easy.

27

Alex moved swiftly to set up a meeting with Santo Bonocante. With Wellford's permission, Captain Diaz's attorney arranged for him to be released on his own recognizance.

Tony picked up the phone in Scaglione's Seafood Market. He was second in line only to Santo. He was both a killer and a trusted and able capo.

"This is Tony. Whadda you want?"

"Tony, this is Capt. Alex Diaz of the *Corrina*. I was hoping to speak to Mr. Bonocante."

"Well, maybe that can be arranged. Hold on."

Alex waited nervously on the other end, lining up the message that he had been told a dozen of times. There was a long pause, and then finally a gravelly voice came on the line.

"This is Santo. Where are you, captain?"

"Yes, Santo. I know it's you; I've heard your voice before. I was hopeful you might meet with me to discuss an important business matter."

"Well, what is it? I'm a busy man. Right now, I'm wondering about a shipment I gave orders for you to deliver in Cartagena. What happened, captain?"

"I can explain everything," Alex began. "I was hopeful you and I might set up a meeting to share some common interests, perhaps at Licata's. Is that favorable to you? By the way, may I call you Santo?"

"You know, you got a lotta balls asking for a meeting and trying to get all familiar and shit when I still don't know what the f—— happened to my shipment! You work for me, you little bastard, and don't you forget it! If I want to meet you, I'll tell you where and when. You got that?"

"Sure, Mr. Bonocante. Good-bye."

Alex hung up feeling unvarnished by the cretin's words. He thought, *I wouldn't give you the sweat off my balls if it weren't necessary to kiss your ass.*

A week later, Alex waited at Licata's just after sundown. The room was dimly lit as usual. Only a few nearby candles gave off enough light to recognize even a familiar face. Alex had arrived early, hoping to put Santo at ease. In this way, Santo's men could case the joint to decide if it was a setup. Lately, Santo couldn't be too careful. He was aware of the FBI snatching his cargo. Since then, Santo decided to divert future shipments back to Port Tampa. As for his ex-captain's fate, that remained to be seen.

Seeing Tony had finished frisking Alex, Santo emerged from the darkness. He was wearing a full-length coat. He came to the table and turned immediately, allowing Tony to remove his coat. It was easy to see it was an expensive Burberry camel hair coat.

Santo announced, "I don't know; sometimes this place gets too cold for me. Maybe, I'm getting old."

Alex offered, "Please, do sit down."

Alex kept his eyes on him, watching where his hands went. He felt a little more at ease when he chose to place them on the table in front of him. Even though it would have been considered bad form by most of Santo's underworld colleagues to whack a person in Licata's, nevertheless, Alex didn't forget for one second who he was dealing with.

"I'm pleased you could take this time to meet with me," Alex said. "I know how busy you are. I wanted to speak to you about an important matter that concerns both of us. I feel it is something we can agree upon, and then both of us will benefit."

Santo replied smugly, "I'm still sittin' here. So, tell me what it is you gotta say, my captain."

Alex spoke hesitantly at first, not wanting to upset Santo. "Recently, I diverted a former shipment of yours, because I thought we were going to be highjacked."

Santo's eyes narrowed briefly in the flickering candlelight. For a scant second, he looked up at Tony standing by his side. There was only an instant of wonderment in Santo's eyes. Tony slowly nodded his head, affirming the shipment could have been in jeopardy. Word on the street told him of competitors trying to break into his lucrative drug ring.

"I'm sorry to hear that. Did I know these guys?" Santo asked.

"Well, yes. I believe you've heard of them."

Santo was unwilling to let him off the hook so easily. "Is that a fact? Tell me where you got that idea."

Alex played the game just a little longer, hoping to gain some advantage in his negotiations with Santo. He'd been well coached. The FBI was well aware of Santo's so-called competition.

"I don't have every detail yet, but I understand they're younger guys and they left one of your men in critical condition over in Port Tampa."

Santo continued to feign interest.

Alex blew out his cheeks, shaking his head slowly from side to side. "That's part of what I wanted to discuss with you. They were operating behind my back. They acted against us when they redirected our cocaine shipment to Tampa in spite of my specific orders to recall it."

"Why would they want to do that, Alex?" Santo questioned.

"Because, Santo, they got tipped off somehow by an informant that the feds were waiting to bust that shipment as soon as it arrived in port."

"Oh, yeah? Who was the informant?"

"Well, I'm sure they will not reveal that source to me, if you don't mind, Santo."

"Okay, let it be. You know I don't interfere with your side of the operation just so long as everything goes smooth on my side—you know, according to plan. Do you get my meaning?"

"Sure, I do, Santo. In fact, that is why I asked for this meeting. You see, I'd like to change the site of our next shipment to Tampa's main terminal. After that last bust, Port Tampa's too hot. I didn't want to change things, unless I got your blessing first. Also, I'd like your permission to change the timing of our delivery schedule. I think we have to shake things up to keep the feds off our ass."

"You know, Alex, okay, you made your point. When you've got a new time and place, call Tony at this number. Let him know all the details, okay?"

Alex took the card from Santo's hand. He could scarcely believe how easy it was to make the necessary changes. Now, all he had to do was get the information back to Agent Wellford. What the feds did with it, he couldn't care less. He was getting out of the cocaine business. Alex decided not to order. He'd gotten what he wanted, and now he felt the need to be away from Santo and his men. The whole restaurant scene gave him gas.

"I'm going to leave you now, Santo," Alex said. "I have some other important business, if you don't mind."

"Yeah, well, that's up to you. Just keep in touch, you got that, all right?"

"Sure, Santo," he agreed. "You have my word on that. Good night."

The following day Alex took a cab to Ballast Point. His plan was to meet with Agent Wellford at the pier. He felt extreme caution was needed in keeping Santo's men off his tail. If they even suspected a double cross, he wouldn't be meeting anyone ever. In this case, all was secure. A sparkling bay with a long pier was the only backdrop for his meeting. Alex was dressed in his best blue leisure suit and sipping a Pabst Blue Ribbon as he awaited his federal accomplice. He was ticked off when he received his associate instead.

"Where's Wellford," Alex demanded.

Junior Agent Daniels replied, "He's been detained. All you have to say can be entrusted in me."

"Is that so? Well, I'll tell you something. *My* ass is on the line here. Am I cuttin' it pretty clear here, junior? Or, did anybody entrust you with that news? The time I meet with Wellford is the time he'll get his information." With that, Alex marched from his table in disgust.

"Agent Wellford, please; this is agent Daniels calling."

Wellford came on the line after a long pause. "Where are you, Daniels?"

"I'm at the meeting place," Daniels responded. "Alex left in a huff. It seems he prefers your company to mine."

Wellford was annoyed, but managed to hide it. "Pack it on in, Daniels. I'll have to rearrange my schedule to meet him personally."

28

There were signs of renewed activity when agent Wellford met with Alex. Again, Alex chose the relatively secure surroundings of the Ballast Point Pier. At his outside table, Alex sipped on a PBR. It was 10:15 a.m. Wellford arrived late enough to see the avid fishermen already far down the pier, so there were few other anglers close at hand. The morning mist had long since burnt off, and the Tampa skyline was clearly visible a mile away to the northeast.

"Sorry, I'm a little late," Wellford said. "It's difficult getting out these days."

"Better late than … whatever. Would you like a beer?" Alex asked.

"No, thanks. I'll have coffee."

With a wave of his hand, Alex called a waitress over. Ordering coffee, he decided to dispense with further pleasantries.

"Here it is. I've met with Santo. He assures we can still work together. I can call for a future meeting with his capo, Tony Scaglione."

Agent Wellford's mouth tightened when he heard the name. Unpleasant dealings from the past rushed into his mind. "Do you have any knowledge as to where this meeting will take place?" he asked.

"Sure, at a fish market," Alex responded. "I believe you already know about Scaglione's."

"Yes, that would be an excellent place to meet. We have a wiretap in there. Of course, it depends on where you sit."

"Well, I can't guarantee we'll actually stay there or where we're gonna sit, for that matter."

"When you do meet, try to steer the conversation toward shipments in the future. I want the mafia out in the open when this goes down, or there's no deal. Understand? We intend to let as many as two shipments go by at the new location to build up some trust between you and Tony. Everything should be wrapped up in three months, if all goes according to plan. Do you want a weapon, Alex?"

"Definitely not," Alex said. "Every time we meet, they frisk me."

"All right, just let me know as soon as you arrange a time and place, okay?"

Alex said, "It's a deal, señor."

Later that same day, Alex gritted his teeth as he dialed the number for Scaglione's Seafood Market.

"Yes, this is Captain Diaz. Is Tony there?"

"Just a minute. I'll check."

Tony picked up in his back office. "Hello, Alex. How you doin' over there? Are you keeping safe?"

"I'm doing fine; thank you, Tony. I called to see if we could set up a meeting. When can I come by your place?"

"Yeah, I guess that's okay. Hows about eight o'clock?"

"Eight will be fine, Tony," Alex agreed. "I'll see you then."

"You got it."

After hanging up, Alex immediately dialed Agent Wellford's number to report in.

"Hello, may I speak with Agent Wellford, please? This is Captain Diaz of the Bonocante Shipping Company."

"One moment, please. I'll transfer you to his extension."

Wellford picked up on the first ring; he was just leaving the office for the day. "Agent Wellford. What can I do for you?"

"This is Alex. I've been in touch with Tony. We set up a meeting for eight this evening at the market. I thought you might want to know in advance, in case your people want to be tuned in tonight."

"Very funny, Alex. Listen, it's good you called anyway. I meant to tell you—pay close attention when you meet with Tony. They must have found our tap. We no longer have a tap—that is, unless you'd like to wear one."

Alex said, "No, thanks. I'll give you a full briefing afterward. By the way, before we get this underway, I want it in writing that my first mate and I will be in the witness protection program when we're done with this business, understand?"

Wellford bristled. "I thought we had an understanding at the outset, Alex?"

Wellford wasn't accustomed to being spoken to that way, especially not by an informant. By the same token, Alex wasn't used to speaking to business associates this way.

Wellford continued, "Meet me tonight at the Old Fort Restaurant on Platt Street after you finish with Tony. I'll be waiting in a booth in the lounge."

"All right, I'll be there," said Alex.

At the appointed time, Alex arrived for his meeting with Tony. He dimmed his headlights in front of the seafood market. Most of the day's business had ended hours earlier. He pulled around in back of the building. When he reached the back door of the market, he knocked three times followed by two as he was instructed. The door was thrown back quickly by a carny-like man in knee-high rubber boots. A man wearing a large rubber apron led him down a narrow hallway. Alex's first whiff inside was an assault to his nostrils. The smell of dead fish created a complex unpleasantness of its own, but when mixed with the strong floor cleaning agents in the wet tiled walkway, it took his breath away. The diminutive doorman led him through the distasteful stench toward the office.

Alex tried joking about the smell. "You know, a guy could get bumped off here a week ago, and nobody's goin' to know the difference. You know what I mean?"

The little carny man looked over his shoulder at Alex with a very curious expression. Further down the hallway, an office door appeared, which the little man held open for him. Once Alex stepped inside, he was thankful there was air conditioning. At least it seemed to mitigate the stronger fumes of afterhours cleanup in the seafood business. He found Tony sitting in an office chair. His walls were festooned with scantily clad women on outdated calendars.

Tony swung out from his swivel chair to greet him. "So, good, let's get down to business," Tony suggested. "Sit down, take a load off."

Alex was only too happy to get it over with. As he took a seat, he noticed the telltale lump beneath Tony's coat. He briefly reminisced about what someone once said.

Any man who does business with an armed man is either desperate or feeling mighty lucky. He wondered which he might be at that pivotal moment.

"So, the boss tells me you got details on an arrival." Tony began.

"Yes. I contacted my sources." Alex confirmed. "The next shipment can arrive on the fifth of May at the dock opposite warehouse number six at the main terminal in Port Tampa at 3:00 a.m. Your men should be in place at exactly 3:30 to receive it. Your men should be set to move the product. It's gotta go quick from ship to shore. All, of course, with security provided by your men."

"Don't worry about my men; they'll be well equipped. Let's just keep the calls between you and me down, and we'll be okay. You got real questions between now and then, give me a call and we'll work something out, okay?"

Alex got up from his chair and extended his hand to close the deal, anxious to leave.

Tony only said, "The way I see things, it's as good as done. I'll see ya."

Alex withdrew his hand and turned to leave the building, as soon as possible, without arousing any suspicion. His next stop was only blocks away. When he pulled into the parking lot, he noted the go-go girls dancing in the lit up front window of the Old Fort Restaurant.

Such a seedy departure from the fine old traditional Spanish restaurant that used to do business on this very site, he thought. *Once, on this very site, there stood Tampa's first fort back in 1823.* Alex heaved a sigh. *Is nothing sacred anymore? Such a place to have to meet with an FBI agent. Aye, mi Madre, what's this world coming to?*

Parking in back, so as not to be seen, Alex left his car in the lot as he wondered why a straight-up agent like Wellford would chose such a spot for a rendezvous. He entered the front door and headed straight for the lounge, hoping his business would transpire quickly. Locating Wellford in the third booth on the right, Alex slid in and began speaking secretively.

"All right, let's get on with it. This place disgusts me. Here's the low down."

Wellford held up his hand, forestalling any further conversation. "Hold on there, amigo. For one thing, we never say 'here's the low-down,' and another thing, this place is where your kind of people do business all the time, am I right? Look around you. There's gambling like running the numbers and bolita, white slavery, and teen prostitution to name just a few things your drug shipments have financed all over Tampa. Oh, and let's not forget kids who get their first taste of coke free just to get them started, compliments of Santo Bonocante and that creep you just met."

"Yeah, I have to work in some pretty sleazy joints, and there'll be more to come. So, captain, tell me, how far am I from your own port of call? Or, did you think you'd just traipse in here and fill my head with dates and meeting places, and waltz out holier than thou? Take another look around, Capitan Big Shot, before you go shootin' off your mouth. This is the side of Tampa you and your amigos dealt with. Now, tell me what you gotta say. I'm ready to listen."

Alex was learning that he had to pay his way in the witness protection program.

Wellford said, "All right, let's hear it from the start. Don't leave out a thing. Every detail could be important. When you're finished, write it all down exactly as you remember it. Then, you're going to see another agent and tell him all over again. You got that?"

"Si, intiendo."

"Then I'm leaving here first. You'll follow at a safe interval. Just make sure we're not seen together. After you meet the other agent, you'll hear from me again, okay?"

Captain Diaz bowed his head, looking diminished.

Another meeting was scheduled with Tony Scaglione, after the first went off without a hitch. This time, Alex arrived at Scaglione's with the exact number and unit weight of the incoming shipment. Tony was ready to engage his crew. Off-loading would proceed at 3:30 a.m. sharp. The weather provided a low-lying fog shrouding the dock that morning. At assigned secure locations, the FBI was ready to observe the entire operation.

Tony met one more time with Alex, after that delivery for the payoff. This time, he insisted on meeting at a new location in north Tampa. It seemed unusual to Alex. He thought he smelled a rat. The place Tony picked was a liquor store called Char Pal's. It was on the north side of town near Busch Gardens. When Alex informed Wellford of the rendezvous, he seemed a bit suspicious, too.

Wellford asked, "Did he say why he wanted to meet there?"

"You know him. He has a limited vocabulary."

"Sure, so what exactly did he say?"

Alex repeated what he'd been told: "We'll meet at Char Pal's parking lot at eight o'clock tonight, right?" He then added, "What can I say? The man's direct."

"Okay, there might be something more to it. I'll have a couple of men posted there just in case, so don't worry."

"That's easy for you to say," Alex noted. "I'm the one who has to get in the goon's car and accept a briefcase chock full of money. What if he's changed his mind? Maybe he wants to make a deal. What do I do if he asks for a bargain?"

"Look, Alex, all you have to do is take the briefcase and leave. Don't even try to count it. Don't even look at it. Especially, don't make waves, okay?"

Alex glumly replied, "Yes, I understand. What else can I do for you?"

"Well, first you make sure you haven't been followed, and then, meet us in the back of the dog track parking lot. Do you know where that is?"

Alex shook his head in dismay.

"Everybody knows where the damned dog track is. It's the only one in town for Christ sakes!"

Meanwhile, Tony Scaglione had reason to be suspicious. Tony couldn't put his finger on it, but something was happening on the streets. Something he couldn't account for, since the first shipment off-loaded at Tampa's main port. There were some low-key busts. Some of his people in the distribution line were arrested. It wasn't a full-scale takedown, yet it was enough to get his attention. As a precaution, he shook things up a little, just in case. It was his reliance on these same tactics that kept him in business longer than most in the dangerous game of moving drugs.

Alex arrived in a black 1959 Ford Galaxy 500 sedan in the back parking lot of Char Pal's liquor store right on time. As he turned off his lights, the back door of the store swung open. It was obvious someone watching identified him quickly. Now, a medium-built man approached his car. Alex rolled down the window, ready to engage him in conversation. The man, dressed in a dark suit, walked with a decided limp. He seemed winded as he reached the car and leaned on the window. Alex noticed his breath smelled of strong drink when he leaned in.

He spoke in a hoarse voice. "The boss wants you to come inside."

Alex replied, "Sure, I'll be right there."

Now, he wished he'd packed a gun. He walked toward the back door, feeling naked. The man in the suit opened the door and allowed him to pass. Alex found himself in a small, narrow hallway that led to an office. The door was open, and he found Tony playing cards with several other men.

"Hey, Alex, come in, and take a load off. I'm almost finished with this lousy hand."

Tony looked him over atop his cards for any telltale signs of a hidden weapon. His partners did the same. Eventually, Tony ended up folding.

"Come on, Alex. Maybe if I give away some money, my luck will change."

Tony stepped to the rear of the room where the store safe was located. Bending over the large gray steel box, he spun the dial back and forth until the tumblers clicked into place. Pulling back the heavy door, he produced a briefcase containing $1 million. Reaching across the space between him and Alex, Tony handed over the briefcase.

"There you go, Alex, your take—one million dollars."

Alex accepted the case without a word. He turned to leave the smoke-filled room. One of the card players called out after him as he reached the door.

"Hey, ain't you gonna count it first?"

Every man in the room, except Alex, burst out laughing. Alex simply smiled wanly in reply.

Tony was still laughing as he waved him off. "You see, that's outta respect, somethin' maybe you guys oughta learn."

Alex kept walking. Outside, he felt his trousers, making sure he hadn't pissed them. Ten minutes later, he was in the parking lot of the Tampa Downs Dog Track watching an FBI car winking its headlights at him. It was time to make the exchange. Wellford, and another agent, sat in the front seat as Alex approached their car.

Wellford said, "Get in the back, Alex."

"Not much racing tonight, is there?"

"No, we picked a quiet night, Alex. Don't be a wise guy. Let's have the briefcase."

Clearly, Wellford was in a hurry. He didn't like being out in the open exchanging large amounts of cash. His agents would go over the money that night and log every serial number for tracing. Then, as agreed, he would return the money to Alex for payment of the next shipment out of Colombia.

"Okay, my men will have this counted and logged by morning. I can drop it off to you at the pier, if you like."

"Do this for me, instead. Meet me at the horse stables across the street. I'll be parked there in my black Ford."

"That will work. I'll see you there tomorrow morning at, say, ten o'clock. Does that suit you?"

"Yes." Alex looked both ways, and then, stepped from the agent's car. There was nothing left to do now but head for home. The following day, he was waiting at the stables. It comforted him knowing he only had a few miles to drive back to Port Tampa. It did start to wear on Alex's conscience that his entire crew were incarcerated awaiting the outcome of his gambit as an FBI informer. He had assured only his first mate would also receive asylum in the witness protection program. What would become of the rest of his crew? God only knew. Soon, the FBI car arrived, and the exchange was made.

Captain Diaz was anxious to complete the last shipment, and his part of the bargain with the FBI. All agreed the last shipment should be arranged for by mid-month, at the latest. All he had to do was be sure Tony and his men were in the right place at the right time, and then, the rest would be in the hands of the FBI. This shipment would contain a normal shipment of fertilizer with an ample amount of pure Columbian cocaine, paid for by the mafia from the proceeds of their previous shipment.

The FBI was already using their knowledge of shipping times and places to pull certain dealers in the chain off the streets in Tampa. In their view, it was time to start forming a network of informers to work through the chain of distributors. This was an action they failed to inform Alex about.

By the time the third shipment arrived in Tampa, Tony's suspicions were confirmed by the number of recent arrests. He was struggling with the notion that their security was being compromised on the street. In a brief meeting, Tony confided, "Santo, I'm concerned. I've lost seven dealers off the streets in the past three weeks."

Santo replied, "Don't be paranoid. You know, we lose dealers from time to time. It's risky business out there." He shrugged. "Besides, sometimes you know the good guys get lucky, that's all. Don't worry about it. These shipments are making us a very favorable turn around. Just keep your guard up, stay close to Alex, and try not to worry too much, okay?"

Tony smiled. "Okay, Santo, if you say so. I'll not worry."

Santo stood up and patted Tony on the back. "Maybe you're just trying to get a raise on account of your extra worry. Come on, now, meeting's over. Let's go eat."

By the third week of June, the Panamanian freighter *Miramar*, owned by the Bonocante Shipping Company, was making its way into Hillsborough Bay. Soon, it would dock in Port Tampa; the FBI was already lying in wait. They continued waiting, until the cargo in question was completely off-loaded, before they made their move. Hours later, a radio crackled in Special Agent Wellford's unmarked car.

"Special One, this is Dock Force Two. We've completed photographing the unloading. You can proceed with Dock Force One for the intercept."

It was a clear morning at the docks in Port Tampa, not the kind Tony liked. He made a point of varying delivery times, but it was to no avail. Every detail of the shipment's progress since the *Miramar* left port in Colombia was known by the FBI.

Now, Tony was also shadowed. Agents sat at their listening stations in a van. Their only duty was to monitor Tony's reaction as he learned of the raid. Then, they would tail him to every contact he made thereafter. Hopefully, he would eventually lead them to the top of the food chain. In the meantime, the trap was being sprung on the dock.

There were six stevedores lumping the cargo when the agents revealed themselves from all sides at once. Other cargo stacked high on the dock concealed several agents with submachine guns. The stevedores had just finished loading the truck with cocaine.

Agents came out of hiding.

They shouted, "Freeze, FBI. Put your hands on your heads and lie down!"

All six of the men complied immediately. Agent Wellford remained in his car hidden inside a warehouse. He listened intently, as his radio crackled to life.

"Special One, this is Dock Force Two. We have the suspects in custody. The drug transport truck is secured."

"Special One, here. That's excellent, guys; great work. Tell the guys at the dock exits to keep a sharp eye out for runners."

Just then, a large Buick with four men in it, spun out on a dock ramp coming up out of the shadows. They sped toward the road bordering the port. Its driver raced for the highway. As they approached the point where agents stood waiting on a warehouse roof, the driver floored the accelerator as his companions fired long bursts from their Uzis. Fusillades of bullets went out in the agents' general direction, panging the corrugated steel building all around them.

That was their cue. The agent in charge shouted, "Now! Men, fire at will!"

From their vantage point on the roof of the warehouses, six agents with assault weapons riddled the passing car through the roof until it careened off course and slammed into a dumpster behind a harbor front bar. There was no movement inside the smoking vehicle.

When news of the bust reached Tony, he was furious. Now, the pieces were coming together. His suspicions became reality. Immediately, he concluded the FBI was responsible for everything. Only they had the resources to put together a bust like this. Now, he was convinced another wiretap was in place at the seafood market. Tony grabbed his gun and stormed out the back door.

He didn't dare try to contact the boss. His first action was to head for a nearby diner where he would use a public phone. He kept close watch in his rearview mirror. As expected, a familiar Ford showed up. Two men in the front seat of a custom Fairlane was proof enough for Tony that he was being tailed. Despite the burning hatred in his gut, he decided to ride it out. After all, they had no idea where he was going. It was a cinch they hadn't bugged a public phone in a diner.

Parking his car in back, he went in and nonchalantly ordered a cup of coffee. The two agents behind him figured they'd already been spotted, so they radioed HQ for further instructions. Meanwhile, Tony stepped into the phone booth.

"Hello," said a familiar voice.

Tony said, "Yeah, it's me. I gotta speak to the boss right now. We got trouble."

Cangelosi put down the phone in Santo's den and fetched his boss right away.

"Yeah, Tony," Santo answered. "Where are ya?"

"I'm in a pay phone. I'm being tailed."

"Who's tailing you?"

"I don't know; most likely the FBI."

"What happened?" Santo questioned.

"I got a call from that customs agent we bribed on the docks. He says the whole shipment was confiscated in a bust by the FBI. A lot of our guys were taken prisoner."

A long silence prevailed on the line, and then Santo's voice returned. "Listen, here's what you're gonna do."

In the meantime, Special Agent Wellford was posing before one of the largest cocaine shipments confiscated in Tampa law enforcement's history. The smile on his face belied the fact that the Bureau's actions that day set off a chain reaction of retribution that would reverberate all over Tampa.

No sooner had the bust gone down then Capt. Alex Diaz was on the phone. "Wellford, this is Alex."

"Of course it's you, you stupid bastard," Wellford retorted sarcastically. "You've only called me three times since the bust. What is it I can do for you now, Alex?"

Alex said, "Well, you know my crew is still in jail. They're getting' kinda antsy waiting. It's just that they're asking me all sorts of questions that I don't know the answers to."

"Alex, I've already told you—we have to work out some last-minute details. As soon as I know, you'll know. I promise you. Now let me get back to work."

Alex didn't like hearing that hard click in his ear. After all, he felt he'd done his part. What was coming he felt he had earned. Alex continually felt the pangs of pressure to make all the important decisions. He found himself isolated and put upon, wishing he was free of his heavy responsibilities. He wanted to be the happy-go-lucky captain, the amiable old Alex.

Instead, he found himself forced to man up with a carefully controlled demeanor, forced to conceal his emotions. His crew was too dependent on him. All the while, there was a raging alcoholic anger building within. Inside, he knew he lacked the fortitude and character to live up to his responsibilities. It seemed everything fell on him at once after his ship was confiscated. To him, it all seemed woefully unfair. Even his grubby little soul felt for the men of his unsavory command. He knew even they deserved more than a sellout.

If only Little Eddy were there. He would buy Alex drinks and lend a sympathetic ear to the old *Capitan*. Little Eddy may have been an addict and a scurrilous scoundrel, but he was around in times of need. He lamented, *Alas, poor Little Eddy. You're on the other side of the green now.*

Wellford put down the receiver. *So it begins,* he thought to himself. *Now we're getting death threats from the mafia.*

Wellford stood up and went to his office door. "Daniels, I need you in here right away."

"What is it boss?"

"I need you to get over to Alex's right away. I need you to get him and his first mate, bag and baggage. Take my sedan; it's parked out back. Make sure you get all their belongings and keep an eye out. There's a chance the two of them might get bumped if you don't. The mafia might have already put out a contract on these guys. Get moving. I'm calling to notify Alex right away."

He immediately dialed Alex. "Alex, this is Wellford. Are you and your first mate ready to travel? Never mind that, I told you to be ready at a moment's notice. Now move. I'm sending Daniels over to pick you two up. Don't open your door for anybody else. You got that, Alex?"

Wellford deliberately tried making his voice sound calm and reassuring, as if his call was routine. "Good, Alex. Just call him. Have him meet you there. Daniels is on the way to get both of you. Don't go anywhere else, understand?"

Alex detected a strain in Wellford's voice. "Is everything in order?" he questioned.

"Yes, just do as I say. Good-bye."

Alex smiled as he set down the receiver. It was long in coming, but now the wheels were turning. He felt like a nine hundred-pound gorilla had just bounded off of his chest. He picked up the phone and called his first mate.

"Are you ready? Yes, this is it. I just got the call from Wellford. Come over and wait with me. He's sending an agent to pick us up. Hurry, it's time."

Alex thought, *At last, it begins. Our journey may be to an unknown destination, but it's a new future.*

Capt. Alex Diaz and his trusted first mate Diego left carrying their suitcases to the waiting car. After stowing their luggage in the trunk, they piled in with some smaller bags. Their packing job was complete considering the time they had to finish. It looked like another fine, clear blue spring sky in central Florida—hot by noon but tolerable. Agent Daniels sat behind the wheel as he looked in his rearview mirror at his passengers.

"Well, here we go, boys. I hope you remembered to pack your tooth—"

From outside the building, any gardener could tell the blast could be felt for a quarter-mile around. Small pieces of the car body flew in every direction like shrapnel. What remained in the aftermath was a flaming hulk of twisted automobile chassis consumed in flames with other remnants of the FBI Ford four-door sedan. Nothing else existed except scraps of the three men's bodies. There was complete devastation manifested in one space, formerly occupied by the sedan. Even the tires lay ablaze atop the charred driveway.

In the investigation that ensued, they would recover bits and pieces, like Agent Daniels's charred shield. But for the most part, everybody in the vehicle, according to the cleanup crew, could have fit in a shovel.

The FBI dared not break the news immediately, although it was tough keeping such an explosion under wraps in the port town neighborhood. One hard truth remained for Special Agent Wellford: more than ever before, the local mafia and the FBI were still at war.

29

Frank must have been one of the few pilots who actually wanted to be back in Thailand. He knew from talking to other pilots when he returned to Ubon that there was something big coming. Every visible sign pointed toward rapid expansion of interdiction missions over North Vietnam.

It was now July 1972, and they were on the cusp of a dramatic change in the air war. Frank was assigned a great GIB/RIO back at MacDill, and they trained together for months leading up to the coming campaign. His name was Capt. Mark Rodman, and had recently been promoted like Frank. They remained at Ubon while completing base orientation.

Their first combat mission was escorting B-52s along with Wild Weasels, specializing in electronic countermeasures to suppress surface-to-air missiles. They bombed the fuel storage tanks at Haiphong, setting fires that were visible from 110 miles away. For Frank and Mark, this was the beginning of Operation Linebacker.

Several sorties into North Vietnam followed, but the most gratifying from their point of view came later on July 13.

Frank sounded jubilant on the interphone. "We finally dropped the Thanh Hoa Bridge! There she goes, down in the muddy water. There's nothin' like laser-guided bombs!"

The bridge had been a strategic target since April 1965, consuming 873 sorties and 11 aircraft. Now, it was finished, compliments of the Eighth Tactical Fighter Wing and Frank.

From then on, the scope of the air war changed.

Frank said, "Look at this new expanded target list; it includes the Uong Bi Power Plant near Haiphong and a whole new class of targets we had to avoid before. The gloves are off now. Next, we'll be striking power plants, shipyards, even the Haiphong Cement Plant on a regular basis."

In the next couple of months, Frank and Mark racked up twenty-five missions together. Of course, flying at such a frenetic pace would take its toll on both planes and pilots. Frank led the next briefing for his squadron, and he gave it to them straight.

"Gentlemen, in this mission, we'll meet head on with North Vietnam's air defense effort. Our squadron is likely to be engaged in intensive air-to-air combat, and we expect large numbers of SAM launches. As the saying goes, no guts, no glory."

However, there was nothing glorious in seeing your buddies riding their parachutes right into downtown Hanoi. That scenario began to occur with frightening regularity.

Back at base, pilots were either catching up on sack time or discussing tactics and maneuvers to outwit their opponents in the air. There was the rolling scissors tactic, in which two fighters could be engaged in a tight turning match. The objective was to increase the intensity of the roll, while closing in on the enemy's six. This maneuver involved gut-wrenching, increasingly tighter, high G-turns in an attempt to get a clear shot at the tail of the aircraft in front of you. If done incorrectly, in a split second of hesitation, even the best of pilots could wind up with the enemy taking his place on *their* tail.

Then, there was what some pilots called the drive-by. That is, if they suddenly found a MiG on their tail, they pulled back hard on their stick to slow the craft down considerably. In so doing, it was hoped the MiG would inadvertently overshoot, putting them in the position of pushing the nose down hard and getting on *his* six, instead.

Every pilot had to be in top shape to withstand the heavy G-forces exerted on them during these brief, but violent encounters. This meant more downtime must be spent in physical conditioning—something most pilots loathed.

Frank knew, from experience, nothing seemed more pleasurable than showing up in a clean flight suit at the Officers' Club to relive exploits of the day over a drink or two. This was where Frank spent some mighty unpleasant hours as a squadron commander chasing pilots scheduled to fly next day out of the bar. To be sure, there was no glory in it for Frank.

In the meantime, Frank and Mark continued their own personal mission—getting closely familiar with their enemies ways. For instance, on one sortie returning from a particularly hot engagement, Frank had no missiles left, only their twenty-millimeter Gatling gun was full of ammo.

"What the hell was that?" Frank asked Mark as they streaked over some low mountains southwest of Hanoi. "Something just hit us underneath."

Frank threw the stick over to the left, pulling away from a mountain ridge. Mark looked up from his radar, trying to avoid vertigo, while bracing himself against the building G-forces from the hard turn.

"That, my friend," Mark grunted, "was definitely enemy fire; from the sound of it, forty-millimeter AAA. I think I saw that guy."

Straining for a better look over his shoulder, Mark suspected a mountain fading in the darkness.

Frank said, "Not on our second mission of the day. C'mon, I'm in no mood for games. Let's get that guy."

Frank pushed his throttles full up to mil. Max position. This action injects raw fuel directly into the afterburners, creating an immediate jolt of additional thrust. Having come around one hundred eighty degrees, Frank was looking directly at the muzzle flashes from the offensive batteries on top of the mountain.

Frank said, "Yep, they're definitely training on us. Maybe they don't know it, but their fire is giving me a perfect line of sight to *them*."

Frank reacted by pushing his stick forward, while arming his cannon.

Mark complained, "Ah, c'mon, Frank. Let's just head back; we're almost bingo."

"Don't worry," Frank responded. "This will only take a second, and, then, we'll be RTB."

With growing darkness, Frank appreciated his GIB's concerns. Low fuel and a long mission should have meant it was time to call it a day, but Frank just wanted to end theirs before returning to base. Mark obediently slaved his radar to Frank's target, while simultaneously searching for other hidden batteries on ground mode.

Mark exclaimed, "It looks right on the beam, major. Just use your piper sight and lay it on 'em.'"

Frank flipped the safety off the red fire button and fired. It was almost pure joy to see the illumination of tracer rounds telling him he was pummeling the target. Flaming foliage formed a silhouette around guns and crew as they haplessly increased their firing angle attempting to hit them. For the AAA gunners, it was a case of too little, too late. Just as their craft swooped over, they could feel the concussion of exploding ammo rocking them around. Then, Frank horsed the plane's nose around, until he could see the entire hilltop lit up like the Fourth of July.

Mark cheered. "Holy crap, will you look at that? I guess we won't be hearing from them anymore!"

Frank acknowledged, "Roger that, now let's RTB."

"Hot stuff," said Mark.

Inside of two minutes, Mark came over the intercom. "Frank, we got a problem. Look at your fuel remaining. Do you see what I'm seeing?"

"Damn, they must have hit us for sure. We're leaking like a sieve, Mark."

"Roger that, major."

Frank said, "Depending on our flow rate, we just might make the field on our reserve."

"Negative, remember those gyrations at mil. Max back over the target? We've already used up most of it," Mark replied.

"Go ahead and notify base that we may have to ditch." Frank directed. "They can, at least, scramble a chopper before we have to spend all night in the jungle."

Mark transmitted in staccato fashion. "Ubon tower, this is Bee Sting's flight. We have a low fuel warning light. Our position is approximately 110 miles out on vector 205, over?"

"Ah, roger, Bee Sting. This is Ubon tower. We should have you on our scope in ten minutes. How long do you estimate you can remain airborne?"

Frank broke in. "Ubon, we have sustained fuel leakage from ground fire. Our situation is uncertain. We're requesting a rescue chopper out on our present vector. Over?"

"That's affirmative, Bee Sting. Wilco to that. What is your airspeed?"

"We're at four hundred knots. Over?"

"Keep us posted, Bee Sting. Ubon is out."

During the next fifteen minutes of their flight, neither Frank nor Mark spoke a word. Each of them had enough to think about. Mark was busily trying to work out rate of fuel consumption, while Frank kept his head on a swivel, praying no bogeys would appear. He also nervously mothered his gages, hoping nothing else would light up. Their only consolation was they would be flying southwest soon, over friendly territory. Frank stared at the fuel ladder as it dropped from green to orange.

They heard from Ubon tower, as soon as they showed on radar. Next, they were told the trucks were foaming the runway. Finally, as the gage went red, Frank sighted the control tower ahead.

Frank said, "Mark, we're going to flame out soon. Hold on to your butt. This landing is going to be dead stick."

Mark's voice strained, speaking hoarsely, "Can we at least make the threshold of the runway, Frank?"

"Busy now, don't know for sure. As long as we have … oh, there goes number one. Help on the rudders here, Mark. One good engine is throwing in a lot of torque. Now, she's getting nose heavy."

"This is Ubon tower. You are cleared for straight in emergency landing. No response required."

"There goes engine number two," Frank noted. "You can relax on those rudder pedals now, Mark. We're in glide mode—we've got a flying brick on our hands now."

Frank had to hold the nose high to lengthen their glide path, in order to reach the end of the runway. Too high, the wing would stall, and, then, at their present altitude of three hundred feet, the 55,000-pound Phantom would slam into the earth like a load of bombs.

Frank cried, "It looks like we got the threshold for sure. Here goes. We're not gonna flare; we're just gonna land hard on all three."

Mark puckered up and prayed. "Just bring it in, please, Lord."

That was the last thing he said as, Frank scorched the mains heavily on the steaming hot threshold, a split second before the nose wheel took to the tarmac.

One of the guys in the tower was so excited he shouted. "Nice work, major; very nicely done indeed!"

Frank let the plane roll out as long as the momentum lasted. Popping the canopy, they each waved off the foam and fire trucks.

Frank said, "It feels good to call those guys off, doesn't it?"

Mark replied, "That's funny. I thought I caught a look of disappointment on their faces."

The ground crew were already breaking out the VAT 69, while Frank and Mark received a welcome ride back to their quarters in a jeep. It was a long day for the two weary, jelly-legged pilots.

There were drinks all around at the club that night. Frank kept hearing the rounds bell ringing and wondered where they would get the money to pay the tab. By the time Frank returned to his bunk, he felt blessed to be alive. He should have learned something about combat that day. Instead, his after-action report never mentioned returning fire on any enemy AAA battery hidden on a hill.

As missions slipped by, results from their efforts finally began to show. For years, the U.S. Air Force fought over Nam with one hand tied behind its back. Now, with stepped-up bombing in the North, they got results at the peace talks in Paris. Even the country's leaders, finally saw the light. A blind man could see it. Every time attacks were escalated, the enemy found its way back to the peace table. What a surprise!

Most of Frank's squadron attacks in the latter phase of Linebacker I were directed against three main areas in North Vietnam—Hanoi, and Haiphong. Strike operations were preplanned and usually directed at fixed targets. Most of these, not associated with armed reconnaissance, required approval by the Joint Chiefs of Staff prior to attack.

The bottom line was, Linebacker I operations definitely helped stem the flow of supplies into North Vietnam. This, in turn, limited the operating capabilities of North Vietnam's invading army. In terms of tactics employed and results obtained, Linebacker I was a vast improvement over Rolling Thunder.

Frank's squadron was mainly responsible for disrupting the flow of supplies and reinforcements to enemy units fighting in the South. Laser-guided bombs proved most effective, especially against bridges over the Red River at Hanoi.

They were also able to maintain air superiority over MiGs in this area, because American airborne radar detected enemy interceptors rising from their bases, thus giving them early warning. In spite of all that, going downtown, as it was called whenever they struck targets in Hanoi, was still risky business. The vast array of SAM sights set up around the city made it so.

Frank's next mission took place on October 15, a week before the United States stopped all bombing north of the twentieth parallel.

"Mark, check your radar warning, missile management," Frank directed. "We're rolling in on our target in fifteen seconds."

"Roger that, Frank. I show green on all systems."

Frank said, "On my mark—three, two, and one. We're going in now."

Frank and Mark started to grunt in an attempt to force blood back up into their heads as they loaded on the Gs. Frank steepened his angle of attack further still, until he was squinting at the target. It was an electric power plant just north of Hanoi. Frank released all four of their laser-guided bombs.

Frank said, "That's confirmed. All bombs are away. We're initiating climb out. Watch for SAMs, Mark."

Mark cried, "I've got flashes on the ground now. I've got multiple SAM launches."

"How many SAMs do you see?"

"My scope shows three closing fast."

Frank shouted, "Eject all flares! We're rolling hard over. Hold on."

Frank put his plane in a sixty-degree right bank while maintaining his climb, attempting to make their craft as small a target as possible. Simultaneously, he pushed throttle to mil. Max.

Mark shouted in a shrill voice. "Two. I only see two that took the bait. One's still coming!"

Frank said, "We'll try an accelerated stall. Maybe we can give it the slip."

Frank throttled back, lifting the nose steeper while putting out his air brakes in the climb. They were now ballistic, straight up.

After that, Frank heard Mark shout in the interphone. "Oh God! We're caught!"

The SAM hit them at a glancing angle directly behind the canopy. There was no chance for Mark to eject. Frank instantly pulled the D-handle, instinctively blowing the canopy off. Then came the T-handle; after pulling it, the explosive device under his seat propelled him into the slip stream at three hundred fifty knots. Frank felt the force of ejection beneath, just as a ball of flame nearly engulfed him from behind, where Mark had been. His body felt intense heat, then, just as suddenly, it was gone.

When Frank's chute deployed, he was looking straight down at the north side of Hanoi about three thousand feet below. Frank thought, *This could well be the worst day of my life.*

30

Frank's oxygen mask was ripped off by the windblast, even though it was affixed to his G suit. Fortunately, he was at an altitude where oxygen levels were adequate. Unfortunately, the survival stuff in his seat pack became inaccessible to him when he became caught up a tree. He was at least thirty feet off the ground, and the bad guys would be headed for his area soon. There was no time to lament Mark. It all happened much too fast for Frank to internalize any true sense of loss.

He thought, *I need to use my lowering device.* It was a nylon cord he could attach to the parachute riser cross strap, and then he could unfasten his parachute. After getting out of his chute, he could use the nylon cord to lower himself down.

Frank kept quiet, trying not to hurry. In training, he learned that rushing could cause the cord to bind up and may leave him stuck. With some effort, he did manage to reach the forest floor.

By then, he could tell from the voices of excited hunters, they were very close. Frank remembered from his days of squirrel hunting, how they reacted whenever he came close to the tree. The squirrels would circle, keeping the tree between themselves and him. He did exactly the same when he saw them approaching. Secluded behind the tree, he was hoping they would pass on the other side. They did, and he just kept circling the tree as they went.

Frank thought, *My heart is really pounding. After they pass, I'm heading for that dense area, burying myself under that log, and covering myself with brush.*

After he was well hidden, he smeared his face with mud. From his position, he was able to make radio contact with his rescuers. They insisted he stay put until dark. There were steep limestone cliffs in the area. He was on top of a mountain. There, he realized one misstep could kill him. Sitting still in the night, the sheer terror of his situation came over him in a chilling wave that caused him to shudder in the pitch-black. The triple canopy jungle caused Frank to believe that if he couldn't see them, then they couldn't see him. Yet, the overwhelming sense of fear, deprived him of any sleep.

The first night was cold and damp. He didn't even think of finding something to drink. After a fitful night, he did feel really thirsty. Unfortunately, his only water was up a tree in his kit. He had decided to run a bit after getting down, and now he wasn't even sure which direction his chute was. He decided to forget the chute and try living off the land, by taking moisture from the broad leaves of surrounding vegetation.

The following day, he could hear jets overhead making an effort to rescue him, but the sky was so overcast it was terribly difficult for them to even sight a parachute hung in a tree, much less him.

By the third day, the air force wanted to drop bombs to keep his pursuers heads down, while they attempted a helicopter rescue. The enemy had a small camp not far from Frank, and a couple of times he had to stop using his radio because they came so close to his position.

Frank was using a small hole in the brush for his antenna, which he kept uncovered. When an enemy search party drew near, they had to go around the log he was under because it was so big. He could see a woman soldier walking right by his head. He didn't dare even swallow. Then, two others were near his feet about five feet away. He just froze up completely, feeling the terror within of being caught. Just then, one of the rescue planes flew over real low, and they stopped to follow its flight path. When they did, their eyes came to rest on the small opening Frank had made in the brush for his antenna. Suddenly, the jig was up. The group gestured for Frank to come out, so he stood trembling with his hands up.

They wanted to get out of that area for fear they might be bombed, so they all ran through the jungle. Even though he was weak from lack of food and water, Frank was able to keep up because his adrenaline was pumping. Soon, they broke out on to a red dirt road. Not long after that, a truck came along, and Frank was thrown in the back with two armed guards. Now, escape was virtually impossible. Frank felt he was probably on his way to the Hanoi Hilton. His depression didn't have time to set in, because his captors kicked him around in the truck like he was a soccer ball while he was tied up.

This must be their way of getting back at me for keeping them out in the jungle for days looking for me, he thought. However, when he finally reached his destination, that was when he learned what real torture was all about.

On Frank's first day, he was issued striped cotton pajamas (a standard prisoner's uniform, one size fits all) and a pair of cloth sandals, no underwear. To his great surprise, he was also given a toothbrush. It was so small, it looked more like what he used to apply blacking when he shined his boots. Actually, it was kind of a joke, because they issued no toothpaste. Next, he was taken to a barber where all of his hair was shaved off. At first, Frank thought they might have a use for it. Later, he learned it was just a measure taken to keep lice under control.

He found it unusual, at first, that no one spoke to him. Not one person said a thing that first day; they only grunted and gestured to him. He guessed this was part of the regimen, until he learned later they were under strict orders not to communicate with him. That was reserved for his interrogator. Frank met him the following day.

The interrogator's name was Major Phuc. His green suit with brass buttons and red insignia on his epaulets seemed a bit over-the-top as far as uniforms went. Frank thought, *He must be uncomfortable; he appears to be too hot. The major is taller than the others. Maybe he's Chinese. Yet, his facial features are clearly Vietnamese. His broader flattened nose and high cheekbones make him appear more like the rest.*

Frank was in solitary in a seven-by-five-foot room. Because his health was generally good at the time, he was not seen by a doctor. The interrogator and his special thugs were the only persons he saw or heard.

When Frank was put in his tiny cell, he really did not know what was in store for him. In time, he learned that solitary was a form of torture, in itself.

The guards came for Frank not long thereafter. The first guard was diminutive, yet packed a big punch. Suddenly, Frank received a blow to his solar plexus, while the bigger guard held his arms back. When the punch struck Frank, he felt as if his entire chest was caving inward. The pain radiated out, searing his upper torso. It was followed by a volley of elbow punches to various parts of his torso. When the first guard tired, they changed places, so the bigger one could have his turn at pummeling Frank's upper body. Apparently, that was their specialty. Mercifully, Frank dropped to his knees, in spite of the small one's efforts to hold him up. Frank had passed out. Even though he was beaten thoroughly, solitary was far worse.

The guards left him alone without having said a single word during his entire beating. As time wore on, a dark hole of mental anguish came slowly creeping into his mind. The mind itself, he discovered, created an incredible burden of mental pain. It created a dark fog over his consciousness and robbed him of his power of reasoning. He realized that the mind can persuade life to just ebb away through the beckoning black hole of pain, if allowed. He learned how vital it was to keep his mind as sharp as possible. If he did not keep his mind clear, they would crush him through a steady dose of pain that eroded both mind and body, like the use of some deadly drug.

Despite mental anguish, Frank's body was first to give up. He couldn't keep from passing out, throwing up, or screaming. Frank discovered that the more his body convulsed, the more he could observe it with detachment, as though it belonged to someone else.

Once, in the midst of a torture session, Frank thought he could hear another soldier's voice crying out in a cell close by. At first, he thought, *Wow! Some poor bastard is really getting the hell beat out of him.* Then, he thought, *The guards really messed up this time, allowing my solitary to be broken by his screams so close to my cell. I love it when they get so incensed at a soldier that they abandon their discipline.* Later, Frank came to realize that the soldier he heard screaming was him.

Eventually, Frank found he could intellectualize pain. It allowed him to increase his tolerance of it. However, a new problem manifested itself. It was a way to stay in touch with reality enough to stay alive, but detaching too much would have an insidious narcotic effect that seeped into his sense of reason, dulling the normal danger signals. Sometimes, when pain got to be too much for the physical side, nature took control, and he would simply pass out.

Nevertheless, sometimes the beating continued after he was unconscious. Frank discovered new physical damage, when he awoke, that he was not previously aware of.

Frank learned torture was really very simple. It is a wearing process that just goes on and on until the will submits. To him, it was just a rule that he could never quite learn to live by. Frank felt that was why he survived, among other things. Sometimes, while being tortured, he would make lists. He would base his mental escape on real things. For instance, he would design and build homes. Some were dream houses, others more practical. First, he designed a floor plan. Then, he would build it up in his mind, right down to the last detail. Frank would design it, lay cement, put up two-by-fours, and drive each nail and saw each board. Sometimes, he even made mistakes, so he would have to do it over again.

There were other distractions in list making. He made a list of all the state capitols. Then, he made a list of all the candy bars he could think of. Finally, he embarked upon a list of all the people he ever knew, but stopped for fear he would blurt out their names and possibly their roles in North Vietnam. The oddest part of his experience with the Vs was how they could continue pummeling someone they didn't know, in total silence.

With mental exercise, came resolve. If he could withstand it, he was resolved that this was not going to be the place where he checked out. His isolation lasted approximately sixty days. To Frank, it felt like a damned eternity. Finally, he was moved to another part of the prison.

There, Frank was presented to a roommate. He tried not to show his elation. It was Lt. David Nelson. Frank had trained him back in the states. He learned Lt. Nelson had been subjected to six months of solitary. Frank figured this must be the standard length of time before commencement. David, the poor bastard, being a first lieutenant, had little to tell them, because he knew so little himself. With his captors, that proved to be a problem. When Frank first arrived, he had to wrap his ribs with his T-shirt. His breath was wheezy after experiencing a recent kick fest.

For the rest of their time in prison, they existed in a windowless concrete room that measured seven-by-eight feet. They had boards to sleep on and a rusty bucket for defecation. It was a hot box, in which they could hardly breathe. It was so bad they took turns sleeping by the slit under the door where jailers slid food.

The food itself was used against them like everything else. It was usually a watery green soup and a chunk of tasteless bread. They called the soup weeds. Because Frank's internment lasted during the late fall and winter months, the soup was served stone cold.

Because of his strong feelings about cooperation with the enemy, Frank endured the hardest part of his captivity. This began shortly after he refused to meet with some radical Hollywood type's delegation. He was supposed to interview with them and tell them how well he had been treated. Frank was determined not to participate in their propaganda games. Consequently, his treatment got rougher. It began with long sessions of standing immobile around the clock. Next, he was put on his knees on cement for six hours at a time. This routine went on for days.

Then, he was told to write a war crimes confession, saying that he was sorry he participated in the war. Frank stood up and heard his own voice saying he refused. Then, he was taken to a larger room. Soon, twenty guards lined up outside and took turns beating him to a pulp. By then, he was beginning to lose his power of reasoning.

Hours later, he was confronted with a bowl of water, some stinky rags, and a steel rod. They stuffed one rag in his mouth with the rod and put another rag over his face. Then, they slowly poured water over the rag until he was breathing water vapor. He could feel his lungs tightening up like he was drowning. Frank thrashed in panic as his lungs screamed for air. Then darkness came. Frank passed out, thinking he was drowning. Just before the sensation, his limbs convulsed in all directions. Finally, he remembered thanking God for helping him make a stand against subhumans.

When Frank came to, he discovered he was blindfolded and trussed up in a pretzel position. Leg irons shackled his ankles, and his wrists were tied behind him. Another rope bound his elbows just above the joints. The guards tightened the ropes by placing their feet against his arms and pulling the ropes as hard as they could. Then they tied his wrists and ankles and jammed a ten-foot pole between his back and elbows. After a few hours, the leg irons started to press heavily on his shins. The ropes strangled and burned his skin, causing searing pain that made his arms go numb as they slowly turned black. It was then that he realized he could lose his arms. The stark reality was if that happened, he would not be fit for release. Instead, he would become one of the men who was never repatriated.

Being a hopeless optimist, somehow he knew it was only a matter of time before all POWs in captivity were released. So, Frank reasoned he had to stay whole in both mind and body to qualify for that release. It was at that moment, he decided to start faking his being broken and told them he would talk.

Immediately, they brought in Major Phuc, who seemed ever so glad to see Frank, even though he looked like a bloody bag of chicken bones.

"So, you have decided to confess your crimes?" the major asked.

Frank replied, "Oh, major, I'm sorry. I thought you needed sensitive information about the U.S. Air Force. I did not realize you wanted to talk politics."

Instantly, Major Phuc took a step back and slapped Frank as hard as he could. The major did not conceal his disappointment. "You are an insolent military pilot who kills women and children with his bombs. How can you even dream of playing games with me at a time like this? Now tell me, what sort of information do you have for me?"

As Major Phuc listened, he pulled out a small tape recorder from his kit bag and turned it on. Frank proceeded to tell him all he knew about the inner workings of the North American B-25 Mitchell medium (obsolete) bomber first manufactured in 1939. At one point, during his lengthy confession, the major stopped him. "Are you positive about this information?"

Frank replied, "Yes, major, I am certain of it."

Following a long stare, he nodded his head and started taping again. They finished in about an hour.

Phuc said, "I will take this tape to my superiors for analysis. I hope you are correct in every detail."

Frank figured he had bought some time to heal. At this point, he was desperate to stop his internal bleeding and give his kidneys time to heal. Every orifice of his body was oozing red fluid. Unfortunately, his ruse did not last long.

Oddly enough, his captors decided to get back at him surreptitiously. Frank began to discover small slivers of glass in his bread. Sometimes, there were bits of wire or broken plastic, and, of course, the daily regimen of maggots in his soup increased, as well. He wasn't fooled. Then, it stopped. Instead, they tried one more attempt at propaganda.

This time, Major Phuc arrived with another officer and an already-written confession. Frank told them he would never sign it, even if they killed and ate him.

They both laughed, and, then, Major Phuc taught Frank a hard lesson. He said, "It is easy to die. It is much harder to live. We will show you how hard it can *really* be."

The next few days were all a blur to Frank. The head-banging beatings wore him down to the point where his mental resistance games began to fail him. He was in so much pain, at times he really did just want to die. He wondered where all the training tips had gone.

Then, the hate began. At first, it was like an elixir—a tonic that strengthened him. He found he could curse the guards, the air force, his faith in God—everything he knew, he cursed. However, after a few venomous days, he belatedly arrived at a powerful conclusion. Hate was an insidious, creeping evil, that when concealed in one's heart, ate people alive. Frank resolved to free himself from the vengeful feelings he had been harboring in his heart since his wife and child were taken from him.

Finally, he truly understood that hate and revenge grew on the same tree. Once he buried the old Frank in the grave he had dug with vengeance, he knew he would be able to repent and really live again. That night, Frank experienced a dream, although it all seemed very real.

Frank saw himself on a windswept, wide white beach walking along while watching emerald waves rolling in and out, lapping at the shore. There was the sound of gulls laughing all around. It was such a bright, cloudless day he had to shield his eyes from the sun. He looked down the long stretch of sugar sand and saw a woman and a boy walking steadily toward him. When they drew nearer, he recognized it was Ramsay. The boy seemed very familiar. Then, Frank realized the little blond-haired boy was his. Then, they all stood together alone on the beach, embracing each other. Ramsay was speaking softly in his ear.

"It's time to come home now, Frank. It's your son, Frank Junior."

Frank understood; he cried a tear and gently kissed the boy on the forehead.

Ramsay said, "Come this way, Frank. We're going home."

Suddenly, he opened his eyes and saw a gorgeous blonde flight nurse leaning over him. She was so close he could smell the long strands of her hair touching his face. She was so beautiful. Her name badge read RN Captain Sandy Peacher. Just then, she was speaking to Frank.

"Isn't it wonderful, Frank? We're all going home."

Frank experienced an awesome feeling coming over him. It was then that he closed his eyes and began humbly thanking God for all there ever was and ever would be. Somehow, he knew in his heart he would never be alone again. He looked around himself in the C-141 and saw other men who formed up the angel flight of freedom with him. It was March 3, 1973. They *were* finally going home!

As Frank looked back, he had to reflect. What about the others who had died? Why him? How did he survive the rigors when others just gave up on wanting to live? Many things came to mind that helped Frank understand how he survived. He did, after all, come to understand what was important in life. He embraced a spiritual aura of closeness to God and Jesus Christ, whom he had accepted as his personal savior. They became his family. Also, he and the others held out with a sense of honor and integrity, preserving their sense of duty. He internalized with mature understanding what he'd already been through.

In Frank's final analysis, he realized war is nasty business and brings out the worst in people. When he saw his brothers endure unspeakable cruelty, as they sacrificed all for their comrades in captivity, he came to believe the true nature of man lies in what he does in anonymity. He also realized that a strong moral character requires daily maintenance.

Then, he looked over his seat to see where that pretty blue-eyed nurse went who had first spoken to him. He saw her in the back of the plane talking and joking with some of his compatriots. Then and there, Frank set his sights on her. After all, Frank was a fairly young man. Yes, he possessed some scars that would never show, but he also had a lot of back flight pay coming.

Frank raised his hand, calling out to her. "Hey, can a guy get a drink up here?"

She called back, "I'll be right up there, soldier."

The nurse was very shapely. Frank was emaciated, and he didn't know how she could see anything in him unless she just liked skinny guys.

When she approached, Frank asked if he could buy *her* a drink for a change.

She surprised him with her answer. "Crazy, what are we having?"

He had been away awhile, but certainly not that long. She had a slight Southern accent in her voice that he picked up on right away. "Where are you from?" he asked.

She just smiled at first as Frank poured the ginger ale, and then she commented. "Some of these guys are half wolf. They just have no taste, when it comes to entertaining a premium-quality broad like me." Then, she laughed. "I suppose it's just their way of exercising their freedom on this plane." Only then did she answer Frank's question. "I'm from a small town in Florida. I doubt you've ever heard of it."

"Try me," Frank asked, hoping he sounded hip enough.

"Okay, I'm from Fort Walton Beach, Florida, born and raised."

Recovering from his initial shock, hopefully, before she noticed the wave of tingling excitement pulsating through his entire body, Frank could say little more than, "Wow."

She said, "I attended Fort Walton Junior College and then jumped into the Air Force Nurse Corps. Then, I entered the aeromedical branch as soon as I could. You see, I'm from a military family, and I love to fly. My daddy was a pilot in World War II."

"Is he still around?" Frank asked. "I mean, my dad was a pilot in the war too, but he's gone now."

"Why, yes, my daddy is still around. In fact, Mom thinks he's quite a handful."

Frank said, "By the way, I live near MacDill in Tampa. How would you like to come and visit sometime?"

Sandy leaned back. Frank wondered if she was studying his eyes carefully for signs of ill intent. Then, she sat back farther, crossing her arms and eyeing him with a funny look. She took a long sip of her drink before speaking. "I think I'd probably like that, major."

"How did you know my rank? Your name is—that is, I think it is Sandy something?"

"I'm Sandy, and you're Frank Barrett."

"Hey, that's not fair. How did you know that?"

"Frank, I've got a list of every man on this plane," Sandy noted.

"Well, that's a great way to get to know guys," Frank joked.

She laughed. "Hey now, that's not fair either. It's my job to know everybody's name and rank. It helps me take better care of you guys."

Frank assured her he could be better cared for by her anytime.

"Now, let's not get too fresh, Major Barrett." Sandy looked directly into his eyes. It was the kind of look that fills the soul and causes the heart to skip a beat. There was definitely something happening between them right then and there on that aircraft. Then, she laughed softly.

Frank closed his eyes, giving thanks for all there was once again.

31

Eventually, Sandy took Frank up on his invitation. Frank had a lot of catching up to do. The two of them began dating and enjoyed the bay area like two butterflies caught in a whirlwind. Frank learned Sandy had lost her first husband to the war in Nam. They both figured it was time to put Nam behind them. No remorse, no guilt, and no sadness—they both agreed the future was for those who kept falling forward.

The US. Air Force also had its plans for Frank, which included stationing him at MacDill. It was a reward, of sorts, for what he'd been through. That was fine with him. Following an extensive flight physical, the doctors prescribed eight weeks of intensive physical training in order to get him back in shape for flight status. It was another decision he did not mind.

After months of dating, Sandy told Frank she would like to move to the bay area. Frank was agreeable, because they really clicked. Their relationship had begun with mutual respect and seemed bound to blossom.

Sandy took up a new position in nursing at the Veterans Hospital in Bay Pines, St. Petersburg, Florida. As for Frank, he was slated to continue flight training as soon as he was able. At least that was the plan for the time being.

However, two things became clear toward the end of 1973. President Richard Nixon's Vietnamization Program was winding down the war. Consequently, demand for combat pilots was beginning to wane. That meant Frank might be out of a job training pilots. Conversely,

Sandy's choice of hospitals was experiencing a surge of returning vets from the war. It was clear she would be needed at Bay Pines. Frank needed to make an executive decision.

First, Frank called his old pal Chad, who was still kicking rudder pedals for Pan Am out of Miami.

"Chad, ol' buddy, guess who? And guess where."

Chad's voice registered true surprise. "Frank, I can't believe it's you! I saw your picture on TV a while back. Man, that Freedom Flight was really something else. I was glued to the set. I saw you walk by the camera. You're an honest to Pete hero."

"No, not me, Chad. You know it's those other poor bastards who stuck it out far longer than me. They're the real heroes. Somebody should erect a monument for those guys. I really mean it. Some of the pure hell they went through for years on end, without ever seeing the light of day. Good Lord!

"But that's not why I called, Chad. I called because I was wondering how the job market looks in commercial aviation. Any openings at Pan Am for a good stick like me?"

The long pause on the line gave Frank a telling chill.

"Uh, Frank, I love you like a brother; you know that. I gotta level with you right now, quick and in a hurry. It stinks like you know what on ice. With Nam winding down, they've got pilots falling out of trees. I just saw a buddy of mine take a layoff, and he's been with us for five years. They're taking the low timers first, but I know I'm ridin' the bubble myself. To tell ya the truth, I don't know how long Peg and I can hang on here. I may have to take a different overseas route. It's like Dodge City around here right now."

"Well, I really love the way you sugarcoat it and paint the rosy picture even when the chips are down, ol' pal. You might as well say, 'Stick with *me*, and you'll be wearing walnuts the size of diamonds.'"

"I'm awful sorry, Frank, but what you see is what you get, man. You know me. I'm not going to shine you on, man."

Frank got the picture. "Anyway, the Air Force ain't so bad, after all. What's the worst they can do? Send me overseas? How's Peggy taking the pressure? Is she holding up okay?"

"Oh sure, she's fine. She just doesn't want to leave her job in real estate," Chad said. "She's made a lot of connections, and it's just beginning to pay off. I swear, if they decide to transfer me to another country, it's going to be a bitch of a decision for us. She makes as much as I do." Chad lamented. "You know, it's a crying shame. We busted our humps flying missions overseas for this? Look at you—of all the people who deserves better."

Frank said, "Hold on there, partner. The Air Force isn't such a bad employer, you know."

Chad replied, "I know, but it just seems like we both deserve better for the dues we paid."

Frank assured Chad that he was just checking out the possibilities.

"Well, I wish I could be more positive, buddy. You probably think I sound like it's the end of the day."

Frank didn't see it that way; he was sure he could handle the situation. "Do you remember the lesson we learned in combat?" he asked. "Don't look too hard at the problem; let it reflect back to you."

Chad replied, "Yeah, that one has come in handy a time or two. That reminds me.... Frank, do you remember when you forgot that lesson about mountains being where you find them and not where you think they are?"

Frank said, "Ah, yeah ... you mean when visual references exceeded my aircraft's performance?"

Chad coughed bullshit over the phone, so Frank quickly resumed his aplomb.

"As you were, Chad; as you were, you winged wonder you."

"That's okay, Bee Sting. At least you always brought me home."

Frank thought grimly, *That's more than I could say for my last GIB. Anyway, it's nice to be called Bee Sting—it hasn't been heard in a long time.*

From then on, somehow Frank knew things would get better no matter what he flew.

Frank said, "Gotta say so long for now, Chad."

"For sure, Frank. Just don't make it so long next time."

"Fair enough, my friend, *vaya con dios.*"

After getting the scoop from Chad, Frank knew there was no sense pushing a worm. In other words, if Pan Am (the top airline) had a glut of pilots, so would all the others. So, it was back to the drawing board.

In the meantime, Sandy and Frank got engaged and decided to look for a place where they could live in semiseclusion. They took out a map and narrowed their search to the north side of Tampa Bay. Sandy wanted to be close to her work. That meant the west side of the bay, which was dominated by the city of St. Petersburg. Unfortunately, Frank grew up with a negative image of the city. He had always heard it was the home of the newlywed and the nearly dead.

So, one fine Sunday, the couple headed east on Highway 60 out of Clearwater, Florida, looking for something viable. Frank drove past a sign with an arrow pointing northward toward Safety Harbor at the threshold of the Courtney Campbell Causeway. For some reason, the name rang a bell. He did a one-eighty and turned north at the sign. They soon found themselves winding down a narrow two-lane road skirting the harbor on their right.

It all came back. Frank had visited the little harbor town ahead before. It was with Toni and her parents in her father's boat. Only now, Sandy and he were approaching from the south by land.

On the left there were mangroves, on the right the placid harbor. Immediately, Frank and Sandy were captivated by the quaint sense of seclusion afforded by the seldom traveled road. Frank secretly hoped they wouldn't see Toni where they were headed.

They did see occasional passersby, but considerably less traffic than the rest of the bay area. Eventually, the mangroves gave way to well-manicured lawns and large homes that appeared on rising slopes. They were encountering hilly countryside, which was somewhat unusual for

Florida. Frank figured that being above the harbor accounted for the increase in elevation.

They both enjoyed seeing the sun sparkling off the harbor now and then, as they rounded each bend in the road. It was a beautiful day for cruising in Frank's sky-blue Mustang with the top down. As they drew near the town, most homes appeared to be older. Some were built in the old Spanish hacienda style with terra-cotta tile roofs. These were both charming and pleasing to the eye, as were the surrounding live oaks gracefully draped in gray Spanish moss.

In town the road changed to brick-lined pavement, which gave the town the flavor of a bygone era in Florida history. It was almost as if Sandy and Frank had taken his Mustang into a turn-of-the-century village. They stopped at an interesting-looking spa fashioned after a Grecian bath. It was ornately decorated with columns, marble statuary, and shaded outdoor benches, which appeared particularly inviting.

The entire Main Street was deliberately built to fit that same turn-of-the-century look. Sandy and Frank were quite taken with the whole scene of small shops and eateries. When they discovered the huge gazebo in the center of the beautiful town park, they found themselves attracted to the sleepy little town.

Frank decided to walk Sandy up that same ancient Indian mound where weddings were held on top. They learned it was just on the outskirts of Safety Harbor, and true enough, they found Philippe Park. It was only a quarter mile further on the main road out of town.

They climbed a pathway nearly three hundred feet to the top. According to county parks information, the mound was made from oyster, conch, and other shells deposited over the years by the Calusa Indians, a Paleo-Indian tribe that inhabited Florida as far back as pre-Columbian times. Sandy and Frank found it interesting that this quaint little harbor town had such ancient roots.

Frank brought his camera for a chance to catch Sandy where many a bride had posed on her wedding day. Instead, she chose to perch upon a huge limestone landscaping and beautification rock. In her blue shorts and sleeveless white blouse, along with those curvaceous legs, Frank thought she could put many a bride to shame. As he tightened his focus, he couldn't help observing she had the right hips for a great cannon ball the next time they hit the pool.

"C'mon, Frank, take the picture already. This rock is getting cold."

Frank took the shot and leaned on the rock, while he waited the sixty seconds for the Polaroid to develop. When he peeled off the developer, the picture appeared in living color, as it were.

Sandy liked it. She held it in her hand while she talked to Frank. "You know, this place is within easy commute of both our jobs; plus, the quiet living and city convenience seems to make it the right place for us."

Frank said, "I agree, so let us make our next stop the local realtor's office."

The couple quickly found it not far away, just like everything else in Safety Harbor. As they came up the steps of Gardenes Realty, they met an elderly gentleman coming out.

He held the door waving them in. "If you're lookin' for Howie, he's out back watering the dog."

Sandy and Frank each looked puzzled at his remark. Entering, they found an oak rolltop desk dominating the front portion of the building, with a narrow office stretched out behind it. The imposing desktop was littered with colorful brochures and a plethora of loose papers engendering a general look of dishevelment before them. An alleyway formed between stacked file boxes, which led to the open back door. Sunlight streaming in gave the impression that was where Howie had gone to water the dog. Frank had his own idea of what that meant. But Sandy, he could tell by her curious expression, wasn't quite sure.

As it turned out, Frank was wrong. Sandy peeked around the open door and spotted Howie Gardenes with hose in hand. He was, literally, watering the dog. Howie held the hose on Jack, his black-and-tan miniature dachshund, while he danced playfully, under the steady stream.

"Hold still now, Jack, or I'll never get that stinkin' stuff off."

Howie was the seventy-three-year-old, semiretired, sole proprietor of Gardenes Realty. Florida-born, he knew everyone worth knowing in Safety Harbor. A devout Methodist and thirty-third-degree Mason, he also fancied himself the local historian.

Currently, he was busy washing kitty litter and cat scat off Jack's nose. He'd received a snoot full from one of his favorite spots—the florist shop's cat box. Just then, Howie caught sight of Frank and Sandy. He straightened up, still holding the hose.

"Oh, hi, folks. I didn't know we had company."

Sandy and Frank came down wooden steps into the alley, as he stretched out his shaky hand.

"I'm Howie Gardenes, but I guess you figured that out for yourselves. You'll have to excuse me. Jack, here, has a taste for sandy patties, at least that's what I call 'em. I just can't figure him. Every time he gets a chance, he heads off to that cat box down the alley behind the florist's shop. I tried to get 'em to move that blamed thing, but they won't. He's a good dog otherwise, but when it comes to cat boxes, he just won't take tellin'. What can I do for you?"

"Mr. Gardenes, I'm Frank Barrett, and this is Sandy. We'd like to talk to you about some local real estate."

"Are you interested in buyin' or sellin'?" Howie asked.

"We may be interested in buying a house."

Howie gave Jack one more squirt, and turned off the hose. "In that case, come into my office, folks. I got somethin' ta show ya."

The couple followed Howie, and Jack followed them back to the rolltop desk. Howie pulled out a top drawer and produced a color issue of current listings.

"Please, make yourselves comfortable," he said. Howie motioned to a small loveseat, in a cramped alcove near his desk. Sandy moved several stacked magazines, and they sat down to peruse the listings while Howie looked on. Meanwhile, Jack occupied himself with a chew toy on the floor nearby.

Howie asked, "How much were you lookin' to spend?"

Frank replied, "Mortgage payments aren't a problem, because both of us work. When the present home of mine sells, there should be enough for an ample down payment."

Frank looked at Sandy, and her eyes told him they were making the right moves. After all, it was her telling eyes and caring heart that brought him to love her in the first place. Frank figured with her looks and strawberry hair, he was way ahead already. She once told Frank she wanted him to teach her how to fly. It made him feel like a man with no complaints.

"Howie, let's put it this way. We could be comfortable paying for a fairly new 2,500 square foot home. We'll pick out some models here that we like, and you work out the details. Then, we'll be back to take some tours. Fair enough?"

Howie pushed his straight silver hair back over his head and grinned. "I like a man who can make up his mind." Readjusting his tie, over his soup-stained shirt, Howie leaned forward with an outstretched hand. "Fair enough, Mr. Barrett."

"Just call me Frank."

Howie said, "The rest, to paraphrase Shakespeare, will be left to the eye of the beholders."

Frank and Sandy said their good-byes to Howie, while Jack cocked his head and wagged his tail as if to say, "You'll be back."

As Frank and Sandy departed down the winding road, it seemed just as much fun as coming into Safety Harbor; only this time, they each wore an expectant grin on their faces. With the top down, on a clear, sunny, spring afternoon, everything seemed idyllic. Soon, they were back at the causeway intersection, where they had first turned north.

As Frank pulled out into the right lane, he was suddenly sideswiped hard on his side, by a bat-out-of-hell red sports car, coming from behind them! The sudden slam sent Sandy hard up against her door, in spite of her seat belt! Frank's hands jarred off the steering wheel, as he struggled to regain control. His training kicked in automatically. Keeping his wits about him, he rapidly assessed the damage.

Making rapid side-to-side movements of his wheel ... okay, now the vehicle is still in control, gauges reading normal. What hit us? Where is it?

Instinctively, Frank checked out Sandy. To him, she looked a little shocked. Her pupils were slightly enlarged, and she was breathing rapidly. Outwardly, she appeared uninjured, but terrified.

"Thank God, you're not hurt," Frank cried.

Looking ahead, he could just make out a red, low-slung sports car weaving in and out of traffic rapidly, as it faded into the distance. The brazen offender was running for it!

"What the hell was this?!"

Frank pulled the car off on the easement. He leaned out of the car to check his front and rear tires on the left. They seemed okay. Quickly checking his rearview mirror for oncoming traffic, Frank suddenly burnt rubber as he rapidly accelerated up to highway speed.

For the first two miles, Sandy seemed to be in shock. Frank wasn't gaining, but he was certainly in the chase. Sometimes, Frank caught sight of the red car in the distance as they rounded a bend or when the other car became balled up in traffic. When Frank's own speed crept over ninety miles per hour, Sandy suddenly started screaming.

"*Stop! Stop! Stop the damn car, Frank! I want out!* If you want to kill yourself, go ahead! Let me out now. I mean it, Frank!"

Frank glanced over and saw a look in Sandy's eyes he knew he did not ever want to see again. It was primal, almost animalistic. What was going on behind those eyes spoke volumes about her instinct for survival. In an instant, Frank steered off the highway, again stopping on the easement. He reached down and yanked up the emergency brake lever, while gripping on the wheel and pumping the disc brakes hard. The car skidded straight to a stop.

With all the control he could muster, he spoke. First, Frank calmly told Sandy he loved her. Then, he raised his voice and said, "*Now get out!*"

As her door slammed, Frank resumed the chase with tires squealing, as he punched the 289-cubic-inch Mustang throttle to the firewall. In his rearview mirror, Sandy grew smaller, as she stood helplessly like a child in a blue cloud of burnt rubber. Frank wondered if he was wrong. A split second later, he thought, *Ah, hell no, this guy needs justice—now.*

Pushing his Mustang up past eighty, Frank hoped that he wouldn't find irony in receiving justice himself for speeding. Then, he got lucky. Two miles down the road, there he was. The SOB was sitting at a stoplight. Frank was shocked he hadn't already run it. Did the man even know he was after him?

As Frank drew nearer, he made out what he'd been chasing. It was a once-gorgeous, candy apple red, metallic '66 Shelby Cobra, complete with roll bar, speed stripes, and scoops—the whole package. Except now, it had a huge, rumpled aluminum right side very similar to his Mustang's rumple on the left. Even the chrome exhaust pipe was crushed. Frank's first thought was, *It's such a pity defacing two beautiful sports cars.*

His next thought was to get the guy off the road before any more damage was done. When the light changed, naturally, the driver was off like a jackrabbit. Apparently, he was none the wiser of his collision with Frank. Frank's conclusion was he must be drunk. As the wayward driver pulled ahead of all other traffic, Frank continued his pursuit. Now, it became a little easier for him to keep pace in the heavier traffic. They raced through a series of long, winding curves on State Road 686 heading south. Then, Frank realized they were getting close to St. Petersburg/Clearwater International Airport. The road now bordered airport property, which was fairly remote on the north end of the airport.

Previously, Frank thought only mangroves populated the acreage in that area. Yet, he witnessed his quarry take a sudden ninety-degree left on to an oyster shell road and disappear between the mangroves. Fortunately, dry oyster shell leaves a dusty trail that's easily followed. So Frank tracked the car a quarter mile down the twisting little road. Two forks came up, but Frank could still see which way the car had gone. At the end of the road, much to his surprise, there was an ample asphalt parking lot. Across the lot was a small stand of cypress trees, and nestled among them was a wood-framed bar and grill named Pilot's

Cove. Frank never knew the place existed. There, the mangled Cobra sat without a driver. Now, came a moment of decision.

Frank was still in hot pursuit mode. Trotting up to the heavy, wooden double doors, he pulled. To his surprise, the door opened. Frank entered a darkened lounge pervaded with the scent of Old Spice and beer. It seemed to be a well-appointed lounge with a well-stocked bar, polished dance floor, and grand piano. Anyone could see, but for its rough-hewn exterior, this was a swank place.

Frank waited for his eyes to adjust from the bright sunlight outside. To hasten the process, he applied the night-vision technique taught in survival school. Lightly pressing his index fingers into his eyes brought forth a chemical reaction called visual purple. It augments visual adjustment to dark environs. As soon as he was able, he looked for an exit door, figuring the driver was trying to give him the slip.

Instead, he heard a voice come from across the dance floor in the shadows. Frank refocused and spotted a tall, slender gentleman standing still across the room.

"May I help you, sir?" The man spoke with a discernible accent, which Frank's brain immediately recognized as mideastern seaboard United States. *Perhaps Virginia, maybe even Maryland,* he thought. The voice came again from the shadows, this time more challenging than cordial.

"I said, may I help you with something, sir? The bar does not open until five, but you're welcome to wait while they restock."

"Ah, thank you, no, sir. Actually, I was looking for someone who might have rushed in here awhile ago."

"Was he driving a red Cobra?" the gentleman asked.

"Yes, his car is still in the lot." Frank confirmed. "Have you seen him?"

"Truth be told, that's my car, but the driver is indisposed. What do you want with *him?*"

Frank cursed under his breath. *What wouldn't I want with him?* he thought to himself. *For starters, he might have killed Sandy and me six miles back. That would be something to discuss.*

Frank stood still, feeling the tremors of rage building inside when the man spoke again.

"I am Curtis Selway. And you, sir, are?"

"Major Frank Barrett, USAF," Frank said. "I'm looking for the driver of your car."

"My apologies, sir. As I said, he is indisposed at the moment. Did I understand you correctly that you're a pilot with the USAF?"

"That's right, an F-4 flight instructor." Frank went on to explain that he and his fiancée were sideswiped up the road by the driver of his car, and he intended to settle the matter.

The atmosphere between them was charged by the absence of the accused.

Curtis raised his voice. "Randy, get yourself out here now! I'll not stand by one more time watching you screw the pooch while people's lives and my reputation are at stake."

Randy produced himself from the shadows behind the bar with a hangdog look of shame on his face. He wavered there while Frank contemplated what to do with his sorry ass.

Curtis interceded, trying to placate. "Major Barrett, you *do* have my most profound apologies. Randy, here, used to be my corporate pilot."

Randy tried to protest. "Now, just a second, Curt. I was ready—"

Curtis interjected, "You were nothing. As I was saying, now, you see, I must find another pilot. You can't imagine how difficult that will be on such short notice. Yet, I must. It never ceases to amaze how those to whom much is given can ball it up so royally when so much is expected of them.

"You see, major, I needed Randy sober. He needed to be ready to fly out of here right now. As you can see, he's too drunk, and it wouldn't be the first time. Please sit down, Major Barrett. Let's discuss remuneration for your damages."

Frank felt that it was, at least, a step in the right direction. As for Randy, he'd been summarily dismissed from a lucrative position on the spot. *Punishment enough for now,* Frank thought.

Frank said, "Unlike Randy, you seem a gentleman who is willing to make amends."

At that, Randy spun away from the bar and stormed into a back room. As Frank sat down, Curtis Selway emerged completely from the shadows. Sitting opposite Frank, Frank could see Curtis was well dressed in a custom-made silk suit and tie. He reminded Frank of pictures he'd seen of Howard Hughes, in his early days as an intrepid aviator, right down to the mustache. He cut a handsome image but something more. His demeanor exuded a certain energy within.

When he spoke again, it wasn't about remuneration. What he said totally took Frank by surprise.

"Major Barrett, I'd like to make you an offer. I've been looking to replace Randy for some time now. I can't trust his judgment any longer. His drinking has become more than a minor inconvenience to me. Would you consider flying my jet for me today? You see, thanks to Randy, I'm in a bit of a jam. I simply must be in California in a matter of hours. Unfortunately, the only travel arrangements I made were with my own jet."

Frank was stunned. He came there to settle a score. Now, he was being offered a position, on the spot, as a high-paid chauffeur. It struck Frank as being highly irregular, to say the least. Yet, his mind jumped a step toward accepting.

I'd have to discuss it with Sandy, he thought. *Then there's the USAF.*

Just then, all thoughts of entertaining Curtis's offer fell away. Frank asked if he could take his card and get back to him. Presently, he felt a crucial need to get back to Sandy, who he'd left stranded on the roadside.

"I'll be here for thirty minutes more. Beyond that, I shall have to rescind my offer."

Snatching the business card from his outstretched hand, Frank bolted for the door, leaving him with a parting assurance. Frank promised he would be back.

Frank left Pilot's Cove in a cloud of dust, hoping Sandy would speak to him again. The decision ahead would be up to both of them.

As Frank sped on, thoughts of a civilian career as a business jet pilot swirled in his mind. He had to admit, it was a truly attractive offer compared with the shrinking future in his current service life. Quickly, his thoughts shifted to Sandy and how he could convince her to go back with him to Pilot's Cove.

The good news was, she waited for him there by the roadside, knowing he would return. When he did, she was glad that he hadn't succumbed to revenge against the driver. As he slowed and turned around, Frank had to think of something that would convince her he was not going to submit to vengeance again. As he pulled alongside, he said, "Sandy, it's not a problem anymore. You can trust in more sober judgments from now on."

Sandy had been waiting and wondering what he would say to her. What he said sounded right. Also, his winning smile came through to save the day. As she got in with him, he began to explain to her what had transpired up the road. She was spellbound by his story. Suddenly, she told him something he did not expect.

"I saw you in a dream," she said. "You were flying a different plane—different from all the rest—and you were very happy. I could see it in your eyes. I feel this new venture is right for you, and I want to be a part of that dream."

Frank did return, and with a complete aircraft checkout, he flew Curtis Selway to his destination in California. In fact, a bit of a tailwind got Frank there on time, firmly ensconcing him as a corporate pilot in the employ of Curtis Selway. Resigning his commission wasn't difficult. Besides, it heralded the vision of new horizons for him and Sandy.

Epilogue

All that we are is the result of what we have thought; it is founded on our thoughts and made up of our thoughts. If a man speaks or acts with an evil thought, suffering follows him as a wheel follows the hoof of the beast that draws the cart.

—*Dhamapada,* collection of ancient Buddhist poems

GLOSSARY

AAA—antiaircraft cannon battery

B-66 ECM—electronic countermeasures jet aircraft

Big Charlie—a Chinese national in the Vietnam War

Bingo—condition where fuel is limited to a return to base only

Chandelle—climbing 180-degree turn

EC-121—propeller-driven airborne early warning radar surveillance aircraft with combat control over MiG interceptors as electronic countermeasures aircraft

Gomers—slang for strong enemy pilots flying without the aid of hydraulically assisted controls

Grayout—condition of impaired vision brought on by high gravitational forces

Green-up—warm-up of a radar-seeking system

Hoyaldras—fried bread

IP—intersection point on a bombing run

SAM sites—surface-to-air missile SA-2 guideline missiles

Tet—Vietnamese lunar New Year's festival celebrated late January or early February

TFW—Tactical Fighter Wing

Vector—a compass heading to be followed by an aircraft

VFE—do-not-exceed speed

Wild Weasels—F-4 aircraft equipped with radar suppression for SAM sites